T3-BGM-324

CHANDLER PARK LIBRARY
12800 HARPER
DETROIT, MI 48213

SWEET TOMORROWS

KIMBERLEY WHITE

Genesis Press, Inc.

Indigo Love Stories

An imprint of Genesis Press, Inc.
Publishing Company

Genesis Press, Inc.
P.O. Box 101
Columbus, MS 39703

All rights reserved. Except for use in any review, the reproduction or utilization of this work in whole or in part in any form by any electronic, mechanical, or other means, not known or hereafter invented, including xerography, photocopying and recording, or in any information storage or retrieval system, is forbidden without written permission of the publisher, Genesis Press, Inc. For information write Genesis Press, Inc., P.O. Box 101, Columbus, MS 39703.

All characters in this book have no existence outside the imagination of the author and have no relation whatsoever to anyone bearing the same name or names. They are not even distantly inspired by any individual known or unknown to the author and all incidents are pure invention.

Copyright© 2000, 2007 by Kimberley White. All rights reserved.

ISBN-13: 978-1-58571-234-2
ISBN-10: 1-58571-234-5
Manufactured in the United States of America

First Edition 2000
Second Edition 2007

Visit us at www.genesis-press.com or call at 1-888-Indigo-1

DEDICATION

To my parents, Leon and Geneva, and all the
ancestors who came before me.

ACKNOWLEDGEMENTS

My family has been very supportive through this process. There are too many to name individually, so let it be said that I appreciate Christopher Judson, Brandy and her family, Leon Jr. and his family, grandma Lewis, the nieces and nephews, all of the aunties and uncles, my cousins, and extended family.

Thank you to my first readers Michelle V. and Karen O. My writing partner, Charisse Walker, spent many hours helping me get it right—Good luck on your novel, Peaches Pawns. Montell, your words always give me the push I need to turn on the computer.

Many people on the writing circuit have given me encouraging words and invaluable support. Thank you to all of the writers who autographed my books with a smile and a friendly word; Herb Metoyer and The Detroit Black Writer's Guild; all the bookstore owners across the country who support black writers.

Readers, I hope you enjoy my work. Stay tuned for more. Please e-mail your comments to: kwhite_writer@hotmail.com

Eric Jerome Dickey, the inspiration you provide is breathtaking.

To my special friend, Batman, otherwise known as page ____: With you around, many more sensual novels are to come.

CHAPTER ONE

Instead of waking up terrified in a cold sweat, Talya felt as if she was embraced by strong, muscular arms. Maybe, after nine months, she was beginning to relax and live again. Maybe the terror was going to start to dissipate.

Holding on to the memory of the dream was important to Talya because it was so unlike the others. There was no sequential story. The dialogue could not be recalled. But the dream did leave Talya with feelings that were very distinctive. The emotions involved were so strong that she felt safe and loved, but when she awoke she felt scared and lonely. It was so realistic that Talya could feel the heat of the sun burning her bare shoulders.

The dream consisted of only one scene: Talya sat at a white lawn table shielded from the bright sun by its umbrella. Her lover approached from behind with a smile, wearing only swimming trunks. He rubbed her shoulders as he leaned down and whispered in her ear. She threw her head back and laughed at his words. This man brought her incredible warmth. He made her feel cherished and loved. And then she woke up.

Talya tried to keep the warmth of the dream with her while she worked. She replayed it again and again in her mind while sitting behind her desk. The room was hot and stuffy. She did not have enough seniority at the bank to have earned a large, bright corner office. The sun lit the tiny work place through the only window in the room, to the right of her desk. She glanced over at the file cabinet near the door and made a mental note to purchase another plant to liven up the dull room. The bulletin board was crammed with messages and memos. She would reorganize the board after her last client. She kept her desk clear of clutter and well organized, but most times the unwanted papers ended up on the bulletin board. She told herself that she needed to remove the clutter just as she had cleared the turmoil from her life nine months ago. The warmth of the dream began to slip away as the memories of her last lover crept into her head. That life was left behind, nine months now, and she refused to even think about the past.

Talya's daydreams were interrupted when Kathy, the receptionist, entered the small room to announce the last client of the day. She never knocked before she walked in, despite Talya's request for her to do so. Kathy had worked for the bank many more years than Talya and felt she was above knocking to obtain permission to enter.

Talya stood to greet Robert. He was her first client six months ago when she started at Brunstown Bank as a financial manager. They worked so closely that he also became a good friend.

"Good morning, Talya." Robert rushed to Talya's desk to embrace her outstretched hand. His small frame and quiet mannerisms were misleading. His good looks were subtly hidden behind his black rimmed glasses. His intelligence was not so easily hidden. Robert was the vice president of finance for Weston Realty Company and answered directly to the owner of the company. It was the sixth largest African-American owned real estate company in the country.

"Good morning, Robert." Talya mocked his tone, trying to make him smile. He was much too serious for his age. She always lit up when Robert came for their monthly financial reviews, and she liked to make him feel as good.

Robert pushed his black-rimmed glasses up on his nose with his finger, trying to hide his smile, "Talya, this is my boss, Meridian Weston."

Talya noticed the gentleman standing behind Robert for the first time. She recognized the name immediately. His name was on all the checks she deposited for Robert. He was the owner of Weston Realty Company. Talya's hands became clammy as she wondered if his presence was due to some huge mistake she had made managing the account. She tried to wipe her hand on her skirt unnoticed. "Nice to meet you, sir."

Meridian took her hand. He gazed directly in her eyes which unnerved Talya. She noted how young he appeared to be. She always pictured him as a balding older man who wore neat but outdated suits. He was completely the opposite. Meridian was tall and slim but muscular. His hair was curly and faded with military precision. He wore the shadow of a mustache and beard. Talya knew his suit cost more than all the clothes hanging in her closet by the way it fit him with sharp cuts and rounded corners. The royal blue fabric of his suit against his caramel-colored skin made a definite statement. The sweet smell that slowly filled her office belonged to him.

Meridian held Talya's eyes a second too long. He noticed her uneasiness and smiled down at her. "Yes, nice to meet you."

Talya did not expect his voice to be so deep and syrupy either.

Robert explained Meridian's presence at their meeting. "I'm going on vacation for three weeks with my wife, and Meridian will be handling all of the company's finances in my absence."

"Wouldn't you prefer that I work with your team of accountants?"

Meridian answered, "Ms. Stevenson, I learned a great deal from my father before taking over this business. The most important being to manage my own finances. I would never leave total financial control of Weston Realty in the hands of a team of accountants."

The harsh response to her question made Talya glance over at Robert for support.

Meridian continued, the harshness of his tone replaced by a lilt. "I have neglected to learn all the details needed to accomplish this; now, with Robert going on vacation for such a long period of time, I'm up against the wall." The corners of his mouth moved upward into a friendly smile.

Talya relaxed the tension in her back that made her sit ramrod straight in the chair. She imagined running one's own company left little time to make bank deposits and review financial statements.

Robert shifted in his chair. "Meridian will need your help managing things while I'm away. I've briefed him on what we've been doing, but he will undoubtedly have many more questions."

"Mr. Weston," Talya said, "I'm not sure if I am the one you need to meet with. I can have my manager speak with you." Working with Robert managing routine financial matters was one thing; working with the owner of the company to manage the entire business was another.

Meridian sat up straight in his chair, planting his feet firmly on the floor in front of him. "Robert speaks very highly of you, and most importantly, he trusts you. I will speak to your manager if you wish but I insist on dealing only with you."

Talya looked over at Robert who avoided her questioning eyes by nervously pushing his glasses up on his nose. They had joked over lunch about their bosses in the past. Robert always described Meridian as being determined, almost rigid, when making business decisions. His character assessment of Meridian made Talya believe he was an older man. From the weary expression on Robert's face, this matter had been discussed between them, and all had been decided before they came to her office.

"Mr. Weston—"

"Yes?"

"I'm happy to hear that you have so much confidence in me, but I really think you should have my manager assign someone with more seniority to work with you."

Meridian rested against the back of the chair, never taking his eyes away from hers. "I have made my decision.

Unless you're refusing to work with me, there's no reason for me to speak with your manager."

The intensity of his eyes told Talya that any further attempts to persuade him to talk with her manager were useless. She relented and flipped open her planner. They scheduled their first meeting and quickly concluded their business.

The possibility of losing Weston Realty Company because of a mistake she might make prompted Talya to speak with her manager. As expected, he would assign the task of working with Mr. Weston to an accountant with more experience. Weston Realty was one of the largest accounts at the bank, and he did not want to take any chances with losing it. He thanked Talya and hastily dismissed her from his office. Talya would have loved to have been granted permission to handle the important task, but the manager had given her an opportunity when she came to him without experience seeking work, so she did not object to his decision.

Not many people were willing to help her then. She had lost so many jobs because of the problems He caused at her workplace. She still couldn't bring herself to speak His name. Strange how He would insist that she work and then make her quit or get her fired every time she started a job. Because of this, she always remained detached from her co-workers. Some people labeled her as a quiet person; others called her a snob. The truth was, Talya was afraid to become emotionally attached to anyone for fear that He would find out and hurt them too.

Talya had worked so hard to obtain her bachelor's degree, and He never allowed her to work in her field of choice. She didn't understand it at the time, but being away from Him gave her time to think and figure things out for herself. He had not been able to meet the challenges of academic life and, therefore, never obtained his college degree. He took another route in life, which seemed to make Him happy, but He was always resentful of what she had accomplished.

Talya removed a thumb tack securing several outdated announcements onto the cluttered bulletin board. She used images of the dream to push away His angry voice sounding in her ears. The words were so cruel. He made her regret finishing college. It was as if her success resulted in His failure. She tossed the old announcements into the trash can near her desk. If she could only rid herself of the memories as easily.

Robert stuck his head in the door of Meridian's office. "Did you need to see me before I take off?"

Meridian sat at his oversized mahogany desk going over legal documents he should have signed a week ago. The stereo filled the office with the soft sounds of jazz music. "Yeah, come in." He pushed away the papers.

Robert came in and wandered over to look out of the windows that opened the office up to the city from ceiling to floor. Although he worked in a spacious and well decorated office, it did not compare to Meridian's. Meridian's was equivalent to the size of the entire living room in Robert's condo. The decorator used shades of silver and black to provide a soothing yet elegant atmosphere. The aquarium and the piped-in jazz music allowed clients to relax while they negotiated deals. The bathroom was fully equipped with a shower, tub, and anything else a wealthy bachelor might need for dating after work.

"Why didn't you tell me about the woman at the bank?" Meridian called Robert's mind back into the room.

Robert walked over to the black leather sofa and sat down. "What woman?"

"The financial adviser, Ms. Stevenson."

"Talya. What about her?"

"She is gorgeous." Meridian emphasized every word.

"Yeah," Robert said smiling, "she is also very good at her job."

Meridian pushed his chair back from his desk. He stood and stretched his long, lean arms out from his body. He was tired of reading papers and trying to understand legal lingo. He wanted a drink, then he would return to business. He walked over to the black glass bar trimmed with silver metal and poured himself a drink. He held the crystal flask up in Robert's direction.

Robert declined the offer. "Rena will nag me if she smells liquor on my breath when I get home."

Meridian nodded his understanding before sampling his drink. "The manager of Brunstown Bank called to tell me he was going to assign one of the senior accountants to take over my account."

"Really? I hope I haven't caused Talya any trouble."

"I told him we would only deal with Talya, or I would be forced to remove my business from his bank."

"I suppose he agreed."

Meridian nodded. "From everything you've told me, she's a sister working hard to establish a permanent place in the business world. I don't want to interfere with that. I should be doing something to help her. You know what my father always said, 'Once you make it, you have to reach back and bring one more person with you.' Besides, you're comfortable working with her so there really is no rational reason to make any changes."

"The only reason I can think of is that you're becoming involved. The manager has never once met with me. I don't even know what he looks like."

Meridian took a slow drink from his glass. "What do you know about Talya Stevenson?"

"She started at the bank six months ago. I like working with her much better than the last guy. She's very talented. Dedicated to her work."

Meridian gave Robert a look that categorized his annoyance. He was interested in her personal affidavit, not her professional credentials. "You know I'm asking about her, not her resume'."

"We go out to lunch quite a bit, but she has never confided anything to me about her personal life. I only know she's single, no kids." He joined Meridian at the bar. "Why are you so interested in Talya?"

"I was thinking about asking her out to dinner." Meridian took a long drink from his glass so that he could

avoid Robert's stare. He braced himself as it burned its way
down his throat.

"Meridian, she's a friend of mine. Don't treat her like
your other women."

"What's that supposed to mean?" Meridian knew just
what that meant. He had a weakness for women. He dated
a lot but never became serious. He wined them and dined
them and slept with them if he had a mind to. The women
went out with him to see how much they could get. He
dated them to fill a void in his life. No one ever got hurt.
The unspoken rules were understood by both parties. He
kept all his relationships distant and short, making sure no
emotions were ever involved. Another valuable rule he
learned from his father: "Never get mixed up in love affairs
that could affect the assets of the business. And God forbid,
don't have children out of wedlock OR before the prenup-
tial is signed."

"Just don't take her for a ride."

Meridian put his hands up in surrender. "Point taken."

Meridian looked forward to his private conferences
with Talya. He found himself making up excuses to meet
with her. He asked her question after question in an
attempt to prolong their appointments. Meridian became
absorbed in her words as she explained the financial jargon
he should have already known. He moved closer to her to
examine balance sheets. He told her jokes trying to ease the

mood and catch a glimpse of her smile. Meridian saw more than a casual dating experience in Talya Stevenson.

Something about her entranced him. Her good looks went unnoticed until one examined her closely behind the splattering of tan freckles on the bridge of her nose and across her cheekbones. The only make up she wore enhanced her sultry brown eyes and reddened her full lips. She was very charming and moved with a grace that made him cognizant of her femininity. The stylish cut of her mane framed her face. Not one hair was ever out of place. The radiating smile she gave Robert at their initial meeting had made Meridian want to melt. He wanted Talya to smile that way when they were alone together. She should only gleam for him.

After meeting Talya, there was no way he would give up the chance to work with her to meet with a boring old man. Supervisor, bank manager, or senior accountant, he didn't care. Thoughts were beginning to form in his head. He wanted to see how far this chance meeting could go.

"How does your family feel about you working late with me?" Meridian asked in an attempt to personalize their conversation. They were sitting together in his office having their fourth conference.

"I don't have any family."

"No family?" Meridian looked up from the stack of papers in front of him and focused on Talya. "Where are your parents, brothers, sisters?"

"I'm an only child."

"That's something we share." Although Talya seemed uncomfortable with the line of questioning, Meridian tried to learn more. "What about your parents?"

"They're dead."

The finality of the statement kept Meridian from asking any further details about her parents. "I'm sorry."

"It was a long time ago."

Meridian watched the solemn expression that passed over Talya's face. Even as she spoke of a personal tragedy, her voice remained soft and sultry. It sounded as if she was in the throes of passion. She should not be allowed to speak so seductively outside of the bedroom. Meridian wondered if her using the soft bedroom voice should entice him. Or torture him. Whether purposeful or not, she was succeeding at doing both.

"I'm sure someone is at home waiting for you." Meridian searched for more information.

Talya kept her eyes glued to the documents in front of her, but Meridian noticed how uncomfortable she instantly became. The comment had been innocent enough, why did she swallow hard enough for him to see her throat bob up and down?

"No, I'm a career woman."

A silent sigh of relief. "We've been at this long enough. The numbers are all running together."

"Don't worry; you're catching on." Talya started to gather the papers and put them into her briefcase.

"Can I drop you off at home?"

"No, I have a car." Talya awkwardly placed her briefcase in one hand and her purse in the other before moving to the door.

Meridian followed closely behind Talya. She was in such a rush to leave him. "How about a drink?"

"No, I better get home. I have a full day ahead of me tomorrow."

Talya's polite, businesslike attitude at their meetings drove Meridian crazy! Every time he tried to move the conversation to a personal topic, Talya quickly brought it back to spreadsheets and account balances. She became animated only when she advised him on managing his assets. He had other things on his mind that he wanted to manage. He repeatedly reminded her not to call him Mr. Weston. He watched her intently as she spoke, but she never noticed. Meridian's frustration with being subtle grew. Giving up on starting a relationship with her never occurred to him, but his methods thus far did not yield the results he wanted.

It drove Him nuts. Where could Talya be? She had never, ever stayed away this long before. She usually realized how much he needed her and returned on her own after a day or two. He might have to clean up his act a bit before she found her way home, sweet-talk her and buy her a gift, but she came back. A few times he had to find her and bring her back. He grunted as he bent his knees and lifted the barbell containing two hundred pounds of weight to his

middle. "I guess I'll have to bring her home again." He
inhaled and lifted the barbell above his head.

CHAPTER TWO

"Date number ninety-nine." Jennifer popped out of her apartment when Talya put her key in the lock of her own apartment door.

Talya put down her briefcase and waited to hear this new dating experience. Jennifer reminded her of the person she had once been: dynamic, strong, full of energy.

"I went out with this guy that I met on a lunch run for work one day. He was so short he came right here." She raised her hand in a karate chop up to her breast. "He took me to some fancy restaurant to impress me. And it did. I ordered fifty dollars worth of food all by myself. Anyway, he thought that the meal included a free dessert, which I would provide. He was all over me in the car on the way home. Do you know that when I told this jerk he was not going to be serving me up for dessert he started to bug out? Hands everywhere. So, do you know what I did?"

Jennifer's hands were waving wildly in the air as she spoke. Talya shook her head trying to hold back her laugh until the story ended.

"I jumped out of his car when we got a block from my apartment."

Talya could not contain her laughter any longer. "You did not."

Jennifer held up her hand in the air giving the Girl Scout's pledge of honor. "True story."

"You are so crazy." Talya unlocked the door of her apartment, and Jennifer followed her inside.

"Working late or dinner date?" Jennifer flopped down on the sofa while Talya turned on the lights in the apartment.

"Work."

"As always with you. When are you going to get a social life?"

"You and I go out all the time." Talya sat next to her on the sofa.

"I mean with a man."

Jennifer always encouraged Talya to create her own dating adventures. They met and instantly became friends the day Talya moved into the building. There were only four apartments on the eighth floor, and they were next-door neighbors. The other two apartments were occupied by married couples. The couples were cordial in the hallway or on the elevator, but their interests were very different so they never became friendly. Jennifer and Talya were both single, the same age, with some of the same goals.

Jennifer arrived at Talya's door the first night of her move with a chocolate cake and a pint of chocolate ice cream. There was no way they could sleep after eating all of that chocolate. They sat on the floor of Talya's apartment and talked for hours. Talya did not have any furniture other than a kitchen table with chairs and a bed. When she ran away from Him she took only her clothing and what money she could find hidden in the house. Jennifer assumed that Talya was starting out and could not afford the costly rent of the downtown apartment and the expense of new furniture. Over the months that followed, the women spent many days at discount stores and specialty outlets furnishing Talya's apartment. Talya's chest swelled with pride when she came home to her apartment because she purchased everything herself. She started with nothing, and now had a beautifully decorated home.

"Hello." Jennifer waved her hand in front of Talya's face. "Where are you?"

Talya rubbed her eyes. "I think my client is flirting with me. He drags out our meetings so that work that should take one hour takes three. Robert and I usually meet once a month. I've met with Meridian four times in three weeks. Sometimes I catch him looking at me. Staring at me, really."

"Is he handsome?"

"Yeah, I guess so."

Actually, Talya found him very attractive, but she was not ready to admit that to herself yet, let alone Jennifer. Every time Meridian moved next to her to examine the documents she presented, Talya's breath would catch. His conversation with her came easy to him, and he made her want to relax and talk about anything other than business. He asked about her—her life, her thoughts—which gave her some sense of importance.

"Is there a problem?"

"The problem is that I don't want this to get out of hand. I don't know what, if anything, Meridian is up to. I could lose my job if I mess up on this account."

"Do you know what this sounds like? It sounds like you feel guilty about your attraction to this guy. There's no great conspiracy theory behind his attraction to you. You're a good-looking, intelligent woman." Jennifer stood and moved to the door as she spoke. "If he's handsome and he's flirting with you, why don't you flirt back? Maybe you'll get a date. You better get back out there and start dating or else you're going to end up old and alone." She opened the front door. "I've got to go get ready for my date. See ya."

Jennifer unsuccessfully tried to uncover the reasons for Talya's lack of dating. Talya never said anything more than that all her concentration stayed on furthering her career. Jennifer didn't seem to buy that excuse, but she never pushed too hard for an explanation. There was too much hurt in Talya's past to give Jennifer all the details behind her aloofness with men.

Talya hadn't dated since leaving Him. Not one date. He monopolized her thoughts. Either she missed him because she was lonely or she was hating him for everything he put her through. She decided when she removed herself from that situation that she would never invest her heart in another man. The hurt took too long to get over. Better that she invest in her future security. Learn everything she could about her career. Put away money for a rainy day. Go back to school and get her master's degree. She wanted to spend time healing herself and moving toward the future. Dating had no place in her life. She learned to be content with that fact until she met the owner of the Weston Realty Company.

Talya never spoke of Him to anyone. Not since leaving the shelter. The counselors were helpful. They taught her words like power, independence, respect, self-love, and dignity. The counselors were the ones who referred her to Brunstown Bank for an interview. They helped Talya work through uncontrollable emotions while she saved enough money to move in to her first apartment. The counselors encouraged her independence as she shopped for a car to get to work. Talya stopped attending the counseling sessions at the shelter when she realized that rehashing her history with Him made her feel worse. She knew she needed further healing, but for right now forcing herself to forget the pain was work best for her. That's why Meridian's flirtation made her uneasy. He rekindled memories of her past relationship,visions that carried too much pain to handle.

In order to start another relationship she would have to take a self-assessment, as her counselor called it. She would take out pen and paper and write down the adjectives that described who she was. Then she would have to list the qualities that she wanted in a man. Finally, she'd search her heart and be honest about what level of commitment she needed in a potential relationship. Those things were too hard to do. She had spent so much time trying to re-create herself and forget her past. To dredge it all up again meant new agony.

And how was she supposed to trust herself to know just what qualities she needed in a man? She had been so sure with Him. That was nothing short of a nuclear disaster. Confusion swept through her when she started to speculate on the words she would put down on the paper to describe the perfect mate. The only word that kept recurring to her was Meridian. Crazy, foolish thoughts. Working so closely to him the past few weeks had caused her daydreams to go too far. She pushed away the vision of his handsome face and went to dress for bed.

Meridian rolled onto his side and looked over at the woman asleep next to him. He never took his dates back to his home. He tried to remember the woman's name or what hotel they were in. He could not. She was pretty enough, but silly; she giggled the entire night over every little thing. If he didn't know better, he'd question if she was even of legal age. He lifted the sheets and stole a glance; they were both naked. Now he remembered. A little too much to drink, a curvaceous body, and he could not resist. He looked to the bedside table to read the time from the red glowing face of the alarm clock—it was too late to drive an hour and a half back to his home, so he would stay the night with the stranger. On his way to the bathroom he searched for evidence that he had been sober enough to remember to protect himself. To his surprise, he found two opened condom packages next to the bed.

"Is there something wrong?" the girl asked when Meridian returned to bed. She was asleep before he could answer.

Meridian became annoyed with himself as he watched the woman sleep. He hoped that he could get away in the morning without going to breakfast with her. He still could not remember her name. An overwhelming sense of dissatisfaction filled him. He was disgusted with himself. This kind of relationship never bothered him before meeting Talya. The void he used the woman to fill had only grown larger.

Something about Talya Stevenson caused a jolt to flow through his body when he thought of her, which was very often. The void faded when he talked with her and shared her knowledge. His wealth did not impress her. The numbers on his balance sheets never fazed her. She was interested in doing the best she could to help him manage his company's finances. Meridian usually dated women who swooned over his looks and his money. Did the fact that Talya didn't seem to notice him make him want her more? He discarded that idea; he'd had his share of women who offered a challenge. As he looked at the silly woman sleeping next to him he realized he needed someone special in his life. He wanted someone that needed him for love and support and not his money. He saw something extraordinary in Talya.

Talya looked up from the papers in front of her and watched Meridian pacing across the silver-gray lush carpeting of his office. He started at one corner of the room and traced a straight line through the carpeting to the opposite glass wall. He'd been in a sulking mood since she arrived. She wondered if it was something she said or did. She gathered a stack of papers and struck them against the table. She made one last noisy smack on the tabletop hoping to get Meridian's attention.

He turned on his heels to face her and closed the distance between them with long strides. "I'm sorry. I've been distracted today."

His syrupy voice gave her goose bumps. "That's okay. How do you think the past three weeks have gone? Do you feel you have a good grasp on things?"

Meridian's brow rushed upward at the innuendo he could easily apply to the statement. He had to stop himself from saying what he wanted. "You tell me. You're the teacher."

"I think you learn fast. Robert will be proud of the report I give him."

Meridian stuffed his hands into the smooth wool fabric of his pants pockets. The bright smile again. Was it for him this time, or did she only smile when Robert was involved in some way?

"Are those the final numbers?" He pointed to the papers Talya was holding against her chest.

She nodded, placing the papers down on the table in front of her. The deep timbre of his voice made even that simple sentence sound seductive. Instead of sitting in his original seat, Meridian walked around behind her chair. He leaned down, placing one hand on the arm of her chair and the other on the table in front of her.

Talya's breathing became choppy as she felt Meridian's body weight push against the back of her chair. The sounds coming from his throat could be taken two ways. Talya tried to convince herself that they were sounds of understanding as he read the figures. Not moans of desire. The heels of her shoes pushed into the carpet, if she swiveled the chair around at that moment—Meridian leaned down farther. His beard rubbed against the side of her face.

The phone on his desk chimed causing them both to jump as if caught in the act of doing something wrong. He was about to press his lips against Talya's face when the interruption came.

Meridian tore himself away from Talya and went to his desk, snatching the phone from the cradle.

"My secretary has ordered us lunch." Meridian returned to the table.

Talya pushed her chair away from the table as he approached. She had made it through three weeks without giving in to her fantastic fantasies; now was no time to crumble. She stood to stretch and returned to her seat only after Meridian sat down.

"I shouldn't take up anymore of your day. I'm sure you have a lot of work to do."

"Nonsense. Lunch is already on the way. We only have a little more to finish up. We'll eat together, and then I'll let you go." Meridian sat forward, his voice lowering a little. "That is if you don't have anything else you need to show me."

Talya's lips parted, but no words came from her. What did he mean? Did he know how sexy he was and how racy his words seemed? She reminded herself that if she could get through this last day, everything would return to normal.

Robert returned from vacationing with his wife of two years refreshed and ready to catch up on the work that had piled up on his desk. Tension filled everyone working on the top floor of the office building. It didn't take long for Robert to hear the employees in the break room talking about Mr. Weston being on a rampage. He was overly critical of all the work that passed his desk. He canceled several meetings that week without rescheduling. He even got into a shouting match with a messenger the day before Robert's return. This was out of character for the easygoing boss the employees were used to working for. Meridian had a reputation of being pleasant and treating each employee with respect. There was speculation among the employees that a deal had gone bad and a large sum of money was lost. Others believed the business was being taken over by a large conglomerate. Still others believed the young executive was having a nervous breakdown from all the pressure of running a multimillion dollar company.

Robert spoke with Meridian's executive assistant and then entered his office. "Boss, do we need to discuss some problems in the office?"

Meridian looked up from his desk, annoyed with the interruption. "What?"

"I hear you've been really hard on people around here. Is it the workload? You know that I can take some work from you and reassign—"

Meridian gave Robert a pointed look that stopped his flow of words. He slapped his pen down on the desk. "No, it's not that." He spun his chair around and looked out over the city. "I didn't realize how bad I've been. I'll apologize to everyone at the next department head meeting."

Robert sat on the corner of the desk. "What's up?"

Meridian swung his chair back around to face his friend and most trusted employee. "You would never believe me."

Robert looked at Meridian over his black-rimmed glasses and waited for him to continue.

"Talya is driving me nuts."

"You're right; I don't believe you. Did something happen while I was on vacation?"

Meridian shook his head. He stared off in the distance as he always did when he was contemplating his thoughts and the words he would use to express them. "Nothing happened. I've been trying to get her to notice me. I've asked her out casually for lunch or dinner, but she always refuses. Strictly business with her." He drew in and released a deep breath. "You know me, Robert. I never cared if a woman stayed or if she went. But ever since that first day in Talya's office, well, I can't stop thinking about her."

"Are you being straight with me? You don't think of Talya as just another conquest?"

Meridian shook his head again. "This is different. I want to spend some time with her and get to know her. I can't deny that I find her attractive, but it's more than that."

Another day filled with dead ends.

Rizzo stood at the head of the bench to spot the one hundred and fifty pounds of Jason's lift. "Why don't you just wait for Talya to come back? You said yourself she always does."

It had never been this hard to find Talya the other times she left. She was getting better at the game. But Jason was tired of playing. He would have to go another route, but he would find her. No matter what obstacles were placed in front of him.

Jason laid his muscled back on the bench and gripped the bar containing the weights. "It's been over nine months. She's never stayed away this long before." He lifted the weight with little effort. "I think she must be hiding out with someone. There's no way she could have survived by herself all this time."

Rizzo helped him lower the weight back onto its cradle. "I don't know, man."

Hearing the doubt in his friend's voice, Jason sprung upright on the bench and turned to face him. "Are you going to help me do this or what?"

Rizzo stared into his friend's angry face. He had dealt with his temper since they were little. "I never said I wouldn't help you find her. I'm just saying—"

"Thank you," Jason spat before he rose from the bench and headed toward the locker room.

CHAPTER THREE

Talya sat with Jennifer at the airport waiting for her flight to begin boarding. Jennifer had all the information she needed to pick her up the next evening when Talya returned from her business trip. Being a major hub, the airport was buzzing with business travelers on their cell phones, punching data into their laptops. Talya had come a long way since the shelter six months ago. She hadn't reached the level of success the travelers around her were boasting, but she was on her way. Concentrating on her future might pay off after all.

"Dating adventure 147," Jennifer said, breaking the silence between them. "I sat next to this handsome businessman on my flight to Florida last year. And we'll just say that those little blankets they give you on the plane have more than one purpose."

Talya looked around to see if anyone in the crowded airport was listening. "Did you ever see him again?"

Jennifer used a blunt nail to scratch the scalp under her short, curly hair. "Don't even know his name."

They looked at each other and laughed.

"You seem nervous," Jennifer remarked.

"I want to prove that I can manage this account effectively. It could lead to me getting larger accounts at the bank. The truth is that I don't know enough about real estate to be completely comfortable on this trip, and I don't want to blow it."

"Meridian knew that when he asked you to accompany him to the meeting. I'm sure he wants you there for what you do know and not what you don't." Jennifer raised a skeptical brow. "But you know that, don't you? This is about something else."

"I don't know what you're talking about." Talya tilted her body forward and scanned the airport for Meridian. She looked down at her watch.

Jennifer laughed. "Umm-huh, just as I thought. You're nervous because you're going to be sharing a flight with the client who keeps flirting with you."

"This trip is only about business." Talya nudged Jennifer's arm with her elbow. "Here he comes. I'll introduce you."

Jennifer blew a quiet whistle between her teeth. "If you keep this trip all business, you need your head examined."

Meridian hurried up to Talya as quickly as his lean legs would carry him. Their flight was already boarding. He intended to arrive early so that he could spend time talking with Talya. Instead, he got stuck on the phone talking with his mother, listening to her latest escapades in her globe-trotting lifestyle. He briefly talked with Talya's friend, whom he found charming and funny; then he rushed Talya onto the plane.

Meridian was negotiating with developers who were building a subdivision outside of Chicago. He wanted to acquire new property at a reasonable price and sell it to corporations to use for temporary housing for their employees. Robert pitched the idea to him months ago. This meeting would be to finalize price negotiations and sign the contracts if everything went as expected. Normally, Robert would have accompanied Meridian to this meeting, but he was needed at the office to handle other important deals. Meridian jumped at the opportunity to call the bank manager and request Talya's assistance. The bank agreed to allow Talya to accompany Meridian to Chicago, and she was off on her first official business trip. Meridian explained to her on the flight that she would be responsible for crunching the numbers and presenting the final check when the contracts were all signed.

Talya checked into her hotel room and immediately changed into a business suit she purchased especially for the Chicago meeting. The gray skirt fell midway between her thighs and her knees. The matching jacket wrapped snugly around her small waist. She selected a burgundy blouse to wear underneath it, but when she looked in the mirror she decided to wear the jacket alone. The pumps, earrings, and necklace had been chosen by Jennifer, who had good taste in clothing and furniture. When Jennifer entered college initially, she was going to become a designer. Dating adventure number eighty-six explained why she changed her career focus and became a dietitian. Talya checked her hair and makeup in the mirror. She reviewed her records and practiced the answer to every question that might arise. When she felt confident, she jumped on the elevator and went down to the conference room to await the start of the meeting.

Talya listened closely to every word said by the businessmen. She felt intimidated by the much older, more experienced, wealthy white men. It was apparent that they had never met Meridian face-to-face by their expressions when they walked into the room. Meridian showed no signs of intimidation. Although his lawyer was present, Meridian conducted the meeting. He spoke eloquently, and his knowledge of real estate law was indisputable. He was, by Talya's standards, the most intelligent man in the meeting. Meridian's easygoing personality put the men at ease with him. His soft-sale style of negotiating yielded a settlement that was fair and equitable to all those sitting at the enormous table. An agreement was easily reached, and Talya handed over a check finalizing the deal. Everyone shook hands and left the room.

Meridian closed the door behind his lawyer. "Yes." He threw his hands up in the air. "I thought I blew it there for a minute."

"You were great." Talya could feel his enthusiasm bouncing off of the walls. "I don't believe they ever had a chance with you. You are a master negotiator."

"Thank you, but Robert did most of the negotiating before we even got to this point. I could have never pulled it off without Robert, my lawyer, and of course, you. Thank you." He bowed to her with an elaborate flourish.

Talya smiled and gathered the paperwork left on the table.

"Let's have a drink to celebrate." This time he was reasonably sure that the smile was directed at him.

"I don't know—"

Meridian cut her off. "You have to have a drink with me. I can't celebrate alone."

Meridian and Talya went down to the bar off the hotel lobby. The bar was filled to near capacity because the hockey playoff game was being shown on the big-screen television. The waitress found a table near the rear of the bar, abandoned since it was not within the view of the game. That suited Meridian fine. He wanted to talk with Talya without too many distractions.

The soft, dark lighting cast a shadow of romance on Meridian and Talya as they sat across from each other in the secluded area of the bar. Meridian never shared as much about himself with anyone as he did with Talya that night. They talked for hours about everything from business and politics to their childhood experiences. He enjoyed talking with her. She listened closely to every word as if she was genuinely interested.

Meridian followed her sultry eyes with their every movement. The only time his eyes left hers was when he wanted to sneak a peek at the cleavage left uncovered by the jacket she was wearing. She caught the direction of his gaze several times but he gave her his most innocent smile, and she looked away. He wondered if she could be as shy as she seemed or if she were teasing him. He wanted the chance to find out what was rolling around in her mind.

"You haven't mentioned your wife or kids," Talya said, pulling his eyes away from her chest.

Meridian's eyebrow quirked at Talya's question. He was the one that always gave their conversations a personal tone. He could not believe that he never let her know he was available. Maybe that was why she never showed him any interest.

He lifted his beer to his lips. "I'm single; never married. No kids. I'm living the bachelor life." He hoped he left her with no doubt about his freedom to become involved with her.

Talya watched the bottle disappear between his moist lips. "I hope you don't mind me saying that I was surprised by how young you are. You have accomplished a great deal."

Back to business. Okay, let's get it all out of the way. "I'm thirty-five and have been running Weston Realty Company since I turned thirty-one."

"How did you become so successful at such an early age?" Talya thought about how, at thirty, her life was only beginning.

"My father died four years ago from prostate cancer. The business was equally divided between myself and my mother. My mother showed no interest in running it so I, having been groomed by my father since I was fourteen, took over the business. My degree in business administration coupled with my father's guidance well prepared me for the challenge of handling the real estate company.

"My mother keeps a house up North but spends most of her time traveling or volunteering with charity organizations."

Meridian accepted the challenge to continue the family business. He reviewed operations and made major changes in the philosophy of the company. He started actively acquiring land and houses to expand the business. Before he knew it, the business began to flourish. His mother let him handle the company without any interference as long he turned a profit. What was once a small real estate brokerage house transformed into the sixth largest African-American owned real estate company in the country.

Meridian ordered another round of drinks. "How did you choose the path of your life?"

Questions like this threw Talya off balance. It was an innocent enough question to the person asking, but to Talya it was enough to start the spinning sensation in her head.

Talya shrugged. "I always knew I wanted to do something in finance, maybe something with the stock market. I had a teacher in high school that sparked my interest in the field. The rest is history."

"You left out some major history in that story." He knew from Robert that she had only been with Brunstown Bank for six months. What had she been doing between college and starting there? Meridian saw the backdrop of her freckles glow with redness. "But I won't pry."

Meridian kept Talya at the bar much later than he intended, but not as long as he would have liked. They were so comfortable with each other they never ran out of subjects to talk about. He was swept away by Talya's soft and dreamy voice. He found himself watching her movements. The suit she wore fit her curves perfectly. He wanted to reach out and touch her face. He pictured himself pressing against her breasts with his arms wrapped around her waist caressing her behind.

Before they realized, four hours had passed by.

"Again, I'm sorry for keeping you up so late." Meridian handed Talya her briefcase as they stood outside the door of her hotel room.

"Don't worry. I'll sleep on the plane." She opened the door to her room and turned to say good night. "I want to thank you for giving me this opportunity."

Meridian looked into Talya's eyes as she spoke, not hearing anything she said. He considered pushing her into the dark hotel room and peeling off all of her clothes before they made it to the bed. He discarded the idea, afraid that his aggressiveness would scare the shy woman in front of him away forever.

He felt the jolt again followed by an overwhelming urgency to seize an opportunity that he might never get again. Talya's eyes followed Meridian as he took a step closer to her. He bent his knees slightly and pressed his lips against the flesh at the bottom of the V opening of her jacket. Her cleavage had been flirting with him all evening. He put his arm around the small of her back and kissed her lips quickly. He expected Talya to push him away but, when she did not, he kissed her again. Meridian watched thickly lashed lids slowly close over Talya's sultry brown eyes. He used the tip of his nose to caress her cheek and then her neck. She wore a musk fragrance that made him want to linger there. He kissed Talya's neck, and her head fell slightly back. Meridian retraced his path and moved his lips against hers. He encouraged her with his tongue to receive him.

Talya's head began to spin, and everything went black. The flash of blackness disappeared as quickly as it came; it always did. She had grown accustomed to her body's response to highly stressful situations and learned to adapt to cover up its effects. She had let things go too far. She stepped away from Meridian and backed into her room. She gently closed the door so that they did not have to discuss the awkward moment between them. It had been too long since she had been in such an intimate position with a man. She wanted Meridian to kiss her over and over but, at the same time, she remembered. She remembered the fear and pain that so easily took over the love and caring. She could not put herself in that situation again.

It was always the first kiss that did her in. If it were incredible she was hooked. She rested her back against the closed door and tried to catch her breath. The queasy sensation in her stomach and the goose bumps on her arms made Meridian's kiss earn a permanent place in her memory. The kiss struck her as two points better than magnificent.

Meridian's private line rang waking him from his daydream. "Yes, Mrs. Braden?"

His executive assistant announced his two o'clock appointment. He glanced over at the clock. Fifteen minutes early. It was his last appointment of the day, and he hoped it would go quickly so that he could leave early. There were some things he needed to take care of.

"Hello, Mr. Percy. Have a seat." Meridian shook the man's hand.

Mr. Percy nervously sat down in a chair in front of Meridian's desk. He'd worked in the mailroom for the past ten years and had never missed a day of work. He prided himself on that fact, and it was the first thing he shared with Meridian. His hands were ragged, and he picked at his nails to relieve his tension. The uniform he wore was clean and neatly pressed. Meridian respected a man that took the time to make sure his uniform was presentable. Many of the blue-collar employees in his company did not.

Meridian wanted to move the conversation along so he cut in on Mr. Percy's story of the day he was hired by his father. "What can I do for you, Mr. Percy?"

"Well, Mr. Weston, this is a sensitive subject that I need to talk to you about." He continued to pick at his nails.

"Whatever it is will remain between us unless you give me permission to discuss it with someone else. Please be open with me."

Mr. Percy stopped fiddling with his fingernails and looked up at Meridian. "I've got a sickness, and the insurance people sent me this letter saying they won't give me any more benefits." He handed Meridian the worn piece of paper.

Meridian read the letter to confirm what he had been told. "I'm not sure why you came to me with this. I can have my assistant make you an appointment with the benefit manager."

"I'm coming to you because of the reason they stopped my benefits."

Meridian waited for him to continue.

"Mr. Weston, I was diagnosed with the HIV sickness three years ago, and I'm starting to have some medical problems. The insurance won't cover me because they found out. I'm coming to you because I know you're fair, just like your father, and I know you won't stand for it."

Meridian batted his eyes several times trying to gather his thoughts. This subject was way too heavy to handle in a fleeting moment. He did feel the insurance company was unfair, and he wanted his employees to be happy. It was important that they be well compensated for their work. He heard his father's voice: "Always treat the employees with fairness and honesty, and they will be loyal to you and the company."

Meridian formed his words carefully. "Mr. Percy, I am sorry to hear about your health condition. I would like to look into this matter and see what the insurance company's rationale is for its decision."

Mr. Percy rose from his chair. He was doubtful that anything would come from his meeting with the boss.

Meridian read his expression and wanted to offer him some reassurance. "Make an appointment with my assistant to see me in one week. I should have a solution for you by then."

Mr. Percy perked up. "Thank you, Mr. Weston."

Meridian looked over at his clock. He gathered his papers and rushed out of the office before he was detained again. He maintained the open-door policy his father had started when he began the business. It kept him grounded. His employees always knew that there was a recourse to settle any disputes in the company. It was a good practice, but sometimes the policy made for long days. Meridian took the private elevator down to the garage. He normally used the same elevator his employees used, but he was in a hurry and didn't want to spend time making small talk with people he didn't know well.

Meridian used the remote in his hand to open the hatch of his Navigator. The early-evening wind chilled him. A faint blanket of snow was on the ground, making him choose the Navigator as the best option for his hour drive into the city. He tossed his briefcase in the back and slammed the hatch closed. When he started up the engine the radio blasted the sounds of a jazz trumpeter in his ears. It made him jump, and he cursed himself for not remembering to turn it off that morning. His mind was on other things; time to rectify some of them right now.

Meridian rushed through Talya's office door with Kathy close behind him.

"Ms. Stevenson, I'm sorry."

"It's okay." Talya stood to greet Meridian. She expected him to confront her sooner or later. Meridian did not seem to be the type of man to let things fade.

Kathy stood watching their interaction.

Meridian turned to Kathy and excused her. "Thank you."

Kathy looked between Talya and Meridian one last time before she left, closing the door behind her.

Meridian removed his black leather gloves as he spoke. "I'm not going to cause a scene here. I only want to talk to you. You won't return any of my phone calls, so this was the only way for me to talk to you."

Talya ignored the swirling in her stomach and remained professional. "How can I help you?"

"It's been a week since we returned from Chicago, and you won't take my calls. What's going on?"

"It would be best if I dealt with Robert. Or I could have my manager reassign your account."

Meridian walked around the desk and stood in front of Talya. "Don't blow me off like I'm just another client."

"I'm sorry about what happened. I should have been more professional."

Meridian studied Talya's soft, dark eyes and saw something hiding inside. Her voice was cold, but her eyes were very warm and inviting. Maybe he was pushing too hard. Maybe Talya felt boxed into a corner because of their work relationship. He wondered if she knew how much he was worth. Once a woman learned about his wealth they always changed.

Meridian took a step back from Talya. He noticed her posture relax just a bit. "I would like to get to know you on a personal level. I have two tickets to the black-tie premier of the Auto Show this Friday and I'd like to invite you to come with me."

"Meridian, I—"

He stopped her words in mid-sentence. "Think about it and give me a call. Tomorrow?"

"I—"

Meridian held up his hand. "Call me tomorrow."

Talya thought it best not to call Meridian. He would figure out her answer by her lack of a response. Mixing business with pleasure would surely cause problems. She did not have time to invest in a man that left her stomach queasy and the hair covering her arms on end after his kisses. If she ever decided to have another relationship she would do it right. She still needed to complete her self-assessment test.

Meridian realized Talya could only reach him at the office because he never gave her his home telephone number. What was the use of technology if he forgot to use it when he needed to? He could have given her his pager, cell phone, car phone, or home office phone. He forgot. He asked Mrs. Braden to have the answering service put Talya's call in to his home if she should call after hours. She never called. For some reason he could not give up. He rationalized that she was too busy at work to call the very next day. There were three more days until the Auto Show, so he would give her a little push and wait to see what happened.

Talya greeted Robert with her usual smile. Robert embraced her hand tightly.

"What's going on? Is it your birthday or something?" Robert asked after making small talk and noticing all of the roses decorating the tiny office.

"Don't tease me about this, Robert." Talya eased into her chair and pulled it up to her desk.

Robert opened his briefcase on top of his lap and began leafing through papers. "What are you talking about?"

"You don't know?"

Robert looked up over his glasses at Talya.

Talya went inside of the drawer of her desk and handed Robert a small yellow envelope across the desk. When Robert opened the envelope two tickets to the Auto Show fell out, along with a personal note from Meridian.

"My boss sent you all of these flowers? He must have it bad over you. So you're going to the Auto Show this Friday? I've asked Meridian for those tickets every year, and every year he…"

Talya cut in. "I'm not going." She explained her decision to Robert but found she was really trying to convince herself.

"I've never interfered in your personal life, but I do consider you a friend, so I'll offer you some free advice. Go out with him. Meridian is a good guy, and I have inside knowledge that he really is taken with you. Being friends has not tainted our professional relationship. There's no reason to think Meridian and you couldn't have both. Meridian has too much class, and so do you."

Talya remembered the kiss outside of her hotel room in Chicago. Meridian's full lips grazed over the top of her swollen breasts. His mouth was so possessive. For a split second she found herself parting her lips to let his tongue explore her taste, and when he finished she wanted to do the same.

Robert broke in on her thoughts. "It sure would be nice for us to have something to talk about other than business all the time." He went back to shuffling his papers.

The flowers must have done the trick, Meridian thought. He clapped his hands when he listened to Talya's message. She still used her business tone with him. "I'd be happy to go to the Auto Show with you on Friday. Please call me, and we'll make arrangements to meet…" Replay. Replay. Replay.

Talya and Jennifer spent hours driving from mall to mall shopping. They were up against a deadline. They had to find the perfect dress, shoes, purse, and accessories for Friday night—all in one day and on a budget. Talya questioned her decision when she realized how much of her savings she would have to spend to look like she fit in with the wealthy VIP's that would be in attendance. Jennifer talked her into splurging on a dress and pair of shoes for the once-in-a-lifetime event. Jennifer had accessories that Talya could borrow. Now, they needed to get Talya to a beautician at the last minute. Jennifer scolded her friend all day for not giving her more notice of her plans.

Meridian pulled out the piece of paper on which he had written Talya's phone number. He entered the number into his electronic data bank. He took a seat behind the desk in his home office and punched the numbers into the speakerphone. He would call to confirm their date for the next evening. He wanted to make sure there would be no last-minute change of heart.

If Talya had been at home, she would be sitting in the living room laughing at black-and-white reruns on television. Without her there, the house's creaks and moans sounded like the detonation of a bomb.

Rizzo suggested that Jason try the shelters for abused women dotted discretely around the city. He tried to explain to the withered old woman protecting the door that he needed to find Talya desperately. He wasn't like the animals the other women knew as their husbands and boyfriends. He loved Talya more than anything in the world. He never found the right combination of words to make her step aside and allow him to search the premises for his missing girlfriend.

Talya's disregard for his love for her forced him to have to teach her a lesson when she stepped out of line. No matter how awful things became between them, he never enjoyed the rage she pushed him into. Afterward, when she lay bleeding, battered, and bruised, he found it difficult not to feel her pain. Not her physical pain, but her mental anguish. Many times he cried into her breasts as he begged for forgiveness.

Jason cursed himself for going too far. His last frenzy made Talya run from him so far that she could not be found. Jason buried his face in his pillow. "No matter what,

I'll make it up to you Talya. I know you still love me. Everything will be all right once you come back home."

CHAPTER FOUR

"Do you mind if I crash on your sofa tonight? I know I'm not going to feel like driving all the way home tonight," Meridian called from the private bathroom in his office to Robert.

Robert closed his briefcase. "No problem."

"Do you think I'll impress her?"

Robert stood and gave Meridian the once-over. He believed that when dating someone special you always had to make a good impression with the way you dressed and carried yourself. He pushed his glasses up on his nose and walked a circle around Meridian. The suit was new. He was wearing black-on-black; the cut was sharp. The tailor told Meridian it was the latest style. He assured Meridian that no one else would be wearing the exclusive Hugo Boss design this early in the season. Robert stopped to check out his shoes. The shoes should always be shined and without scuff marks. He guessed the shoes were new too.

Robert nodded. "I think Talya will be impressed. You must have spent a bundle."

"Just following your example." Meridian walked back into the bathroom. He went to the cabinet over the sink and got out his comb, brush, and texturizing styling gel.

"My wife would never let me spend that much on a suit."

"I meant to ask you how things were going with you and Rena."

Robert appeared in the doorway. "Better since the vacation but we still have a ways to go." Two years into their marriage and an unmistakable distance began to grow between him and his wife. He hoped that it was just a phase married couples go through, but he wanted to keep it from becoming something more serious.

Meridian broke into Robert's thoughts. "Too much you think?" He stood behind him with a bouquet of flowers.

"Maybe. Her office already looks like a funeral home."

"First dates are murder." Meridian pulled one rose out of the bouquet. "Take these to Rena."

"Will you stay until he gets here?" Talya asked Jennifer. She had not been this nervous about a date since prom night.

"Sure." She fluffed and patted Talya's hair into place. "Are you nervous?"

Talya nodded. "It's been years since I've been out on a date."

"Just be yourself and have a good time."

Talya sighed. She didn't know how to be the happy, outgoing person she used to be before she met Him. It took a lot of work to mold herself into a new person with new attitudes. If dating again became a real possibility, she sure wasn't going back to being scared and timid like she was with him.

Jennifer stood back and looked Talya over, from the pile of curls structured on top of her head to the sheer footing of her pantyhose. "Listen, this guy already likes you, so that's half the battle. There's no way he would be taking you to a three-hundred-and-fifty-dollar-a-person VIP event if he didn't. All you have to do now is see if you're compatible or if he's a total jerk."

"I'm not sure I remember how to act on a date."

"If you get stuck for something to say or feel awkward, touch his arm lightly while you look away in another direction."

"What?" Talya laughed at the thought of her being bold enough to do that.

"Let me tell you about the first date I had with the Reverend..."

Jennifer's only recurring dating partner was the reverend of her church. She happened to attend church the day the new young and handsome reverend took over the congregation. She decided to volunteer to help with the church's medical screening program that day. The reverend left his medical practice to follow his heart, and he would be heading the program. Jennifer, being the only dietitian in the church, quickly volunteered her time.

The first Saturday of the program she showed up dressed in her most sexy business suit. She also monkeyed around with the wires under the hood of her car so it wouldn't start after they were finished working. Dating adventure number one hundred and seventy-eight explained how she knew what to monkey with. The reverend offered to drive her home. They went to grab something to eat and then ended up alone in her apartment. She was nervous about dating a man of the cloth so she remembered a piece of advice someone had given her, and she kept touching his arm at just the right time. She let her hand linger on his arm after laughing at one of his jokes, and he took her hand in his. She closed her eyes and he kissed her politely on her lips.

"Think about what worked for you on your first date with your last boyfriend," Jennifer offered.

The first date with Jason was burned into her memory. How many times did Talya wish she could step into a time machine, travel back in the past, and change the night he asked her out for the first time? If she could do it all over again she would refuse his charms and walk away. Then all of the pain and horrible memories would not be with her now. Her path in life would have been much different. A lot of mistakes would have been avoided.

A collective cheer went up the minute Jason and his friend stepped into the dorm party. When they showed up at a party, everyone knew they would have a good time. The women adored them both. The men admired the body-building giants who were popular in local circles. Talya thought Jason was gorgeous. His friend Rizzo approached her first, but her eyes were glued to the man moving through the crowd greeting everyone as if he were a celebrity. By the time he made his way over to them, she had been captivated by Jason's charm and not by his friend's words.

Jason stood only inches taller than Talya. She remembered how tightly he held her in his big, hard arms, almost crushing her. He told her he went to the gym to work out every single day. He was proud of his body and worked hard at building his muscle mass. Dark skin, as dark as burned chocolate, had never attracted Talya before, but he changed her view on that philosophy. His nose was small and straight. His eyes were the darkest brown she'd ever seen. When he kissed her, fireworks exploded inside of her stomach, making her his for life. Talya never guessed the things that attracted her to Jason would be the very features that signaled his rage and forewarned her of his wrath.

Jason was compassionate and attentive to Talya on their first date. She spent most of the evening in awe of the good-looking, charming man that made her the envy of all of her friends. He focused all of his attention on her. He wanted everything to be just right for her.

Jason was a perfect gentleman that night. A gentle giant that wrapped her vulnerability inside of his muscled strength and guarded her with his life. After seeing a movie, he walked Talya to her dorm room and left after one kiss that reignited the fireworks inside of her stomach. He called her as soon as he got home to tell her good night. Things did not change until a long time later. Talya was so deceived by that first date....

The doorbell chimed, causing Talya to jump and lose her memories. "I don't think I can go through with this."

"Girl, don't be crazy. You'll have a good time. Get your shoes; I'll answer the door."

Talya looked at herself in the mirror, all dressed up, questioning what she could have been thinking to accept Meridian's offer. Her insides were scrambled. She was intrigued and attracted to Meridian, but at the same time afraid of him. She no longer trusted her judgment when it came to dating and investing her emotions in a man. After all, things were so good between her and Jason at first. How could she know that it wouldn't work the same way with Meridian Weston? She was being paranoid; he had never given her any sign of being a violent person. She would have to start dating sometime, why not with someone as perfect as Meridian?

For months, she had resigned herself to focusing on work and never taking another chance with a man. Meridian walked into her life, and the possibility of experiencing the warmth of her dream became real. When he was near, she wanted to run to him and let him take away all of her fears. She took a deep breath and said to herself, Jason is not here. Jason will never be in my life again. I'm going to go out with this nice looking man and have a good time. I'm not truly over Jason until I can live like normal people.

Jason slammed the phone back onto its cradle. She had to know where Talya was hiding. The two had been as thick as thieves in college. There was no way Talya ran away without telling her best friend where she was going. She just disappeared one day. Went to work and never came back. He looked everywhere for her.

Girlfriends. Jason hated them. They were nothing but trouble. The girlfriends were always whispering into his woman's ear, giving her useless advice. That's why he insisted that Talya stay away from her. She didn't need any friends. He was all she needed. He could control her better when there was no outside interference.

"Now what do I do?" Jason went into the kitchen and retrieved the large can of weight gain powder off the top of the refrigerator. He went to another cabinet to get the blender. In his mindless haste, the blender slipped from his fingers and landed on the tiled floor, smashing into pieces. He crossed the kitchen to grab the broom.

"I need you here, Talya. I miss you so much," He said aloud to himself.

"Damn." He plucked a sliver of glass from his middle finger. "This would have never happened if you had been here where you belong." He ground his teeth together. "Wait until I find you."

CHAPTER FIVE

Jennifer came into the bedroom and closed the door behind her. She ran over to Talya, grabbed her hands and started jumping up and down. "He is fine. He didn't look this good at the airport. If you don't go, I will."

Talya smiled while secretly asking herself why Meridian had interest in her. She didn't know what his intentions were with someone like her, but by the way he kissed her, there was definitely some attraction on his part.

After taking another deep breath, Talya walked into the living room.

Meridian felt his pupils dilate at the sight of her. Her covert beauty could not be concealed this night. Describing her as attractive would not do justice to what he saw standing in front of him. If they ever developed a relationship, he would never let her wear a dress that looked so perfect or make up that pulled out all of her inner beauty for every man to see. The dress hugged Talya's waist. The style was simple but elegant. The outline of her thighs and behind made the most intimate parts of Meridian's body respond. She wore heels that were three inches easy, and they made the muscles of her calves flex enough to be noticed. If the opportunity ever arose, he would kiss and caress every inch of her calves before he took her into his arms to seduce her.

Meridian walked over to help Talya put on her coat. "You look very good."

"Thank you. You look very handsome yourself."

"You both look great," Jennifer spoke up. "You make a very handsome couple. Now get out of here; I'll lock up for you."

The opening night of the Detroit International Auto Show was one of the biggest events of the year, and no expense was spared by those participating in the exhibits. The convention hall was filled to capacity with more than seventeen thousand spectators who each paid upwards of three hundred dollars for the honor of attending. The entire cost of admission tickets went to charity, so Meridian never thought twice about his yearly desire to attend the show. Every foreign and domestic auto dealer had a display of their current and upcoming model cars. The elaborate displays took up to nine weeks to complete. The futuristic exhibit of concept cars brought many praises from critics worldwide. The most popular dealers had people lined up for a chance to sit inside of their cars and hear the sales pitch. A well-known soul band from the early eighties provided live music while the crowd buzzed around the convocation.

All of the politicians, recording stars, television stars, and media parading around the convention center did not faze Meridian. His attention remained focused on the delight Talya seemed to get from being surrounded by the majestic decor and elaborate choice of foods. It made him feel good to see her enjoying herself. They walked every inch of the convention center to see all of the new cars, stopping only to take a break to grab something to eat.

Meridian was shopping for a new Corvette, so he focused a lot of attention on getting the details of the car's availability date. He noticed Talya seemed embarrassed when he discussed the sales price with the company representative. He took the salesman's card and promised to call the following week. Talya lightly touched his arm when he asked her opinion of the cars, and he felt the jolt again. He didn't want to be too bold and scare her off, but he took a chance and removed her hand from his arm and held it tightly. When Talya's gait slowed, and she started to have trouble keeping up with his long strides, Meridian suggested they leave.

Once they were settled in, Meridian pulled his BMW away from the curb. "Did you have a nice time?"

"Yeah."

"You sound hesitant with your answer."

"I had a good time, it's just that I felt out of place around all of those important people. It's not a circle I usually travel in."

"I hope I didn't make you feel uncomfortable." He adjusted the temperature gauge to fight off the bite of the cold night.

"No, you were a perfect gentleman."

Meridian smiled. "Are you hungry or anything?" He was trying to find a reason for the night not to end.

Talya patted her stomach. "No, I ate way too much in there."

"There's a restaurant up the street that stays open all night, maybe we could get some dessert."

Talya's feet tightened inside of her shoes. Sharp pains ran across the top of all of her toes. Her arches ached. She could have killed Jennifer for making her wear three-inch heels to a convention center. She wasn't sure if she would be able to walk to her apartment door. Meridian lifting her and carrying her from the elevator flashed in her mind.

"I really want to get out of these clothes." She giggled. "Truthfully, my feet are killing me."

Meridian hid his disappointment and put on his turn signal, easing into the traffic flow on the freeway. "I shouldn't have made you walk as much as we did."

"No, it's not your fault. I shouldn't have worn such high heels."

Boy, was he glad she did.

Meridian didn't want the evening to end this soon. He hoped he wasn't too obvious as he drove a hair below the speed limit. He thought about getting lost or taking side streets all the way to her apartment but he did not want her to think he was some sort of pervert. She lived downtown near the convention center. Two exits after entering the freeway, they were pulling off. Within minutes they were driving through the parking structure of Talya's building.

Meridian watched Talya put her key in the lock. Should he say goodnight and turn away now? Could he steal more of her time tonight? Where had the cocky confidence he had while out on other dates gone? Why did the bashful woman with him make him feel unsure about his every move?

Talya turned to him. "I don't know how to thank you for tonight. I had a really good time."

Meridian felt the same urgency come over him he experienced outside the hotel room door. "You could thank me by inviting me in for a while."

Talya studied his face, finding no answer there. "I'm not—"

Meridian held up his hand to stop her. "Only to talk. We didn't get any time alone tonight." He saw that she was trying to decide. "One hour? I'll rub your feet."

Talya found herself stuck in his deep, syrupy voice. Not to mention the bright, innocent smile he gave her. She could imagine him wearing the crown of class flirt in high school. "One hour, and then I have to call it a night."

Meridian made himself comfortable on the sofa while Talya went into the bedroom and changed her clothes. He found the remote control and flipped through the television stations. He took a look around Talya's apartment. Before their date, he was only able to take in Talya. His father always told him that you could tell a lot about a woman by the way she kept her home. His father said, "Son, when you pick a woman to settle down with, make sure she can provide you with a clean and orderly home."

The olive-brown sofa sat in front of a huge antique oak chest. Talya neatly placed three small blue flowerpots with lush green plants in the middle of the chest. All around them were candles of different shapes, sizes, and fragrances. Meridian sank down into the comfort of the feathery sofa. The matching armchairs side by side to the right of the sofa were covered with a flower pattern in shades of brown, red, and orange. The end table next to him was covered with a contrasting table skirt, a lamp, more candles, and a stack of picture books. Meridian smiled when he noticed how everything had its own perfect place.

He stood and walked over to the three tall windows lined up frame to frame. He pulled back the off-white sheers to observe the view of downtown. He imagined Talya sitting at the desk in front of the window working. Every paper on top of the desk was neatly placed in individual stacks. He smiled when he saw the bulletin board hanging on the wall next to the desk that held scattered papers stacked on top of one another. How could her desk be so neat and the bulletin board so messy?

A quiet tap at the door distracted Meridian. Talya did not answer when Meridian called her name so he went to answer the door.

"Hi, Jennifer. Talya's changing her clothes."

Jennifer stepped into the apartment and closed the door. "I hope you don't mind, but I need to check on my girl before I go to sleep."

Meridian smiled at her loyalty. "Do I look like some sort of nut or something?"

"We girls have to stick together. Plus, I have to warn her not to have sex with you on the first date."

Meridian threw his head back, laughing at her candor. They probably walked together in the mall having the same type of conversations he and Robert had at the bar.

Jennifer laughed with him. "At least not unless she swears she'll give me all the details in the morning."

"Well, if we come to that point in our relationship I better give her something to report."

They laughed together again.

"I like you, Jennifer," Meridian said before finding his place on the sofa.

Jennifer left as quickly as she came. Talya appeared from the bedroom wearing an oversized gray jogging suit. The makeup had been removed, and all of the freckles on her nose and cheeks were visible again.

Meridian looked at the diamond face of his gold watch as she joined him on the sofa. "That took exactly fifteen minutes, so I expect you to add that onto my hour."

Talya smiled. "Done."

"I'll be damned!" Jason mumbled under his breath.

"What's up, man?" Rizzo stopped next to him in the crowded movie theater lobby.

"Look over there; ain't that my girl?"

Rizzo craned his thick neck around. "Talya? Yeah, her hair is different but it looks like her."

Jason was glad he came to the movies after all. He grumbled at first when Rizzo wanted to drive forty minutes away to the new movie theater in the suburbs. Yeah, it was her. He would know Talya anywhere. He loved her more than life. He pictured her face and wondered where she was every single second of the day. All this time, all the phone calls, and BAM! he ran into her in a movie theater.

"What do you want to do?" His friend watched Talya move through the crowd. "Should we snatch her?" he asked without hesitation.

"No, I want to do this right." It was too risky to cause a scene in the movie theater. The police would be there before he had her inside of the car. Besides, he wanted Talya to come back to him of her own free will. He needed her forgiveness for everything he had done. He knew what to say to get her to come back home. They had played out the scene many times. If that didn't work, then he would have to take more drastic steps.

Jason changed his movie ticket and told his friend he'd catch up with him later. He sat in the back of the theater and watched Talya with some woman; they were friends. This was a girlfriend he had never met before. One he hated already.

God, Talya was more beautiful than he remembered. Graceful and innocent to the point of being naive. He had to have her back.

Minutes before the chick flick ended, Jason came up with his plan. He slipped out of the dark theater and casually strolled to the theater where Rizzo watched an action movie, being careful not to attract the attention of the usher standing nearby. He needed to find out where Talya had run to. Rizzo mumbled about having to miss the end of the movie, but he went along with his friend. Talya and the girlfriend were gabbing too much to notice Rizzo pull out of the parking lot behind them.

The girlfriend drove to an expensive apartment building downtown. Jason figured Talya must be hiding out with her. He racked every corner of his brain trying to recognize this new friend. Maybe she had gone to college with Talya.

Jason returned to the downtown apartment two evenings in a row, waiting for Talya to exit the building. She never did. The next time he came in the early-morning hours. He sat in his car, accompanied by Rizzo, conducting their version of amateur police surveillance. Jason had nodded off in the passenger's seat when Rizzo shook him awake. He bolted upright. His friend pointed out the window and without a word, started up the engine of the car. Jason was on edge, afraid Rizzo would lose sight of her car, but he kept silent. They had done this many times before; they would not lose her.

They parked across the street from Brunstown Bank. "She's been in there a long time, Jason."

"I know." He paused to think. "Go in and see if you see her."

His friend looked over at him briefly. His lips curled upward into a devious grin before he jumped from the car. Jason watched the front door of the bank without blinking. Several minutes later, his friend jogged across the street to the car.

"Well?"

"Well, she's not in line; she works there." He flipped a business card between his finger. "It didn't take long to talk one of the honeys behind the counter out of a little info."

Jason snatched the card. He laughed. "I owe you one, Rizzo."

"You owe me too many to count when it comes to you and Talya."

Talya curled up in Jennifer's chair with a bowl of cereal. The food had become a staple with her busy work schedule. "So what dating adventure do you have to share for fourth dates?"

Jennifer sat on the floor at her coffee table cutting out pictures of food from magazines. She pasted them on fluorescent poster boards according to food groups. She planned to use them with the younger kids at the church the next Saturday.

Jennifer shook her head. "I can't think of anything. I'll have to look through my journals." Jennifer came home after every date and recorded the event in her journal. She started doing this in high school and had stacks of journals in the top of her bedroom closet. "Maybe you can go make your own adventure and share it with me."

Talya joined her on the floor to help search the magazines. She leafed through the first one in the stack. "How's the reverend?"

"I didn't see him all weekend. Even after church on Sunday."

"Why not? Did you have a fight?" Talya picked up the scissors and started to trim a picture of a fruit basket.

"I think he wants to have sex with me, but the guilt of committing adultery is getting to him."

Talya stopped cutting and waited for Jennifer to elaborate.

"We got into it pretty hot and heavy the last time he was here and he—you know—in his pants." Jennifer nonchalantly told Talya.

Talya covered her mouth and tried to hold back her shock. "For real?"

Jennifer nodded, concentrating on the work in front of her. "I told him no big deal, but he was embarrassed about the whole thing. I'll call in a few days and talk to him about it. He was so upset about it he'll probably pray for me over the phone and insist I get baptized again."

Talya giggled. She flipped past several pages of the magazine until she found another picture.

Jennifer looked over at her friend. "You are going out with Meridian again, aren't you?"

"I'm not sure." It was only a matter of time before Jason would find her, and then she would have to run again. No use in starting anything serious with Meridian. After experiencing the tranquility that being away from Jason had given her, she could not go back to that roller-coaster ride of emotions and physical pain.

"What kind of answer is that? This guy is gorgeous, rich and crazy about you. How could you even consider brushing him off?"

"I'm not sure that I'm ready to be involved in a serious relationship."

"I know, you have to concentrate on your work," Jennifer said sarcastically. "Listen, tell me honestly, do you like Meridian?"

Talya closed the magazine and placed it on top of the table in front of her. The question brought back memories of their date. He was so handsome. His kisses melted her like ice cream on a hot day. "I like him," she admitted.

"Then please, give yourself a break. You need more self-confidence. Stop philosophizing about relationships and jump into one. Maybe your future is with him, and you won't ever have to concentrate on your work again."

Talya wanted to slam down the phone, but her hand was gripping the receiver, and she couldn't move.

"Precious? I missed you." He was humble.

"How did you get this number?" Talya's heart was pounding. How did he find out where she worked? She felt the urge to run in the bathroom before she relieved herself at the desk. It was the same feeling she would get while hiding in the closet for hours, afraid to come out and use the bathroom because Jason sat waiting for her outside the door with the small shovel from next to the fireplace.

Jason ignored the question. "When can I see you?"

"Don't come around here, please. It's over between us for good this time." She could not stop the trembling in her voice.

"It's not over between us until I say it is." Jason's tone remained humble.

"I'm seeing someone else." Talya hoped it would make him go away to think she had moved on with her life. In reality she knew that with Jason resurfacing in her life, her short reunion with the dating scene was over.

"Tell him it's over because I'm back in the picture now. I'll forgive you for that since it has been so long." He wouldn't make a big deal about it just yet. They would settle those issues once he had her back at home. Then they would have a long talk about her recent behavior.

"Please don't call me again. It's over." Talya put the phone down.

Kathy buzzed her line announcing another phone call. Jason had called right back. Talya slammed the phone back down when she heard his voice.

The wave of darkness passed through her mind, taking with it a little piece of her memory. It was all starting again. Jason had found her. Believing that her calendar was empty for the day, she grabbed her purse and hurried into her manager's office. She apologized for having to leave early and explained she was too under the weather to stay. Her pale, wide-eyed appearance convinced her manager, and she left for the day.

CHAPTER SIX

Robert tapped the face of his watch. They were both timely people; Talya was never late for one of their meetings. Granted, this was a rare occasion for her to come to his office, but she had agreed when he told her about the large volume of work he needed to complete. He dialed her at the bank. Kathy told him she'd gone for the day. Now he worried. Maybe something happened on her ride over to see him.

"Meridian," Robert said over the phone, "I need Talya's number at home. We had a meeting scheduled for thirty minutes ago and she's still not here."

Meridian straightened his back. "Should I go check on her?"

"No, I'm sure she's all right. I just want to call her to reschedule."

Meridian could read the truth behind his friend's voice but he did not question him further. He rattled off the treasured phone number. "Let me know if something's wrong?"

"Yeah, I will."

Talya had completely forgotten their meeting. It happened sometimes. The darkness swooped down on her and snatched something from her mind. Her head could only hold a certain number of thoughts, and when it was full, something fell away. When fear or stress invaded her head, something was lost. It was like blacking out while fully awake. No doctor or counselor could tell her with any certainty if it was because of stress or because of the injury.

Talya knew that it started that day in the kitchen. She had lost the memory of why they were arguing and what led up to the accident. The only thing she remembered was waking up on the floor in front of the refrigerator with Jason standing over her. He looked scared. Her face ached. After that, she had the tendency to lose pieces of her life.

Jason yanked the phone from the wall and hurled it across the room. "She better recognize just how good she had it with me." His voice echoed off the walls of the house. No one was there to hear his words or quiver in fear of what his anger might bring. There was no way he would allow Talya to disrespect him that way. The past was the past. He hadn't beaten her for almost a year. It didn't matter she'd been gone away from him for that long. They loved each other, and just because he had to discipline her sometimes didn't mean she had the right to leave him. That wasn't a good enough reason.

Jason took heavy steps across the living room. He stopped in the middle of the floor when he saw a picture of Talya on the mantel over the fireplace. "I tried to be good enough for you." She always made him feel inadequate. He had tried hard to complete college like all of his siblings, but it wasn't the scene for him. If not for the fact that the college was trying to build a wrestling team, he would have never been admitted with his high school record. He tried and failed. His future was in pro body building, maybe WWF wrestling.

The body building arena he could conquer. Whenever he and Rizzo returned from a big competition, usually victorious, he tried to share his happiness with her, but she always made him feel less than her. Insecurity, Rizzo had labeled it. That's when he realized that he had to show her. Show her that when he thought something was important, she better think it was important too. He was not a loser, no matter what the rest of his family called him.

Jason moved to the mantel and gently lifted the silver-framed picture. He had been pleasant when he spoke with Talya, but she tried to make him feel inadequate again. He wanted her to listen to his apology and forgive him for the last beating. She brushed him aside as if he had never meant anything to her. She mentioned another man. That was a small obstacle that he could take care of if she couldn't. He wanted her to come home of her own volition. He needed that cleansing. Obviously, she wanted to do things the hard way.

Survival skills were second nature to Talya. Jason's phone calls made her plan of survival resurface. Like a robot, she methodically placed clothing into a suitcase and hid it in the back of her bedroom closet. She withdrew enough money from her bank account for a plane ticket, hotel room, and food and slid it into a discrete inside pocket of the suitcase. She checked twice to make sure that all of the important documents she needed were also inside of the pocket. A duplicate set of car and apartment keys were added to the survival kit. She needed to talk to someone about Jason in case she needed to call for help and couldn't reach a phone. She decided against that part of the plan. She did not want to endanger anyone else.

Now came the worst part, the waiting. Whenever her line rang at work she lifted it with dreaded anticipation that it would be Jason again. Time passed, and he did not call again which lulled Talya into a false sense of relief. Maybe he was contemplating his next move. Maybe he had finally gotten the message.

Talya inhaled deeply, and she relaxed when Meridian came to mind. She smiled as she punched figures into the calculator on her desk. She had the opportunity of a life-time right in front of her. When she was with him, things were different. He gave her the encouragement she never received from Jason to succeed at work. He listened to her when they talked as if her words held some merit. His remarks were kind. His touches were tender. He always greeted her with a smile. Their interactions were filled with emotions she did not know she still possessed.

Talya marked her place on the expense sheet with a well-manicured nail. She used her other hand to continue to punch numbers into the keypad of her calculator. Meridian had a pull on her heart. He made her believe that there were men in the world that would put her best interests in front of their own wants or needs. He treated her as if she were a rare jewel when they were together. When they were apart, he always called to ask how her day was going. Days she could not have lunch with him, he sent her a meal via delivery service. Fresh flowers filled a vase on the corner of her desk every day. After the trauma of her previous relationship, his small acts of consideration meant all the world to her.

Why shouldn't she have someone as wonderful as Meridian in her life? For so many years she had been made to believe she was inferior and not worthy of being loved. What if she and Meridian were meant to be together? Talya's mind wandered to a dreamy future. Losing her place on the balance sheet, she cleared the calculator's readout and began to crunch the numbers again.

The door to her office swung open. "Your next appointment is here." Kathy bluntly announced before disappearing in a swirl of red. Did she categorize Talya as stuck up? Whatever she thought, she definitely resented her working at Brunstown Bank.

Talya ignored Kathy's hostility as usual. "Robert, how are you?" She smiled as he took a seat in front of her desk.

"I should be asking how you are. You worried me when you missed our appointment. Meridian bugged me all day about you."

Talya watched as he settled his briefcase on the edge of her desk and began searching for the bank statements he had prepared for their meeting.

"I'm sorry. I wasn't feeling too well that day. Once I went home, I climbed into bed and didn't wake up until the next morning."

Robert never looked up from inside of his briefcase. The lies came so easily. After years of explaining bumps and bruises, she could spin a tale that Dr. Suess couldn't match. The rule being keep it simple. The simpler the lie, the less likely someone would question it.

Talya took the statements and attached checks and began punching them into her computer screen.

"Things going well with you and Meridian?" Robert asked.

Talya's fingers never lost their rhythm.

"That smile tells me everything I need to know." Robert's deep chuckle filed the room. "I see he's still sending flowers." Robert tilted the vase of white roses toward his nose. "He's got it bad for you."

Talya's fingers froze above the keyboard. The most innocent statements triggered the most vile memories. *He's got it bad for you,* Rizzo pleaded with her as she sat on the edge of the stretcher in the emergency room with her dislocated shoulder in a sling. *Give him another chance. He feels really bad about what he did.*

"Talya?" Robert's hands were planted on the surface of her desk, his face inches from hers.

"Yes? I'm sorry?"

Robert pushed his glasses up on the bridge of his nose. "Are you sure you're feeling better?"

Talya nodded and began typing the numbers into the spreadsheet again. Jason's phone call had affected her more than she realized. Do I leave? Is it best to stay put? If he knows where I work, why hasn't he come here to force me back home? Is it possible for someone to change as drastically as he would need to change to become a good person? He had done it before; changed from a dream into a nightmare.

"Hello, Mom." Jason's stress left him when he heard the sound of her comforting voice. The mellow sound of her southern drawl always warmed him and put him on his best behavior. She was more of a mother to him than his own.

"Is this Jason?"

"Yes, ma'am."

"You sound like something's wrong. How's Talya?"

Being a city boy made it hard to understand the words she spoke as they flowed together in one long sentence. "That's why I called. She took off again."

He rushed on when he heard her gasp over the phone line. "I found out where she works, but I'm having trouble convincing her to come home. You know how she forgets things, I'm worried about her being out on her own. She won't even give me her home phone number."

"I'm sorry, honey. Talya has always been too independent. I've told her myself that she should learn how to take care of you and your house and give up on those wild dreams she always had."

"I know you're in my corner, Mom. Wouldn't have been together as long as we have been if you weren't helping me to hold it all together." His voice involuntarily cracked as he remembered her numerous acts of kindness.

"If there was anything I could do—"

"There may be something you can do...."

CHAPTER SEVEN

Meridian arrived at Talya's door Valentine's Day night with two-dozen yellow roses in a beautiful crystal vase. He thought the vase would go well with the decor of her apartment, and it did. The gift was a gesture of the natural kindness that Talya was beginning to realize Meridian possessed. She threw her arms around him to thank him. Meridian took the opportunity to hold her and pull her lushness into him.

Talya stared at Meridian as he drove the Navigator to his house. He was wearing rich blue jeans that outlined his body. The jeans were so snug she wondered why he bothered to wear a belt. They hugged his muscled thighs with every movement he made. Talya had watched him as he walked out of her apartment and felt the urge to reach out and grab his perfectly round, well proportioned behind. And the jeans fit even better in the front. The button-down shirt accentuated his muscular chest and Talya could imagine how it felt to rest her head there. She told herself that she would be bold enough to do that—she wanted to be bold enough to do that.

"How many cars do you have?" Talya asked as the darkness swallowed them. They were driving down winding and twisting roads that were illuminated only by the headlights of the sports utility vehicle. The effortless skill with which Meridian navigated the complicated maze of streets told Talya he was experienced with the direction of travel.

"Three—the BMW, my Corvette, and this."

"Which one do you like best?"

Meridian shrugged. "They all serve their own purpose so I guess I would have to say"—he glanced over to her and smiled—" whichever one you're sitting in."

Talya's eyes sparkled, and her cheeks warmed. She turned to the window. His obvious flirtation was welcomed. She had forgotten how flattering it could be to know a man felt an attraction to you.

"You live a long way away from your office."

"I warned you. You're not afraid, are you? Don't think I'm going to get you out here in this deserted area and take you prisoner, although—"

"Now you are scaring me." Talya hit his arm with a feather-light punch. She wanted to see if the muscles were real.

They drove the rest of the way to Meridian's house in silence. Talya laid her head back on the headrest and listened to the crystal-clear sounds of jazz coming from the stereo. Her body melted into the soft leather of the seat. She felt at ease with him. She relaxed when she was with Meridian. Jason always kept her in a state of nervous antic-ipation that left her unable to eat or sleep.

The darkness made it impossible for Talya to see the house or grounds clearly, but she was able to make out the enormous size of the property by the lighting scheme along its perimeter. She surveyed the elaborate landscape as they drove up the L-shaped driveway. Meridian stopped at the end of the long driveway and entered a code on the overhead console between the sunvisors until the garage door began to lift. Inside were the black BMW and the candy-apple-red Corvette convertible.

"You live here alone?" The house was large; she could see that.

"All alone." He opened the door and helped Talya out of the Navigator. "I came with Robert to see this house about a year ago. Weston Realty was considering purchasing it to sell. Once I walked into the house, I knew I wanted to live here. It's too large for a single man, but I let myself have this one indulgence."

Talya raised her perfectly arched eyebrow, questioning his definition of indulgence.

"Well," Meridian conceded, "this and the cars."

They entered the house from the garage and walked into the kitchen. The large kitchen was any cook's dream. It had been designed with a built-in oven, refrigerator, dishwasher and trash compactor. The brown marble island near the double sink matched the tans and yellows of the kitchen perfectly. A rack of pots and pans hung suspended near the ceiling with hooks and chains over the island. Before Talya could take it all in, an older man appeared.

"Good evening, Mr. Weston." The man lowered his gray topped head in acknowledgment of Meridian and then Talya.

"Mr. Martin, this is Talya Stevenson. Mr. Martin is my cook. If you haven't guessed, I can't cook. I'd have to eat out every night if it weren't for Mr. Martin."

"This is true." Mr. Martin greeted Talya and then turned to Meridian. "I'm glad to see new life in this house."

Meridian became flustered by his remark. He nervously offered an explanation to Mr. Martin's remark. "I've never invited a woman to my house before."

Talya's heart fluttered. Did this mean he considered her special?

Mr. Martin told Meridian everything was as he requested. Meridian gave him the following Monday off and said goodnight. Meridian persuaded Mr. Martin to spend part of his Valentine's Day cooking the dinner for two by paying him a bonus and, since he was so accommodating, Meridian was giving him an extra day off.

Talya watched the exchange between the fatherly looking cook and Meridian. The employee-employer relationship was evident, but Meridian respected Mr. Martin in his tone and his act of thoughtfulness. These qualities were so different from what Talya had grown to expect from a man. She could see herself falling too hard and too fast for Meridian if she didn't proceed with caution.

They walked through the kitchen into the formal dining room. Mr. Martin had arranged two place settings at a table that would easily accommodate twelve. Everything on the table was red, pink, and white in honor of Valentine's Day. Meridian lit the cluster of candles between their place settings and returned from the kitchen with two plates of food. He went back into the kitchen and came out with a Valentine's cake. The icing was white with red and pink borders and decorations. Everything tasted wonderful. After dinner, they took the cake and a gallon of vanilla ice cream into the den to eat as they watched television.

After dinner, they moved to Meridian's favorite room in the house, the den. He spent most of his time there. The room looked like the safe haven of a man needing refuge. There were two oversized off-white sofas positioned back to back. One faced the big screen TV and entertainment center. The other faced a marble fireplace whose hearth occupied the middle third of the wall. Mr. Martin had started the fire before he left. There were chairs and ottomans of various sizes, colors, and textures around the fireplace. The walls were gray on one side of the room and parchment on the other three. Meridian turned off the lamps in the room by the wall switch. He used another switch to turn on the recessed lighting. He wanted to create the perfect mood so he didn't turn them up too high—just enough to see Talya's lips.

"Make yourself comfortable." Meridian put the cake and ice cream on the coffee table and disappeared to retrieve the movies he had rented earlier.

Talya sat on the sofa nearest the television and waited for Meridian. She found herself shifting in her seat in anticipation of his return. Meridian was so easy to be with that there was no reason for her to doubt his purpose. She did not know if she was more worried about his motives or her own. Watching him across the table at dinner definitely gave her ideas.

"I didn't know what you wanted to watch, so I picked several movies."

Talya laughed at him when she looked up and saw him standing in front of her with an assortment of movies. He also held a bottle of white wine and two glasses. She helped him by taking the movies from him and placing them on the coffee table.

"Are you laughing at me?"

"You went out of your way a little bit."

"I think you're worth it." He was embarrassed by his nervousness. He wanted everything to be right for Talya. He hadn't realized that bringing a woman to his house would be so traumatic for him. It meant the end of a way of life and hopefully the start of another. He was ready to go there with Talya, but he was not sure she was on the same page. Maybe he would calm down if he drank a glass of wine.

"Why don't we sit by the fire?" Meridian suggested.

Talya helped him grab everything and place it by the other sofa. She grabbed one of the overstuffed floor pillows and sat on the floor with her back against the sofa. Meridian joined her after he handed her a glass of wine and turned on the stereo.

"I know you went to a lot of trouble for me, and I want to thank you. No one has ever treated me like this before."

"You're always thanking me; stop it." He smiled. "I do these things because I want to. No gratitude is needed."

Now Meridian felt better. A long breath escaped between his teeth, taking with it the rigid posture he had adopted. He put his arm around Talya and pulled her over to him. She smelled like fresh flowers. He ran his fingers along the soft silk collar of her blouse. She was always so feminine and so soft and smelled so good. A true woman. Not a diva: a regular, down south, soul sister of a woman. He remembered the downy feeling of her hair the last time they were together. He placed his chin on the top of her head to see if the softness was still there. This time he also noticed the faint baby powder scent of her hair.

Talya knew what would happen next; he would kiss her. She wanted to kiss him. She had been thinking about it since he licked his lips after biting into a piece of buttered shrimp at dinner. The intensity of his eyes made her aware that he had other things on his mind. The fear she had about her poor judgment of men made her chest tighten. If she was wrong this time she would have to question her ability to make any rational decisions.

"I didn't mean to insult you the other night by asking you…" Meridian let his voice trail off hoping Talya would save him from his embarrassment. During their last date, when their kisses grew out of control, he let his thoughts pass over his lips and had asked Talya if he could spend the night at her place. He had slipped back into his old way of dating women for a brief moment. The second the words became audible he wanted to take them back. It was not the right time; no matter how much his body screamed to sample the hidden passion behind her coy femininity.

"Don't worry about it."

"I'm glad you still wanted to see me." He placed his hand on Talya's thigh. The jolt shot through his fingertips, up his arm so unexpectedly that he almost pulled his hand away. There was something really wrong with him, he thought, or something really right about Talya. He did not want to figure it out right now; he wanted to kiss her. He took away her glass of wine and placed it on the nearest table. He had his eyes on her thighs from the moment she opened the door when he arrived at her apartment. The jeans she wore hugged her body so tightly that he vowed to never take her anywhere again that she could not wear jeans. The only make up Talya wore tinted her lips and her eyes leaving her freckles easy to find. He did not want his lips to miss a single freckle.

Meridian kissed her several times before he felt the urgency overcome him. He stroked her lips with his tongue until he felt the heat of Talya's breath marking his opening into her mouth. He slid his tongue between her lips as slowly and seductively as a raindrop glides down a windshield. The urgency did not subside; it became more intense. He slid his tongue in deeper and deeper trying to feed the hunger. He could not stop the whirling in his stomach caused by the urgency. The only experience Meridian could equate the urgency to was the feeling he got the second before orgasm, but even that was not close to what he was feeling now. It was uncontrollable and made him hold Talya a little too tight and put his tongue a little too far into her mouth. The urgency subsided, and his mind exploded when Talya touched her tongue to his. Seeing that she was giving him the release he needed, he let her take control and move her tongue inside of his mouth.

Meridian had never experienced any sensation so deeply, and he did not want it to end. He leaned back onto the floor taking Talya with him. He held her tightly around the waist while she gave him more kisses. Only after he could not beg her into kissing him anymore did he release her. Then he kissed her nose and cheeks, leaving no freckle untouched. It was just as he imagined.

Meridian knew in his head that Talya made it clear that they were not going to the next level, but his body kept telling him that there was a possibility. He eased her down onto the carpet and positioned himself on top of her. The urgency of the kiss pulled him in like water down a swimming pool drain. He had to go farther and farther to feed the hunger. The sensation would cease if Talya would do her magic, or maybe if he could move into second gear. He was not in control of his emotions when he was with her, and that scared him into trying to satisfy the urgency.

Knowing that emotions and not lust controlled him made Meridian shudder. He could control his lust. Lust would drive him to get what he needed, and then he could walk away. The emotions Talya was awakening inside of him confused him. The void he usually filled with uncommitted sex expanded when their nights together ended. The normal route of keeping himself from falling into the black had not appealed to him. Since the day he walked into Brunstown Bank and met Talya Stevenson.

"Meridian." Talya called his name, bringing him back into himself. She put her hand on his chest and gently pushed him back. He consumed her with his kisses making her feel as if she would suffocate.

"Sorry." He didn't move. "Just kiss me. Please." Her kisses were the only thing that cured the urgency his body felt.

Meridian placed his hands on each side of Talya's face and moved his full, moist lips gently against hers. Talya put her lips against his. He opened his mouth and surrounded her lips with his. Then Talya let her tongue enter into his hot cavern and search the darkness for the source of his urgency. She found it and Meridian's body responded letting Talya know. He didn't let Talya stop soothing his need until she took his hands off her face and turned her head.

Meridian showered Talya's neck with kisses. Most of his body relaxed—excluding the part he pressed against Talya's thighs hoping to persuade her to rethink her original position.

"You're very intense when you kiss," Talya whispered into his ear.

He sampled her freckles. "Only when I kiss you." He moved to nibble her neck. "Overwhelming?"

"Overpowering. Breathtaking."

"Good?"

"Great."

"More?" Meridian looked into Talya's eyes.

Talya closed her eyes. Deep breath. "More."

Talya struggled to admit that she wanted him to kiss her. She hungered for him as much as he appeared to hunger for her. The fear that she would have no one to blame but herself if Meridian hurt her was always present. It made her question the need Meridian stirred in her. She battled with herself over whether she should give in to his seductive kisses or run away from him in the other direction.

Meridian rolled over onto his back, taking Talya with him. He wanted to lie there with his eyes closed and let her take over the fight to keep the urgency from coming back. He lay with his arms at his side and let Talya kiss him. He opened his eyes when she pulled her mouth away and sat up straddling his middle with her shapely thighs. He watched her face as she ran her hands up and down his chest and across his abdomen.

"Talya," he said when he started to throb against the snug fit of his jeans, "I like what you're doing but unless you want to accept my earlier offer, we better watch a movie now."

Talya felt her face become hot. She wished she had the courage to tell him that she felt his heat, and that it was not as strong as her own.

Meridian pulled her body to his and rolled over on top of her. One more kiss, and he'd see how far she would go. He could see that she was wavering. It wasn't like he would be using her. He really liked Talya and planned on spending as much time with her as she would allow. So he saw no harm in trying to coax her into giving in to the feeling.

Meridian kissed her tenderly. First her freckles, then her neck. When he nibbled her neck, her breathing changed. A smooth Erikah Badu record came on the radio, and he hummed in Talya's ear as he licked the inside and gently bit her lobe. Then he kissed her mouth, making a conscious effort to control himself. He felt her softness under him and moved his body over hers.

Talya became wrapped up in the music and the kisses. She let her head fall back into the cushion of the carpeting.

Meridian did not chase her lips. He moved his body next to hers and slowly unbuttoned her blouse. He kissed her chocolate cocoa-colored skin. He knew this record well, and the radio station was playing the remix, which meant he could take his time before the rhythm changed. He loved the bras that opened in the front. He kissed her breasts as he released the clasp. He filled his large hands. Talya took a deep breath when he took her into his mouth. Meridian was bursting out of his pants. His hand found her thigh and then the special place he wanted to see more of.

"Meridian."

No! He wanted to scream. "Yeah?" He breathed into her ear and moved his hand to her breasts again.

"Let's watch the movie."

"Um-huh." He kissed her neck and kept stroking her breasts. He found her lips with his. She kissed him, but not as easy as before. She was resisting. He ran his hand over her tight belly. He used his finger to trace circles on her stomach; big circles, little circles, all around her navel until the tension was gone. He moved smoothly on top of her and pushed against her.

"Meridian, stop."

But the record was still playing. "Listen to the music."

Meridian knew Talya wanted to give in, but was afraid of something, so he tried to put her at ease. He kept moving on top of her. She tried to wiggle away from him but he took her movements to mean something else. He became more aroused and demonstrated this to her.

The blackness came over Talya, and she forgot where she was and who she was with for a brief moment. Jason would come home drunk and climb on top of her....

"Please, stop." She tried to push Meridian off of her.

The sound of Talya's voice alarmed Meridian. The voice that should be reserved for use in the bedroom was quivering from fear as she shoved him off her. He moved next to her on the floor. Talya sat up and straightened her clothes.

"Are you okay?" Meridian ran his fingers through Talya's hair and pushed it behind her ear so that he could see her profile. He could see that she was not. Her hands were shaking as she tried to button her blouse. Meridian removed her hands and buttoned it for her.

Talya moved to the sofa, and Meridian followed. He took her in his arms and she stiffened. You have a fear of intimacy. That's expected with what you have experienced with Jason. It takes time. You'll get past it in time. How long? Talya wished she could ask her counselor. She was attracted to Meridian, and he probably thought her a nutcase now.

"Hey." Meridian used her shoulders to turn her to face him.

Talya rested her head in the comfort of his firm chest.

"Nothing is going to happen that you don't want to happen," Meridian assured her, holding her tightly. More than his strong caresses upset her.

Talya sat up. "I should be getting home."

"Wait a minute. We should talk first."

Talya averted her eyes. Embarrassment and paranoia made it hard to look at Meridian.

"I am very attracted to you, and I think you're attracted to me, but I can't help but notice that you always pull away from me. I'm not talking about sex—I can understand if you're not ready for that. I'm talking about whenever we seem to be getting close to each other emotionally you pull away."

Talya wanted to go home immediately. She did not want to have a heartfelt discussion with Meridian. Confusion swirled around her. Her body wanted him, but her mind would not allow it.

"Is there someone else in your life?"

"No, nothing like that."

"Do you want to keep seeing me? Are you attracted to me?"

Talya nodded. Her body's addiction to his kisses kept her from denying her obvious attraction to him.

"I'm getting some mixed signals from you. What is it? Why do you pull away from me? Why can't you get caught up in what's happening between us and let go?"

Talya sat back against the sofa and stared at the fire. How could she tell him that a crazy man stalked her? Were there any words to explain the fear paralyzing her ability to trust him? No, there weren't. A half truth would suffice. "It's been a long time since I've dated."

Meridian rubbed his hand across his beard. "Why?"

"I had a bad relationship, so I haven't been interested in getting into another."

Meridian sighed. "Is that all? I thought you were going to tell me you were recently released from prison."

Talya could not help but laugh with him.

"Listen, that guy was a fool. I know if you give me a chance, you'll find I'm not a bad guy. Do you think you can do that?"

"I've been trying, but sometimes it's hard. The relationship was really bad."

"I want you to forget that other guy." He let the shadow that crossed her face go unmentioned. "That's his loss and my gain. I really like you, and I want to give this a try. So, unless you kick me to the curb, I'm staying around."

Talya smiled at his reassuring words.

"Now, let's watch a movie before I get into more trouble."

Two movies and two bowls of melted ice cream later, Talya fell asleep in Meridian's lean arms. He shifted, and her eyes sluggishly opened.

"You can stay the night, and I'll drive you home after breakfast—if you want to leave."

Meridian touched her nose.

"No, I better go home."

Meridian used his softest words and most seductive smile to try to persuade Talya to stay. He felt her begin to emotionally withdraw from him, so he reluctantly gave in and drove her home.

"Please, sit with me." Meridian patted the sofa next to him. It was late, and their night together was about to end. "Are you okay? I didn't mean to push you too far." Meridian took her hand in his.

"I'm not ready to…"

Meridian placed his finger over Talya's lips. "I understand." He relaxed and put his arm around her shoulders. They recapped the evening. He asked her out to the movies for the following weekend. She accepted his invitation without hesitation, and Meridian sighed out loud.

"Did you think I would say no?" Talya asked.

"Are you really unaware of the effect you're having on me?"

Talya looked away, feeling her face get warm.

They sat quietly holding hands. A sadness fell on his shoulders. What went on was a good thing, the best thing, but he felt sadness as it came to an end.

Meridian looked over at Talya and brushed her hair away. He spoke softly, noticing that his voice sounded wobbly. "I better be going." He stroked the softness of her hair again. He hoped Talya would ask him to stay with her.

Their kisses were overwhelming. Talya could not even attempt to deny that fact. The emotion was so strong that she wanted to run away, but her legs would not move. She knew that if she stood up, she would stagger, and Meridian would know that she was shaken by his simultaneous tenderness and aggression.

"Did I ruin the night for you?"

Meridian shook his head. "No, you didn't. I always have a wonderful time with you." He looked down at his lap, embarrassed that she might notice how she stimulated him. "I just—" He did not know how to explain. "I've never felt like that from kissing before."

"Is that good or bad?" Talya did not want to tell him that she felt the same way. It would be so easy to persuade her to do something that she might regret later. Sex too soon would complicate things. She was still trying to allow herself to enjoy what she had found in him.

"Definitely good." Meridian pulled her into his arms. "Don't you feel it too?"

Talya nodded, but did not lift her head from his chest.

"Whew." He released a long breath through his teeth. "I would have died if you asked me what I was talking about."

Talya giggled at his honesty.

Meridian continued his firm stroke through Talya's hair. He wanted to kiss her again but knew that he would not be able to leave if he did. He would feel the urgency of his body pulling him to Talya, and then he would have to try to talk her into letting him share her bed for the night. He did not want their first time together to happen because he said the right line, making her give in to him. He wanted it to be more meaningful than that. As he stroked Talya's hair, he hoped she was picturing what their first time together would be like too.

CHAPTER EIGHT

The outcome of their debate didn't satisfy Meridian. The original plan was for him to pick Talya up after work and take her back to his place, where she would dress for the dinner party. Now, she had to work late to clear up an accounting error with an important client.

Meridian and Robert's poker buddies gave a dinner party every month. They alternated hosting the party, and this month Meridian would entertain. The group of friends were all involved in the real estate business in some capacity. They were all in the same age range and developed an informal friendship when they discovered that, as black businessmen, they were encountering the same roadblocks in building up their businesses. They met at a bar one evening and from there they hosted poker parties, dinners, and other activities to network and have fun together.

The group's get-togethers ranged from black-tie formal to bowling and beer. Meridian had spent many hours of planning with his cook, Mr. Martin, and finally gave in to his suggestions for a formal dinner party. At these monthly get-togethers wives and girlfriends were welcomed, but they were banned from the poker parties.

Talya had been hesitant about accepting Meridian's invitation to the dinner party. When he called her office and she was still working, he worried that she might have changed her mind about attending. He worried about her all the time; about every little thing. He pushed the button on his speakerphone, which connected him to Robert's office. Meridian ignored Robert's grumbling advice as he instructed him to escort Talya to his house. Understanding that his good advice was being wasted on his overprotective friend, Robert agreed to bring Talya to the party along with his wife.

Meridian finished up his work week and headed home. Getting out of the city at five o'clock on a Friday was a true test of character. The traffic stood still. Meridian thrust the gearshift of his Navigator into park. He wanted to have enough time to get dressed without being rushed. The stress lines gathering on his forehead disappeared when he remembered his last date with Talya.

A horn sounded, bringing him back into the present. He took the Navigator out of park and inched one car length forward. He dialed Robert from the mobile phone secured to the console between the bucket seats. Robert assured him once again that he would bring Talya to the party and then rushed him off the phone with one piece of advice. "Stop smothering her. I know this relationship stuff is new to you, but give the woman room to breathe."

"Exactly how much room do you think she requires?" Meridian taunted his friend.

"She should be able to take in a breath without you keeping count. Enough space to know that you care and aren't far away if she needs you."

Meridian held his tongue. Robert's wisdom with relationships baffled him. Especially since Robert had only been serious about one woman in his life; and he'd married her.

Meridian checked in with Mr. Martin before barricading himself in his bedroom to get dressed; dinner was on schedule. He stepped from the bathtub and wrapped himself in a lush black towel. He cleared the steam from the mirror over the sink with his forearm and examined his fresh fade and shave. Good thing he had a standing appointment every Thursday after work. He glanced at the wall clock. He still had enough time to relax and grab a quick nap before he had to get dressed. Mr. Martin was orchestrating the caterers and handling the last-minute preparations for the dinner party.

Meridian climbed into bed and covered his nude body with a sheet. Robert might have a point. He would make sure that Talya was comfortable with his associates and then he would leave her to make her own friends. He folded his arms behind his head. The tent in the sheet reminded him of how long it had been since he sought the comfort of a woman. His frequent travels took him to all corners of the country. The stress of negotiating deals, and the loneliness of travel, made it necessary for him to have an available woman in every big city. The encounters were a convenience to both parties, with no pressure and no hassles. These brief encounters had ceased since he met Talya.

The day Meridian walked into Brunstown Bank and met the incredible Talya Stevenson, his life changed and all his old routines became obsolete. No other woman in the world could capture the essence of his urgency and tame it until it dwindled and disappeared like Talya could. His late nights at work were diminishing. He decreased the number of business trips he scheduled. In between every meeting he dialed Talya to find out how her day was going. He had it bad. Meridian rolled over onto his side and closed his eyes. He wondered if his father was looking down on him, laughing at his bachelor-for-life son.

Meridian stood in the archway of his formal dining room greeting his guests. The house quickly filled with his fifteen friends and their wives or girlfriends. He toyed with the idea of calling Robert again as Mr. Martin came into the room and announced dinner would be served in ten minutes. An architect in the group deterred his call when he stopped to discuss a business matter.

Meridian listened intently as the architect told him of an upcoming project. He needed additional committed capital to complete the proposal, and hoped that Meridian might be interested in investing. The architect stopped mid-sentence, his eyes captivated by something across the room. Meridian followed his gaze to find his eyes riveted on Talya. She stood nervously clutching her purse in the doorway of the dining room. The red sequined dress hugged her shoulders, flowed past her round hips, gripped

her thighs and ended at the top of a pair of three-inch red
heels. The deep V cut of the dress stopped at the top of her
flat belly. Her cleavage flirted with Meridian. His feet were
glued to the floor as he watched her shift her weight from
her left foot to her right.

He had never seen a woman look so beautiful. Her hair
was elaborately styled with spiral curls bundled on top of
her head. A few tendrils flowed down at her temples.
Meridian wanted to reach out and push them away from
her sultry brown eyes. He could not see her freckles from
the distance separating them.

"Excuse me," he mumbled to the architect and took a
step to meet her. He stopped and watched the interaction
when Bill approached her. Bill smiled, spoke close to her
ear and took her by the elbow away from the archway.

Meridian adjusted his green-and-tan patterned tie and
shoved his hands into his evergreen colored wool-and-silk
blend slacks. He promised to call the architect the
following week before hurrying through the crowd to reach
Bill and Talya before they left his sight. Typical, predictable,
arrogant Bill Ritter, going after the prettiest girl in the
room. This time he would learn that all gorgeous women
weren't put on the earth for his sole pleasure.

Meridian swooped up Talya's arm, steering her away
from the possessive hand Bill held against the small of her
back. Mr. Martin announced the start of dinner before Bill
could question his actions. Meridian waited until Bill
walked away and the crowd thinned before he leaned over
and kissed Talya's cheek.

"You look great."

Talya ran her hand along the lapel of his suit. The rich color of the material made his caramel complexion glow. "Thank you. You're very handsome yourself."

Meridian ignored the jolt of electricity generated from Talya's touch, placed his hand in the small of her back and escorted her to dinner. Enjoying the formal dinner didn't stop the lively conversation and serious debate. Talya wasn't as talkative as the other women at the party. Meridian knew that after a few more of the dinners, she would be siding with them in all the men-versus-women discussions. He smiled over at her after making a particular point he hoped impressed her and squeezed her thigh under the table. After dinner everyone moved about the house enjoying the extravagant toys that composed Meridian's den and recreation room.

Bill approached Meridian with an outstretched hand. "How's it been going?"

He offered a firm handshake. "I can't complain."

They surveyed the crowd together. "That's quite a woman you're with tonight." Bill took a drink from his bottle of beer.

Meridian looked over at Talya. She was sitting across the room with a group of the wives talking. The topic seemed to engross her.

"She's prime. Not your usual type, but prime. What's the game?"

Meridian turned to him with a raised eyebrow. "There's no game. I like her."

Meridian and Bill were once good friends—until Bill started dating Meridian's girlfriend at the time. It was his own fault. He bragged about their erotic exploits at all of the poker games, and Bill decided he wanted to sample the fruit for himself. The nature of their friendship was rooted in competition. They were rivals. They challenged each other about everything. They always tried to best the other. Meridian forgave Bill, but their relationship remained strained.

Bill returned the gesture of raising his eyebrow. "Yeah, she's sweet. Maybe it's time I try the sweet, quiet type. I might have to throw my hat in the ring."

Meridian's eyes flared, and his voice dropped to a deep, serious tone. "I'm not playing any games with Talya. I'm trying to spend serious time with her."

Bill ignored Meridian's expression. He tossed him a flippant look and walked away.

Meridian never guessed Bill would be the first person he'd share his feelings about Talya with. He meant what he said. He was pursuing something serious with Talya. If he couldn't have a serious relationship with her he would walk away before he hurt her. Her last boyfriend inflicted some serious pain in her life. She didn't deserve that. He would not have any part in any games that might hurt her again.

Meridian spotted Bill making his way over to Talya. The jolt of electricity hit him first, followed by a mixture of gold-laced lust and adulation. The final emotion that occupied him made the pit of his stomach burn, his jaw tighten, his eyes narrow and the tone of his voice drop two octaves. He denied it as he watched Talya toss her head back and laugh at what Bill said to her, but he was indisputably jealous of every man who came near her.

"Earth calling Meridian. What are you thinking about?" Rena wrapped her arm around Meridian's and leaned into his body.

Meridian bent at the knees and kissed her cheek. "I'm watching Talya."

"I like her. We talked earlier about managing my finances. Who would have thought someone could make me plan for the future? She's much better than the bimbos you always bring around. She has more substance, more class."

"So, what are you trying to say?" Meridian laughed.

They talked while Meridian walked Rena over to the bar to get a drink. They joined Robert, and he became so involved in their conversation that he stopped watching Talya. When he looked around he found her sitting in the back of the room alone with Bill. He watched as he tried to listen to Robert's conversation. He hoped that either Talya or Bill would end their discussion and walk away, but that never happened. Meridian didn't want Bill interfering with his relationship with Talya. He thought he had made it clear to Bill earlier that Talya was not to be included in their games. He excused himself from the conversation with Robert and Rena and went to be with Talya.

Women considered Bill a handsome man. They knew about his reputation of being with many women, but it didn't matter. When he came around, they heaved their breasts and began to speak in throaty voices. He was magnetized, and the women's breasts pulled them to him. Meridian asked the only woman he knew he could ask about Bill's appeal: his best friend's wife.

"He's like a song," Rena said, staring out into space.

"What does that mean?"

"It's not just his looks, which are perfect. He has this—this presence that's so overwhelming you get tongue-tied around him. He makes you feel like you're a singer in one of those old juke joints." She started swaying to an imaginary song. "You're standing on stage in a floor-length sequined gown wearing long satin gloves and he's the only one in the place. You want to get onstage and sing a deep—down soul—grabbing song while you take off all of your clothes and then jump down off the stage and—"

"That's enough," Robert interrupted. He refused to bring Rena to any of their parties for two months after that.

Meridian walked up behind Talya and touched her shoulder.

Bill spoke. "Meridian, Talya and I were getting to know each other a little better. I was telling her how much I liked a good boxing match. It surprised me that such a beautiful woman would know anything about boxing. Talya, I'll have to get us tickets to the next big fight in Vegas." He turned to Meridian. "I can't wait until Mike throws his hat into the ring again." His lips curled up into a cocky smile. "You know what I mean?"

Meridian knew exactly what he meant. He had made a direct challenge to Meridian's manhood. He decided not to tell Bill what was on his mind like he wanted to; instead he ignored him. "Excuse us."

Bill stood as Talya rose gracefully from her chair.

Bill took Talya's hand in his and stroked it as he spoke. "You are quite wonderful, and I can't wait to see you again next month. We'll pick up where we're leaving off." One last stroke, and he walked off.

"He's nice—a little flirty, but he's nice," Talya remarked with a curious smile.

"Um-huh." Meridian mumbled. She wouldn't be coming back to these parties for two months either, at least. Strange how all the wives complained about the single women at the parties, but not one said anything about Bill. If what Rena said were true, at least half of the married women had or wanted to sleep with Bill. The wives got together sometimes when the men were playing poker, and they talked just like the men did, and evidently Bill was quite often the topic of discussion.

Meridian escorted Talya during the remainder of the party, separating from her only when she needed to freshen up. Bill insisted on being a threat instead of a friend. He'd deal with him later. Tonight, he had the most beautiful woman in the world on his arm, and he refused to let Bill ruin it for him.

After the party died down, and the last of the guests left, Meridian escorted Talya to his den. Meeting all of his friends tired her. Talya placed her stocking-clad feet up on the sofa.

"I can drive you home as soon as the last of the caterers leave." Meridian closed the door and turned to her.

Talya smiled, too tired to speak.

"Did you enjoy meeting my friends? As crazy as they are, they are my friends."

"I felt out of place at first, but everyone made sure I was comfortable."

"You got along well with Bill." Meridian looked at her over the rim of his glass.

"He's nice."

"How nice?" He placed the glass down on the table in front of the sofa.

Talya shrugged. "Nice."

Meridian folded his arms across his broad chest. "What did you two find to talk about all evening?"

"Actually, he spoke mostly about his friendship with you. He said you shared quite a few of the same interests."

"What did he mean by that?" Lack of trust for Bill, spurred by jealousy, made him continue the line of questioning.

"I didn't have a chance to ask him."

Meridian nodded, running his fingers across the nape of his neck. "Then what did you have a chance to ask him? You spent most of the evening with him, you must have discussed something of importance."

"What do you mean?" Talya sat at attention. Her eyes darted over his face.

"I mean—" Meridian stepped over to the sofa "—you spent a lot of time alone with him. I want to know what he said to you."

Talya swung her feet around to the floor and scrambled to put on her shoes. "I didn't do anything." Her voice became shaky.

"Hey." He watched Talya's trembling hands try to adorn her shoes. "Bill's not as nice as he appears to be. I want to make sure you know he likes to play games."

Talya jumped to her feet and darted around Meridian.

"Where are you going?" Meridian rushed to block her exit from the room. Her eyes reflected her fear. She acted as if she expected him to harm her.

"Talya, wait a minute." Meridian grabbed her arm before she could open the door and run from the room.

The instant Meridian's fingers took hold of Talya's arm, a muffled squeal of distress came from deep inside her chest. The sound reminded Meridian of a wounded animal—in pain and afraid.

"What is it? Are you all right?"

Talya looked up at him as if she didn't recognize him. Worse, a familiar figure she feared. He tried to apologize, but his words upset her more. She tried to pull away from him, almost tripping on the Persian rug under their feet. Meridian tried to secure her arm before she hurt herself. He told her to calm down; she didn't hear him. In one fluid motion, he pulled her into his solid chest and wrapped his arms around her petite body. He stroked her hair and refused to release her until her body relaxed, and the struggling ceased.

"What was that about? I just wanted to apologize. I shouldn't have implied that you wanted Bill."

"I thought—" she said through ragged breaths.

"You thought I was going to hurt you." He placed his palm under her chin and raised her head so that their eyes met. "I would never touch you in that way. You know that, don't you?"

Talya pulled away from his embrace and turned her back to him. "I know." Her voice trembled. "I overreacted."

"Not without reason, I suspect. You're a very quiet, subdued person. You wouldn't react that way without cause. I'm sorry if I scared you. I shouldn't have grabbed your arm so suddenly."

There was a brief knock at the door before it slowly opened. Mr. Martin stuck his head in the partial opening. "The last of the caterers is gone. The cleaning service will be here first thing in the morning. If you don't need me for anything else tonight, I'll be leaving."

"Have a good night." Meridian absentmindedly dismissed him. He waited until Mr. Martin closed the door before he walked up behind Talya. "You're shaking." He rested his hands firmly on her shoulders in an attempt to stop the tremors moving her body.

Talya wrapped her arms around herself in a lame effort to steady her body. "It's getting late."

Meridian moved smoothly around Talya's stiffly erect body until he was facing her. "Every time we get to a hard place between us, you want to run." He moved slowly to unwrap her arms from around her body and took her hands in his. Meridian's syrupy voice deepened with his exertion of authority. "I'm not going to let you run away from me. And don't tell me you don't want to talk about it. I've heard that enough from you, too. If you want this to work out between us and be something real, you're going to have to open up to me."

The room stood still. The house was quiet. Talya looked up into the no-nonsense expression of Meridian's face. He wouldn't let Talya get away with keeping whatever it was inside; it held her back from him. He deserved to know what the problem was so that he could put her at ease. How could he make things right if he did not know the issue? He wanted answers if it took all night. He looked down into Talya's sultry brown eyes and waited for insight on what was keeping her from opening up to him. What happened next threw him completely off balance. She stepped up to him so that her breasts brushed his chest, and wrapped her arms around his middle. She stood on her tiptoes and angled her head to kiss him.

The jolt ran through his body with such force that his limbs twitched as he raised his arms to encircle her. His mouth met her parted lips with a feathery touch, but Talya took more. She kissed him with a hunger that was so out of character for her that he lifted his head to look into her face. Her arms went up around his neck, and she pulled him down to her. He let her kiss him again.

Their kisses grew hotter and wilder. Meridian's fingers found their way to the deep brown strands of hair that were obstructing his view of her freckles all evening and pushed them away. He answered the call of Talya's flirting cleavage with wet kisses and long strokes of his tongue. They could talk another day.

CHAPTER NINE

"Come in, Mr. Percy." Meridian motioned him over to the conference table to sit down. "This is Mr. Uley. I wanted him here for our meeting because he's going to be heavily involved with your case. He's my friend, and second in charge around here. I trust him, and I'd like your permission to fill him in on our last meeting."

Robert stood to shake Mr. Percy's work-battered hand.

Mr. Percy looked Robert over with skeptical eyes. "If Mr. Weston trusts you, then I guess it'll be alright."

Meridian brought Robert up to speed on Mr. Percy's insurance-claim problems. Robert took notes in his over-sized planner, stopping only to look up and push his glasses back on his nose when Meridian told him that Mr. Percy was HIV-positive.

"Mr. Percy," Meridian continued, "I made some calls to the benefit's office, and I'm not happy with the way your case was ignored when you sought help. I want to assure you that will not happen again. I can promise you this because I fired the director of that department and gave someone more worthy the position. I have made an appointment for you to meet with her tomorrow." Meridian slid the appointment card over the shiny wood grain of the table to Mr. Percy.

"Thank you."

"I have given her instructions to correct the situation. She will report back to Mr. Uley with the outcome one week from tomorrow. Mr. Uley will keep me informed of the situation."

Mr. Percy nodded as he wrung his hands under the table. "What if I don't like what they come up with to do?"

"Mr. Uley will take care of the problem. He won't rest until you're happy. I won't rest until you're satisfied with the outcome. If you feel you need to discuss anything with me at any time, you make an appointment with my assistant. I have instructed her to schedule your appointments the same week that you call so there should not be a delay in our meeting."

Meridian relaxed his demeanor as he sat back in his chair. "Mr. Percy, I don't feel you are being treated fairly by the insurance company and I, like my father, won't stand by and do nothing. I'm asking Mr. Uley to help with this because he handles these types of situations well and because I'm very busy. Too busy to give the matter my complete attention; therefore, I need some assistance."

Mr. Percy searched Meridian's face. "Boy, you remind me of your father. I know you'll do right by me." He looked over at Robert. "You too, Mr. Uley."

Robert spoke up. "I think that while we're getting this taken care of we should make sure that Mr. Percy can still receive health care."

Meridian nodded. Why didn't he think of that point? Robert earned his place as his right hand man. He filled in the gaps, caught the things that Meridian missed, kept him grounded when he went on tangents. He wouldn't have made it past the first few months of running the business if Robert had not been there to help him.

Robert went on. "He could bring me the medical bills, and I'll see to it they are paid. That way he can continue to get medical care. We can always recoup the money from the insurance company later."

"Good idea." Meridian commended him.

"I don't want any charity. I only want what I got coming," Mr. Percy interjected.

Robert addressed his remark. "This is not charity, sir, it is what you have coming. The bills should have been paid a long time ago. We need to keep you healthy and at work while we check into this. It'll be harder to win your case if you're off work or hospitalized because of your illness. We need to prove that you're still able to perform your job and that your job is valuable to Weston Realty."

Mr. Percy left the office after he agreed to retrieve the past due medical bills and bring them to Robert the next morning.

"How did he contract HIV?" Robert wondered aloud. "He's an older man. I know the reputations of all of the employees, and Mr. Percy is a hard worker."

"I'm curious, too, but I didn't think it would be right to ask him. I can't see him using drugs. Wild, unprotected sex?"

"I checked his employment history before the meeting. He doesn't take much time off, which makes me rule out drug addiction."

"I guess we're all vulnerable," Meridian remarked before returning to his desk.

"Can you take a walk-in appointment?" Kathy's sour face appeared in the doorway of Talya's office.

"No problem. Give me five minutes to finish up this liability sheet."

Talya quickly scanned her numbers, checking the figures before she saved the data. She had sailed through her work that day. Meridian called her earlier to make weekend plans, and she couldn't wait to finish up the last-minute Friday deposits of her clients. It amazed her every week when frantic business owners clamored to the bank with their revenues for the week. You'd think business owners would be more organized and meticulous with their finances.

Talya stood and rounded her desk when she heard Kathy's heels clicking against the marble flooring. If she could finish up quickly, she might be able to make it to the mall to buy a new dress for her dinner date tomorrow.

"Ms. Stevenson, this is Jason Fulwood. He has questions about opening an IRA."

Before Talya heard his name, she knew the large muscular physique belonged to Jason. All of her nightmares became real. Kathy batted her thickly coated eyes at Jason as he openly flirted with her. He wrapped her up into his charm so securely that Kathy didn't notice the way Talya stumbled backward to find shelter behind her desk. Talya opened her mouth to request Kathy escort Jason to another financial advisor, but Jason closed the door before she could pull any words from their hiding place.

"Precious," Jason spoke in a whisper, "You look really good."

Talya placed her chair between them as he approached. What is he going to do to me? Fear tightened her insides. The darkness came and stole away the time it took for Jason to bolt around the chair and grasp her hands.

"Sit down." His voice sounded sweet, but Talya knew better. To ignore the command would mean triggering his anger.

Talya slowly shrank into the chair. Jason swiveled it around to face him where he sat on top of her desk. He looked like a bank robber dressed in all black. If he killed her, no one would remember any of his distinguishing features. Only she could clearly describe the way his nostrils flared and eyes became slits when he became enraged.

"What are we going to do about this mess you've created?" The musk scent of his cologne assaulted her nose as he twisted her hair around his finger.

"Jason, I—"

He withdrew his hand. Talya flinched, ready to duck to avoid the impact of his blow.

"Do you think I'm going to hit you? Never again. I mean it this time. I want things to be the way they were when we first got together. My temper is completely under control now. That's why I'm not going to drag you out of this bank. I'm going to give you time to realize where you need to be." Jason moved to the tiny window lighting the office. "I took you right after college, maybe you need this time to grow up." He turned to her with an uncharacteristic smile. "I'm willing to wait. As long as it doesn't take too long to get this out of your system." The harsh features of his face returned, his voice became gritty. "And you don't try to run again. I swear, if you try to leave—"

Talya watched his fists curl into tight knots at his sides. His body seemed larger than she remembered. How had she ever survived one of his rages?

"Do you understand what I'm doing here? I'm giving you another chance. I'm willing to work, and you need to make that commitment too. Understand?"

The pressure in Talya's bladder made her afraid to blink.

"Do you understand?"

Talya nodded.

"Don't run."

"I won't."

CHAPTER TEN

"What are you doing here?" Talya instinctively grabbed her hair with one hand and the opening of her robe with the other when she opened the door and found Meridian standing there. She had just gotten out of the shower, and wore a towel wrapped around her wet hair. Meridian laughed. "I came to see you. Who were you expecting dressed like that?" He pointed down to her oversized slippers with the bear claws.

Embarrassed by her homely appearance, Talya kicked the slippers behind the door.

"Can I come in?" He stepped in when Talya opened the door wider.

"You should call before you come over." She wanted to see him so badly; he read her thoughts. She feared seeing anyone more. Jason knew where she worked; he probably knew where she lived. She could be putting Meridian in danger.

"I wanted to surprise you."

"Let me get dressed. I'll be right out."

Meridian leaned down and kissed her cheek. "Don't get dressed for me. What you're wearing is fine, even the slippers aren't bad on you."

"Well, I need to at least dry my hair."

"Fair enough."

Talya turned to go into the bathroom. She didn't realize that Meridian was behind her until she saw him watching her from the doorway of the bathroom.

"Are you going to stand there and watch me?" Talya asked as she plugged in the hair dryer.

"Um-huh." He sat on the edge of the tub and watched Talya dry her hair. Every movement she used to pull the whirling instrument through her dark brown hair made her gown rise to mid thigh. Meridian's eyes darted between the frivolity of flying hair and the rising hemline. When she was done he held her around her waist from behind. He snuggled his nose in her hair and smelled the baby powder.

Talya watched Meridian's face in the mirror. His eyes were closed as he nuzzled in her hair. Every now and then he would stroke her hair and kiss the top of her head. This gentleness she craved after her meeting with Jason. Meridian held her without a word for a long time. He stroked her hair and held her tightly, never trying to take it any further.

Talya was lulled into security and warmth by Meridian's arms. She closed her eyes and let herself melt into him. If she could stay this way forever. If she could surround herself in Meridian's kindness and live forever. She would never fear Jason again.

"Your body feels very good." The short, sheer gown did not provide enough of a barrier between them to reduce the seductive feel of her curves and valleys against his slim, strong body.

A small heat was brewing inside of Talya. He released her, allowing her to regain her composure. "You said you wanted to surprise me?"

"I thought you might want to go to the movies or something. I figured I would stop by and see what your plans were before I drove all the way home." His full lips curved upward under the shadowy mustache.

"I planned to watch *I Love Lucy* reruns and get some much-needed sleep. As you can see, I'm nothing but a party animal." Talya watched Meridian's expression change in the mirror from hopeful to disappointed. She added, "I wouldn't mind some company. Have you eaten dinner?"

Meridian perked up. "I ate at Robert's. If we watch Lucy together it's going to be late when I leave. I don't know if I'll be alert enough to drive all the way home afterward."

"My sofa is a sleeper; you can always camp out there." Talya returned his devilish grin.

Meridian shook his head. "But then I couldn't hold you all night."

"Just hold me?"

"Depends."

"Depends on what?" Talya was enjoying Meridian's sexy teasing. The small space of the bathroom filled with their mutually generated steam. The tall, caramel-colored man standing in front of her wearing a designer suit added to the heat in the room.

"Depends on whether you're going to put those bear claws back on." He shuddered.

Talya hit his well-developed arm with her fist. "You know those slippers turn you on."

That night, Talya held Meridian against her breasts as he slept. She stroked his beard and listened to his soft snoring. His body was slim, muscular, and tight but he felt like silk against her. His suit hung on the back of her chair. He removed his clothes in the dark and slid into bed with Talya wearing only his underwear. He didn't want to embarrass her, he told her. Talya was more embarrassed by the implications of what might happen once they were in bed together barely dressed. But Meridian remained a perfect gentleman. He kissed Talya softly on her cheek when it became hard for him to keep his eyes open then settled against her breasts with his arms around her waist and went to sleep.

She inhabited two worlds. This world where quiet darkness welcomed restful sleep. The other world where darkness meant a memory would slip away. The two men in her life were as different as the worlds that split her time. Meridian, loving and considerate; Jason, possessive and violent.

Her first thought had been to run far away. How far would be far enough? There must be a way to end this. She didn't want to give up all she had worked for. Why should she be forced to? How come Jason couldn't see they were all wrong for each other?

Meridian took in a deep breath and turned his back to her. He wrapped his arms around a pillow before falling back into the rhythm of sleep.

With Meridian, she could snuggle up to his back and enjoy lying next to him. With Jason, she hardly slept. Fearful he would wake up in the middle of the night and start his verbal assault. Questioning her about how she spent her days. Asking if anyone had come to the house while he was at work. The endless interrogations were as exhausting as the beatings.

What could she do to save herself? If Meridian were ever hurt because of her, she would never forgive herself. And Jason would hurt Meridian to prove a point. He'd done it before to men who were nothing more than friends.

"Talya?" Meridian whispered, his voice dry.

She answered by curling up to his back.

He flipped over and pulled her against his chest. "Just wanted to make sure I was really here."

Apprehension filled Talya as she and Jennifer approached the door of the church. The memories of her visit to the church the second time she tried to leave Jason, and the result of his wrath afterward, still made her flinch. She'd had nowhere else to go. She fled to the nearest church as soon as Jason left for work. Her removal of the dark shades hiding the latest bruises to her eyes made the pastor of the small church drop back against the pew. He pulled away, moved his eyes away from her face, and ignored the obvious. Talya tried to describe what went on inside of her perfect little house. He cut her off by reminding her that living together out of wedlock was a sin. He offered to pray for her.

No amount of prayers worked. She could have told the bewildered pastor as much, but he never let her complete a sentence. Jason sat at the kitchen table awaiting his lunch when she returned from the church. He decided that the outside influence of church would only confuse her and that she should never go back. Talya prayed a lot that night, but no one answered her. Not God, not the pastor—and not Jason.

Talya's faith in God and the church had been shaken beyond immediate repair that night. She certainly didn't believe in religion as strongly as Jennifer. Her lack of faith crippled her into staying with Jason for so long. She felt alone and confused. He had isolated her from all of her friends right after college. Her family lived out of the state. He controlled all of her finances. As Talya relived that time in her mind, she became even more apprehensive about going to church.

Jennifer insisted that Talya come along. Lately, the only time Talya and Jennifer saw each other was on double dates. Talya spent her free time with Meridian and Jennifer spent most of her free time with the Reverend. Jennifer even started a new journal titled, "Dating Adventures with the reverend." The reverend was going to be busy after church with marriage counseling, and Meridian was busy putting a proposal together. Jennifer rationalized that they could spend some time hanging out together after church. Talya missed seeing her friend, so she gave in and accompanied Jennifer to church.

The reverend appeared at the pulpit, and the stirring of the crowd died down. He looked large and majestic standing in the front of the church. His eyes searched for Jennifer. A faint smile came across his lips when he spotted her off to the right of the church in the middle of the third pew.

The reverend cleared his throat and began with a booming voice unfamiliar to Talya.

"I overheard two middle-aged women talking in the grocery store yesterday. One was saying that she did not understand how her sister could live in Michigan with its unpredictable weather. She said to her sister that she should move to Florida or California where the weather is always mild. The sister turned to the first woman and told her that those states had to deal with earthquakes and hurricanes."

The reverend paused for emphasis and then continued. "That made me think about the message I wanted to deliver to you today; the morning after our spring revival." He looked around the church and glanced over at Jennifer again. "Michigan is a state where, sure enough, the weather is unpredictable, just as is life, but if you take the time to look around, you see the wonder of the change in colors we are privileged to witness. And just when we think it's too hot, it begins to cool off. And when the snow seems too high to shovel, the sun comes out and helps it to melt."

Someone shouted, "Teach, Preacher, teach!"

The reverend started to pick up steam. "What I'm trying to say to you folks is that life is full of crosses to bear, and when the load seems too heavy, the Lord sends a little help our way. He doesn't do it all for us; He just gives us the tools we need to help ourselves. And like the sister in the store said, we all have our problems. No place or person is perfect. You just have to deal with what you've got."

"Amen!" was followed by applause.

"Today, the morning after spring revival, I'm going to ask you to put your Bibles under your seat and sit back and let go of your worries. Today I'm not going to preach from the Bible. Today I'm going to preach from the book of real life. I'm going to offer you words of encouragement so that those of you who have burdens will open your eyes to the tools God has sent you and encourage you to reach over and pick up that shovel. I'm going to offer you words of encouragement so that those of you who are without burdens right now will recognize that you've been sent by God to be someone else's shovel."

"Amen! Amen!"

The reverend's words touched Talya deep inside of the hidden chamber blocking her heart. She wanted to let go of the pain of the past, but the only way to truly do that was to express the fear and suffering in words. She listened to his words and contemplated telling Jennifer over lunch about her past. She was apprehensive because she knew all the stereotypes and labels. She had heard them all before: "Black women are too strong to be the victim of domestic violence," her best friend said when she tried to confide in her. "Those women are just stupid and must like it if they stay in that situation day after day," one of her coworkers said. "That doesn't happen to people our age," her college roommate declared. Talya wanted Jennifer's understanding, and not her pity.

The only way to come out a survivor is to release the pain, learn to trust, and start all over again without making the same mistakes. Talya wanted to start all over again, so she took a deep breath and placed her trust in the reverend's words and Jennifer's support.

Jennifer held Talya's hand across the table at lunch. She could tell that there was much pain behind her eyes. "What did you want to tell me?"

Deep breath. "My last boyfriend used to—" She dropped her head. "I was in an abusive relationship."

Jennifer's face took on an expression of confusion and then concern. The simple statement explained so much. The shyness, the suspicious nature, the secret past, the fear of becoming involved with Meridian. "Do you want to tell me about it?"

Talya could not believe that was all Jennifer said. She just wanted to help her by listening. They spent two hours occupying their table after they finished lunch. Once Talya began to open up, and Jennifer didn't judge her, the words came easier. She shared the horrors of living in fear of triggering Jason's fury. She described not only the experiences but the emotions that accompanied the pushes, slaps and punches. The words and tears acted as a catharsis for Talya.

Jennifer hugged her. "If you need to talk, knock on my door anytime. I'm glad you're out of that situation with Jason. I know it was hard for you to live through, but I'm glad it brought you to live next door to me because you are the best friend I've ever had."

CHAPTER ELEVEN

Talya's green Saturn handled the curves of the road through, but not with the smooth, effortless motion of Meridian's BMW. The pattern of trees unfolding as Talya maneuvered the twists and turns were only minimally familiar. She drove slowly, not passing the speed limit, as she hunted for the partially hidden dirt road she would have to turn down in the final mile of her trip. This was the first time Meridian had allowed her to drive to his house alone, and she didn't want to get lost.

She smiled with recognition as she turned on the left turn signal. She enjoyed the peaceful drive to Meridian's secluded domain. The work week had been a busy one at Brunstown Bank—a quiet dinner alone at his house would help her to unwind.

Jason had not made another appearance since his visit to the bank. He hadn't even phoned. He wasn't too far away, he never let too much distance come between them. The only thing that could be distracting him would be his body-building competitions. Knowing that her time with Meridian was limited, Talya savored every minute they spent alone together.

The white Audi parked in Meridian's driveway belonged to Robert. Disappointment saddened her when

Mr. Martin escorted her into the formal dining room and suggested she begin dinner without Meridian. A minor crisis threatened a major transaction between Weston Realty and a local brokerage house. History told Mr. Martin that when Robert drove out to solve a crisis, it became a marathon session of negotiations.

"Talya—" Robert came through the doors of the dining room—"I'm sorry I had to interrupt your plans with Meridian." Robert took a seat near Talya at the long table. "He's on a conference call and asked me to slip away to check on you. He feels really bad, but it can't be helped."

Talya grabbed her perfectly arranged plate of unnamable gourmet orange, green, and red foods and navigated her way through the maze of rooms until she found the kitchen. She finished her dinner and her wine as she watched Mr. Martin prepare to leave for the evening. With his encouragement, she showed herself into the den, where she selected a leather-bound autobiography about Martin Luther King from Meridian's bookcase. The hour grew late, and Talya became bored isolated in the den.

Robert ushered Talya into Meridian's office. The buzz of activity in the office directly contradicted the silence engulfing the rest of the house. Their briefcases were open on top of Meridian's desk. Contracts and maps cluttered the table that had been pulled into the center of the room.

Meridian approached Talya with a weary smile. He continued his conversation over his telephone headset as Robert listened in on the extension.

"I'm sorry." He mouthed the words. He pressed his lips to her forehead. Two long fingers covered the transmitting end of the headset. "This shouldn't take more than an hour longer. Can you wait?"

Talya pointed to the compact sofa placed catercorner to his desk. He nodded and answered a question posed to him by the caller on the other end of the headset.

The book Talya brought with her into the office lay discarded on the coffee table in front of the sofa as she wandered from one framed African artwork lining a single wall to the next. Abstract sculptures occupied the space in front of the opposite wall. All the furniture was strategically placed in the center of the room so that its occupants were able to easily view the valuable collection.

Meridian yanked his gold-trimmed pen out of its holder and scribbled a note. "Give them whatever they want." Robert's mouth parted in surprise. The marathon negotiation-discussion-argument-bickering session had gone on long enough. Hours had passed, he missed his dinner date with Talya, and they had made only minor progress. Weston Realty would profit from the purchase even if he paid the asking price for the property. The deal would be profitable to him not only in dollars but in the related contracts he would secure.

Robert watched Meridian watch Talya and Talya watch Meridian. He tactfully gave in to the broker's wishes. He closed the conference call and rushed out of the house, seeing himself to the door.

Although she moved with the quiet grace of a well-mannered cat, Talya's presence disrupted Meridian's thought processes. His eyes were on her as she curled up on the sofa and flipped the pages of the book on her lap. He stumbled over words when he glanced up and caught Talya's eyes locked on him.

Meridian rounded the desk with the unhurried stride Talya had grown attracted to over the past weeks. Everything about him made her take notice. Physically, he was the perfect man: tall, slim, naturally curly dark hair, well groomed, well dressed. His personality was beyond perfect; he was what most women dreamed of being able to have: rich, strong, caring. Talya's eyes roamed over his body. Meridian smiled when her eyes moved from his feet up to his face.

The syrup poured from his lips. "How was dinner?" He gave her a lopsided grin of apology.

"Great." Talya stood slowly. "I couldn't name anything on the plate, but it was very delicious."

Meridian placed his hands into the pockets of his slacks. The freckles were gone again. Undoubtedly, this smile shone for him. "It gets crazy at Weston Realty sometimes," he continued as Talya took a step toward him. "I work too many hours most weeks, but I have a lot of responsibility to keep the business afloat."

Talya watched him closely, fully expecting him to reach up and loosen his shirt collar. He was squirming under her gaze. The smell of his cologne called her to him. She took another step toward him. "There's nothing wrong with working hard."

Talya had watched Meridian pace the length of his office with the intensity of a caged lion. She could almost see the wheels of knowledge turning inside his head as he debated pricing issues with the invisible caller. His knowledge materialized as pure sex appeal. His intelligence hot.

"Hmmm." Meridian stood only a foot away from Talya now. The burgundy dress she wore fused with her shoulders, and her breasts and hugged her waist before it flared out at her hips. He wanted to reach out and touch the fabric. He wanted to take its place next to her body. He restrained himself. His fingers picked at the seam inside of his pockets.

Talya tilted her head up to the brown eyed man standing directly in front of her. They were lost in a comfortable silence as they watched each other. The design dancing across his tie made Talya want to trace it with her fingers. She lowered her gaze to eye level and lifted her hand out toward Meridian.

Meridian stood paralyzed as he watched Talya reach out to him in what seemed like slow motion. Her fingers moved lightly over the pattern of his tie. He couldn't feel her touch; he could only see the sapphire-colored fingernails clash against the checkered pattern.

Talya's sultry eyes were underlined with a dark brown shade that pulled Meridian's attention past the long lashes flickering dreamily up at him. She dropped her eyes to his tie again as she let the palm of her small hand stroke its length.

The black-and-red checkered tie was made of the finest, softest silk. Talya's fingers grazed the gray shirt underneath. The buttons were round and fit snugly into the holes designed to secure them. She traced the exposed seam of the shirt up to its collar, which was crisp, razor-sharp.

The jolt streaked down Meridian's arms, leaving a prickly feeling in his fingertips. His hands dropped to his sides as he looked down upon the top of Talya's dark brown head. She lifted both hands now and smoothed the shoulders of his jacket. Finding the dark gray wool and silk blend jacket had a feathery feel underneath her fingertips, she repeated the motion. A jolt of lightning followed Talya's touch down Meridian's arm as she traced a particular dark pinstripe along its course. She felt his body stiffen and stopped momentarily to question what she was doing. A caramel-colored hand lifted and rested against her face, absorbing all uncertainties.

Meridian's hand moved to her shoulder and then back to his side. He wished he could read her thoughts, but he didn't dare ask. Somehow, questions would shatter what was happening between them. He didn't understand it; he had tried many times to make her realize that he needed her on the most intimate of levels, but words never worked. Tonight, in the serene quietness of his empty house, they were standing as close as they had ever been to verifying that they were attracted to each.

Meridian encouraged Talya with a simple kiss to the top of her head. He inhaled the baby-powder scent before pulling away. She let her mind be cleansed of any thoughts other than what she was feeling at that exact moment. She glanced up at Meridian's parted lips before she reached for the buttons of his jacket. They were snug, and she took her time opening each one with care. When his jacket fell open, she slid her hands around his waist against the silk lining. She leaned in close to his chest and inhaled a deep breath of his manliness mixed with a sweetness she believed was manufactured specifically for him.

Meridian came undone when Talya rested her head against his chest. He wrapped his arms around the smoothness of her body. His mouth found her neck. His tongue played against the hollow of her neck tasting the bitterness of her perfume. His finger traced the cleavage exposed at the top of dress.

His breath was hot against her ear. "I want to be with you."

Talya let her lids close and held them there for the briefest of moments. She let her head fall back and absorbed the electricity of his tongue moving across her collar-bone.

"Do you want me?" Meridian whispered against her shoulder before bringing his head up to meet her eyes.

As Talya answered Meridian with the one word he longed to hear, he bent down and lifted her into his arms. She rubbed her face against the sleekness of his beard as they moved into the hallway, past several doors, stopping only to shut off the lights illuminating the house.

Meridian set Talya upon her feet when they reached the cream and brown interior of his bedroom. The furnishings were maple, and the bed took up the length of one entire wall. The bookshelf was filled with more books on famous black Americans. Two off-white chairs with ottomen faced each other near the small wet bar. The TV and stereo were housed near the foot of the bed in their own shelving. The room chilled with the light wind blowing in from the double French doors leading to an enclosed patio.

"Would you like a drink?" Meridian stood looking down on her.

"No." Talya's voice was husky, her throat dry.

Meridian walked over to the wet bar and turned off the recessed lights over the mirror-backed glass shelves holding an assortment of drinking glasses. He bent slightly to retrieve the remote from behind the bar. He pressed several buttons until the soulful sounds of Maxwell filled the room. He stopped and assessed her from head to toe before he made his way back to her. They stood watching each other until Talya lifted her arms and Meridian simultaneously lowered his shoulders into her reach.

The kiss was explosive. Four eyelids slid closed as they embraced pulling each other deeper into the exchange of desire. Meridian held her tightly around the waist as he took small steps backward to his bed. When his calves touched the side of the mattress, Meridian lowered himself down to the king-size bed. He pulled Talya between the V of his thighs and kissed her breasts as he lifted the dress above her head. He spun her around to undo the zipper, which was making it hard to accomplish his task.

"What happened here?" Meridian asked, tracing the lower right side of Talya's back.

Meridian was not prepared for her reaction. She jumped away from him and pressed the partially removed dress to her chest, covering herself. She stood frozen next to the bed, avoiding Meridian's eyes. He reached out and pulled her by the waist back to him.

"What did I say?"

Talya tried to suppress the urge to run to the bathroom and lock the door. "I'd better be getting home."

"Don't pull away from me. What's wrong?" The urgency alerted him to the fact that his long-awaited chance to become intimate with Talya was slipping away.

"I'm just not ready. I thought I was; watching you tonight—I made a mistake."

"Talya, I don't believe that is true. We've come so far with each other and our relationship. Your eyes tell me that you're ready. Your body tells me that you're ready." He adjusted his hands around her waist. "For some reason you always pull away. Does this have something to do with the ex-boyfriend you mentioned before?"

Talya was trying to make a new start. She wanted things to be different with Meridian. The conversations she had with Jennifer about her past made her believe she was ready. Deep breath. "I told you that I was in a bad relationship."

"And I told you that he was a fool." He pulled her down to sit on his lap.

"It's hard for me to let go sometimes."

"This guy treated you badly, but that's the past."

"I know."

Meridian took a chance. He did not want to do it yet; he planned to wait but he felt the time was right. He buried his head in her breasts. "Don't let this guy keep you from experiencing the love I have for you."

He looked up into sultry eyes the same shade as chestnuts. He could not read her. "Did I just scare you away from me?"

Talya shook her head, too overwhelmed to speak.

"I do love you, Talya."

Talya was flooded with emotions. In one rush she experienced everything from joy to fear. She grabbed Meridian around the neck and held him tightly. She needed the opportunity to have this moment. To experience the unquestioned security of Meridian's love for her. She buried her head against his beard and refused to wonder. The flow of Maxwell's words took her away into a world where fantasies could actually become reality—if only for one night.

"Stand up," Meridian said, freeing his neck of her embrace.

Meridian stood with her, giving her a quick kiss on the lips. He then moved around to stand behind her. The zipper was lowered to the middle of her back, and the dress pooled on the floor around her feet. When it fell to the floor, he kneeled down on his knees behind Talya and secured her around the waist. She felt his hands tracing the markings on her back. His fingertips and then his palms outlined the set of three four-pronged scars on her right lower back. She closed her eyes tight as she imagined how awful they must appear to him. She used a mirror only once to see the markings; they were too appalling to acknowledge ever again. She was humiliated by what they represented. Her humiliation quickly turned to passion when Meridian held her hips tightly and began to kiss the area of her shame.

Talya's body began to heat, and her legs began to buckle with Meridian's aggressive kisses and soft moans. Meridian helped Talya down on the bed. After teasing her lips with his finger, he helped her to lay on her belly. He kissed up and down her spine while he let his hands experience the softness of her body. He told her he loved her as he found the marks on her back and tried to remove them with his tongue. He joined his lips with hers as he used his long arms to rummage through the bedside table. He did not want to stop the rhythm. He moved swiftly and with precision and applied the condom while using his tongue to stimulate Talya's breasts.

Talya wrapped her arms around Meridian's broad shoulders. "It's been a long time for me," she admitted in a whisper.

Meridian's lips were pressed against her breasts. He moved up next to her to fight off the growing uncertainty he saw in her eyes.

"Then you'll enjoy me even more."

Meridian did not realize how hungry he was for Talya—this ultimate form of intimacy—until he lowered himself down on top of her. His urgency began to build, and he felt Talya's hesitancy grow. He stroked her face with one hand while slowly feeding her his tongue. He used his other hand to ready her body for his entrance. He wanted to ease the pain of his plentiful thickness entering her unfamiliar tightness. When he felt Talya was ready, and he could wait no longer, he eased himself slowly into her until he felt the release of her body and her heart as she kissed his neck and rubbed his back. He heard himself sigh from relief. He led her through a medley of rhythms until he found the one that was right for them, and then he concentrated on savoring the place he was exploring.

Meridian whispered confessions of how strong his feelings were for Talya into her ear. She was matching his rhythm as if they had performed this dance many times before. He felt her legs open up to receive him, and her hips rose to meet him. Her body vibrated under his, triggering a new urgency in Meridian. This urgency was so intense that his mind flashed unrecognizable pictures in front of his eyes. His body worked without any direction from him to feed the hunger and end the pain the urgency caused in his groin. Meridian felt his insides empty out as he exploded. He could not let the feeling end, so he continued to move his body around in circles, in and out, even after his thickness tried to recoil. He searched for Talya's mouth and demanded she kiss him. He needed her to take over his body with her tongue to end the lingering urgency that was always there until she removed it with her kiss.

"Meridian." She stopped the probing of his tongue by calling him back to her from wherever his mind went when they kissed. His kisses made her feel as if he were trying to consume her.

Meridian excused himself and went into the bathroom. He looked at himself in the mirror and tried to determine if the urgency was gone from inside of him. It was overpowering and removed all of his control. It frightened him because he was dependent on Talya to fix it and make him better. He looked at himself in the mirror and, although it was not a visible object, he knew it was still there the second she called him from the bedroom. He was not even near her, and the jolt of static electricity pierced his chest.

He felt at that second that he would do anything he had to do to keep Talya in his life.

"Meridian," Talya called again, "are you all right?"

He rejoined her in the bedroom. "I'm fine. How about you?"

She smiled at him and snuggled her back up to him. "I'm fine too."

They were exhausted from their lovemaking and fell asleep in each other's arms.

CHAPTER TWELVE

Before he left for Chicago, Meridian spent the morning meeting with Robert, who would run Weston Realty for the week he would be away. With spring approaching, Meridian would begin to travel more. He tapered down his flying during the winter months because of the constant delays at the airports. During his trip he needed to check the construction progress on the six houses he purchased. Thinking of the upcoming business trip reminded him of the first kiss he shared with Talya outside of her hotel room.

"Bad news." Robert seemed to appear out of nowhere to be standing in front of his desk.

"What is it?"

"Mr. Percy went into the hospital, and the insurance company still hasn't changed its original position on covering people with HIV or AIDS."

The attitude of the insurance company angered Meridian. "I think we've given them enough chances. Let's drop them as our carrier and find a new company right away."

"I agree." Robert scribbled something in his day planner.

"How soon can we get some companies in here with bids?"

Robert shrugged, "A multi-million dollar company looking to cover several hundred employees? They're probably already in the lobby."

Meridian laughed at Robert's attempt to make a joke. He never was one to have a big sense of humor.

"The only thing that might be a problem is breaking the contract with the existing carrier, but there's always a hidden clause."

"Do I need to be involved?"

Robert looked up over his glasses. "I can handle it with the help of the benefits manager. Why?"

"I want to spend some serious time with Talya before I start jetting back and forth to Chicago."

"No problem." Robert smiled. "I'm glad my two best friends are getting along."

Energy sparked his body when he thought of Talya. "We're getting along very well. There's a rough patch here and there, but mostly everything couldn't be better."

"Do you think Talya is the one?"

"The one?" Meridian laced his fingers together on top of his desk. "Do you know that I haven't thought about calling another woman since I've been seeing her?"

"Talya must be special if she has that power over you."

"Hmmm."

"The one. If there was ever going to be the one, it would definitely be Talya."

Meridian called Talya from his car before he arrived at the airport. He maintained a business tone when he left her a message at work giving her the particulars as to where he would be and how she could reach him. *I have to let her* know in case of an emergency, he told himself. Actually, he hoped she would call the second she received the message.

The builder's progress on the houses proved to be satisfactory. The winter weather caused minor delays, but things were moving along as scheduled. Meridian met with everyone involved in the project. In between meetings he hailed a cab and drove around the city looking for vacant property. Keeping busy helped him not miss Talya. After grabbing something to eat at a nearby deli, he settled into his hotel suite and began to review the notes from his meeting.

"Were you asleep? I forgot about the time difference."

Meridian brightened at the sound of Talya's voice. "It's okay. I'm glad you called. How are you?"

"I'm fine. When will you be home?"

"Four more days. I'll call you from the airport right after I get off the plane."

A short hesitation filled the line. "I miss you."

"You do?" Exhilaration warmed him. "Say it again."

Talya giggled into the phone. "You're awful."

"I know. Say it again."

"I miss you."

"See, that wasn't so bad."

They held the line, each submerged in their own thoughts.

"Talya?" Meridian's voice carried a serious tone.

"Yes?"

"I love you. I don't know why I'm finding you at this time in my life, but I know how much I've missed before you came along."

Meridian replayed his conversation with Talya over and over while in his afternoon meeting. She took the initiative to call. He smiled when she told him she missed him. He had been in love once before when he was younger, but it never felt like this. This was good. Powerfully scary, but a good feeling.

Talya curled up in a chair and covered herself with a blanket. She flipped through the work files on her lap and tried to concentrate. Meridian blurted out that he loved her without any warning. They were getting along well, growing closer every day, but she never imagined he loved her. A greedy smile outlined her face as she thought about everything she had in Meridian. When she relaxed and thought about what he meant to her, she could admit her feelings for him were powerful. Could she entertain the possibility that she loved him too?

A faint tapping at the door interrupted her thoughts. She missed talking with Jennifer since their relationships monopolized much of their time. They would probably sit up most of the night sharing their dating adventures.

"Meridian." Delighted, Talya threw her arms around him.

"Do you always open the door without seeing who it is first?" he scolded with a smile.

Excitement fueled her words. "What are you doing here? You weren't supposed to be back for three more days."

"Can I come in?" He was standing in the doorway holding his overnight bag and a huge brown bear with a big red bow.

Talya stepped back to let him pass.

Meridian dropped his bag and the bear on the floor and took Talya into his arms. "I missed you."

Talya marinated in Meridian's strong arms. She awoke in the morning with him watching her seductively.

"Where are you going?" Meridian caught her by the hand.

"I need to brush my teeth and comb my hair."

A low rumble filled the room. "You're beautiful. Give me a kiss." Meridian made her stomach flip when he said those words in his syrup-sweet voice.

Talya lightly brushed his lips before hurrying out of the bedroom. She went into the kitchen and cooked a breakfast of eggs, bacon and toast. She placed the food on a tray with two glasses of orange juice and returned to her bedroom. She woke Meridian with a kiss on the forehead. Sitting Indian style in the bed next to him, she fed him breakfast.

"I'm going to get used to this, and you'll have to do it all the time," Meridian said in between chewing his eggs. "Mr. Martin is a great cook, but it's the little fringe benefits you offer that give you the edge."

"After last night I thought you would be too weak to walk to the kitchen." She grinned over at him and handed him his glass of orange juice.

"I have a present for you."

Talya had already placed the bear at the foot of her bed. Meridian went into the living room and returned with his overnight bag. He opened it on the bed and riffled around until he found what he was looking for.

Meridian pulled out a pair of dark blue sweats. "This is so that you'll always feel comfortable around me."

Talya laughed as she held the sweats up to her chest. "They're wonderful."

Meridian held up a finger indicating there was more. He went back inside of his bag and came out with a silver framed picture of himself. "So you'll never forget about me."

Talya took the picture, kissed it, and placed it next to her bed.

Meridian held up his finger again. This time he pulled out a red negligee that did not have enough material to cover a small baby. "So I'll never forget about you." He tossed it over to Talya. "You can put that on right now if you want."

Before Talya could reply, Meridian held up his finger. He went into the overnight bag pulling out a thick book of crossword puzzles. "So we never run out of things to do together."

Talya could not control her giggles.

"One last thing." Meridian said searching deep inside of his bag. He moved next to Talya on the bed before dangling a gold tennis bracelet encircled by diamonds in front of her. "For you to wear and always know how much I love you."

Now that Talya was given permission to talk, she couldn't find any words to say that wouldn't ruin the tender moment. He fastened the bracelet around her wrist.

"Meridian, it's beautiful, but it's too expensive. I can't accept it."

"Talya, don't try to get me to take it back, because I'm not going to. Asking me to take it back would be an insult. I want you to have it. Just kiss me and say thank you. "

Talya kissed him as requested. They climbed back under the sheets after deciding that they would not be leaving the bed the entire day. Talya settled back into Meridian's slim, muscular arms. She let him strip away every morsel of her confusion and doubt with the stroking of her hair. She relaxed into him and was soon falling asleep again.

Meridian pulled on his pants as he hopped to the door. The doorbell had rang several times. Whoever was there did not plan on going away. Talya never stirred. He hesitated before answering the door to the two uniformed police officers on the other side.

"We're looking for Talya Stevenson," one police officer stated in a dry tone. His partner looked past Meridian into the apartment.

"She's asleep. Is something wrong?"

"Can you wake Ms. Stevenson, please?" It was not a request.

Meridian watched the police officer scribble something onto his notepad.

"Can we come in?" his partner asked.

"Of course." Meridian stepped back and let the two policemen move into the room. "Would you like to sit down?"

The officer looked up from his pad. "We'll stand."

Loud voices obscured by static came from the police radio worn on the first policeman's hip. He adjusted the volume and then looked up at Meridian. "Please wake Ms. Stevenson."

Apprehension weighed down Meridian's body as he retraced his steps back into the bedroom.

Talya pulled on her robe and hurried into the living room with Meridian at her heels.

"Ms. Stevenson?" The first officer asked.

"Yes." Talya stepped into the middle of the room. "Is there something wrong?"

The second officer moved around to stand in front of her with his hand poised over the handle of his baton. "Actually, Ms. Stevenson, we're here to ask you that question. We received a phone call from your mother in Tennessee. She's afraid that you may be in distress. She told us that you disappeared more than nine months ago, and she hasn't heard from you or been able to find you."

Talya glanced over at Meridian before she answered. "I'm completely fine, officer. Is my mother okay?"

"She's worried about you. Like I said, she's been searching for you. When she couldn't find you, she became worried and called the station." He glanced over at

Meridian and then back to her. "Would you like to speak to us in private?"

Meridian's hand went up around Talya's waist. The officer covertly implied that he might be a danger to her. They were speaking in code—Talya and the police officers. What exactly was he missing here? Hadn't they spent the entire morning making love so sweet that he couldn't whisper in her ear as she enveloped him? Why did he feel like he had become the suspect of a crime?

Talya rocked back against his hand. "No, my mother has overreacted."

The officer looked over his shoulder. His partner stood with his pen poised over his pad, giving the situation his full attention. Deciding that the call was a false alarm, he went back to recording the outcome of the call in his notes.

"You should give her a call immediately so that we don't have to come back out here."

Talya stiffened. "I'll call her."

The officer nodded in Meridian's direction before leaving the apartment. A silent warning?

Talya showed the two officers to the door. Her hand was glued to the knob, her head hung low. "There are parts of my life that I haven't shared with you."

Meridian folded his arms across his bare chest and watched Talya's slumped shoulders rise and fall. Talya turned to face him.

He let his arms fall to the seams of his pants. "Share them with me now." The possibility of betrayal bubbled inside of his chest. As Meridian peered into the never-changing smoky eyes of the woman he loved, he wondered how many untruths there were to discover about her.

"You may not want to be involved."

"It's too late for that; I'm in love with you." He hoped she would declare her love for him. When she didn't, he continued. "If I'm involved with you, then I'm involved with every aspect of your life. Why did you tell me your parents were dead?"

CHAPTER THIRTEEN

"Tell me about it," Meridian whispered in Talya's ear as they sat together on the side of her bed. Talya studied the pattern of her robe.

"It's important to me that you do. I want to know about your past. It's the only way I'll understand you better. I want to know that you trust me enough to share everything with me, even if it's difficult for you. We have to be honest with each other, or this relationship isn't going to work. I want us to always be open with each other, no matter what."

Talya hadn't even told the counselors anymore than they'd needed to know. They encouraged her to develop support systems, and she was starting to do that with Jennifer. Meridian would think she was a fool. How would their relationship change once he knew all of her secrets?

"Talk to me, Talya." His bare foot thumped against carpet.

Deep breath.

"The first year with Jason was perfect. He adored me and never stopped trying to prove it. There should have been signs...."

Meridian squeezed her hand. "Go on."

"He could be a little demanding of my time. Asked a lot of questions about where I went and how I spent my day, but I really didn't pay it much attention."

"Things must have changed."

"Everything started my senior year of college. My father died before I started college. My mother hadn't remarried yet, so money was tight for her after she lost her job. I received financial aid and a scholarship, but I couldn't afford the dorm fees. I was about to pack up and go home to Tennessee when Jason stepped in. He told me he loved me and asked me to move in with him. He said he'd work three jobs if he had to in order to keep me with him. He couldn't imagine living without me near. I moved into his apartment the next weekend."

The tension in Meridian's rigid back was unmistakable—it bothered him to hear the details of her last relationship. He stroked the back of her hand as he waited for her to continue.

"The verbal abuse started two months later. Mumbling smart remarks and subtle insults. I blamed it on stress, because he was supporting me and paying all of the bills. I took a part-time job as a waitress at a restaurant near campus to help out. When I came home and told Jason, he was furious."

The scene haunted her as if it had occurred the day before instead of six years ago.

"You got a job without asking me first?" Jason had questioned her.

"I didn't know I had to get your permission," Talya said flippantly and turned to walk away from him.

Jason ran across the room stopping her. He grabbed her arm, swung her around, and met the left side of her face with the palm of his right hand.

Shock froze her where she stood. Jason stared at her without a word, then left the house. He didn't return until late that night, drunk. He brought her flowers the next day and apologized for being such a jerk. He blamed it on the stress of his new responsibilities. He promised it would never happen again, making amends to her for several days. Their relationship became better than it had ever been.

"Then what happened?" Meridian stirred her from her silent reminisces.

"Things slowly began to change again. Jason started to mope around the house, always in a bad mood. I tried to keep him happy, but nothing I did worked.

"I remember the day I received my first paycheck. Jason took me to the bank to cash it and demanded I give him the money. I refused. It was my money. I majored in finance, I could manage my own money....The back of his hand flew up from the steering wheel of the car and landed against my mouth. He wrestled the money out of my hands." She paused when she visualized his angry face. "He tossed a ten-dollar bill into my lap so that I could catch the bus to work because he wasn't going to drive me anymore."

Meridian draped his arm around her shoulders. "What did you do?"

"As soon as we got home, I marched directly into the bedroom and started to pack my things. I would give up graduating from college if it meant taking his abuse. Jason came up behind me while I was in the closet, grabbed my clothes, and hit me in the back of my head. He threw me to the ground by my hair."

Talya flailed her arms, demonstrating their struggle. She could see it clearly. Jason straddled her at the waist then pent her arms to her sides with his thick thighs. "Say you're going to stay." His palm hopped across the left and then the right side of her face. "Say it!"

"I'll stay," Talya said sobbing.

"That's better." His palm came down one last time across her face making a loud slapping sound ring inside of their bedroom. "Now, unpack your clothes, and if you ever talk back to me again, I'll kill you."

The quiet support Meridian gave her as she relived her past contrasted vividly with her time with Jason. Telling him about Jason's abuse eased the burden she carried. His back remained stiff, but he never stopped holding her.

"You told him you would stay?" Meridian clarified.

"I tipped around the house the next several weeks trying not to upset Jason while I tried to find somewhere to go. Jason kept telling me that every couple has their fights and that I was making a big deal over nothing. I tried to bring it up to my friend at the time, but the stereotypes always got in the way. After a while Jason returned to being his charismatic self, and I began to believe he was right—couples went through this all of the time."

"But it's not normal, Talya."

"I learned that too late. By the time I decided I needed to leave, Jason had me too afraid to try and run."

"Run? Why didn't you go to your mother first?"

"My mother." Talya moved across the room before turning to Meridian. "My mother and Jason have a bond that is closer than anything we ever shared. Going to her was completely out of the question."

The incredulous look on Meridian's face told Talya that she had told him enough. She decided against telling him about Jason's rage several weeks after their first fight. She believed they were getting back on track. Talya left work one afternoon finding Jason sitting in his car in front of the restaurant waiting. He was unusually quiet as he drove to his parents' house.

He said his mother wanted to see him, but her car wasn't parked out front when they arrived. She must have been running an errand, Talya rationalized.

Jason got out of the car and started to walk away. "C'mon," he called back to her as he stepped up on the porch.

When she got into the house, Jason told her to follow him into the basement. The finished basement apartment had been his home before he made enough money from body-building competitions to move into his own place. Talya followed, but her racing heart told her that something wasn't right. Jason's long strides got him to the basement before she started down the stairs.

"Get out," Jason yelled at his younger brother. He got up and left not only the basement but the house. He knew the routine."

When Talya stepped off the last step into the basement, Jason turned to her. His dark eyes blazed, and his small, straight nose flared. This was the only warning signal she would receive.

The sound of his palm against her cheek echoed off the basement walls. "Who the hell was that guy you were talking to at the restaurant?"

"What guy?" Talya backed away from Jason. "There was no guy except the customers." Some of the male customers tried to pick up the waitresses, but that was an unpleasant part of the job.

"Don't give me that." Jason grabbed Talya by the arm and pulled her deeper into the basement. "Are you trying to step out on me?"

"No."

"Lying—"

Talya never heard the last of his sentence because his fist connected with her left eye causing her to become dazed. Talya couldn't take the punch of the muscular built Jason, who worked out in the gym every day. She fell back onto the bed; Jason straddled her within seconds. Talya blocked his punches and tried to get up, but she couldn't match his strength. The casual bumping and pushing were gone. He used his total body weight to hold her down. Every punch landed squarely on her face, bringing with it a sensation more painful than the first.

Talya screamed for someone to help her. As he brought his fist down again and again, she believed for the first time ever he might seriously hurt her—or kill her. She cried and begged Jason to stop hitting her. He leaned down and kissed her mouth hard. His lips meeting the ripped areas of her skin sent another stroke of pain through her body. He opened his pants and pushed away Talya's skirt. Talya did not stop him, since she preferred that to the constant punches to the face. When he finished, he told her to get dressed.

Jason kneeled in front of her and held her hands tightly on her lap. He looked down at the floor as he spoke. "I'm sorry. You make me crazy. I don't want to lose you to anyone else. Are you going to leave me? I promise it won't happen again."

Talya felt one of Jason's hot tears run down the back of her hand. That teardrop shattered her will, her heart, and her soul. Jason took possession of the broken pieces and held them for the next six years.

Meridian watched Talya with disbelief as she told him about her past relationship. How could anyone purposefully hurt her? She was so sweet and loving. Experiencing a bad relationship and being in a violent one were two different things entirely. He wanted to ask Talya how she could have endured six years of abuse, but there were more important questions that needed answering.

Meridian joined Talya, wrapping his arm around her slumped shoulders. "How did you get those marks on your back?"

In the fifth year, Talya found a man that would listen to her. The assistant principal at the junior high school where she worked. Jason had long since made her quit her job at the restaurant. They made plans to pick up her belongings from the apartment when Jason left for work. He would loan her money to get away from the almost daily abuse Jason had begun to inflict upon her. On the night she was supposed to leave, she came home early from work to find Jason waiting.

"He knew all about my plan. I made the mistake of trusting my mother again. She called Jason to warn him. I denied everything. He accused me of being in love with my boss. Jason had everything waiting in the bedroom. He stripped off my clothes, held me down on the bed, and pressed a hot fork against my back. He told me that he wanted every man who looked at me to know that I belonged to him."

Meridian lifted her chin. He planted a feather-light kiss on her lips. "But it didn't work, did it? You're finished with him and starting something new with me."

Talya's heart warmed.

Meridian pulled her even closer. "No wonder you've been hesitant about starting a relationship." The night in his den made sense. "Jason obviously didn't realize what he had in you. He was a coward to try to control a woman with force. I'm proud of you for finally getting out of the situation."

"Do you feel any differently about me now that you know about Jason?" Talya asked, hoping the answer would be honest and positive.

"Yeah, I respect you and what you've done with your life even more. It's easy for someone like me to become successful, because everything has always been in place for me. All I've ever had to do was use the resources that I had available to me. I have a strong family who has always supported me."

Talya smiled up at him.

"You've overcome unbelievable odds to become a success. I'm overwhelmed by what you have done in your life both personally and professionally."

Meridian held Talya in the dark silence of her bedroom, wondering if he would be able to find a reason the next morning to leave her bed. What she had shared with him had been a piece of her reality he'd never known lived inside of her. It meant a lot to him that she trusted him enough to tell her about her past. Every time they were together something about her made him love her more and more. He wanted her to tell him that she felt the same way. He could see it in the sultry brown coloring of her eyes that she carried deep feelings for him. He had to believe that. He touched her stomach and then began to fill his hand with her breasts.

"Do you know why I'm attracted to you?" Talya asked, rubbing Meridian's arm.

"Now this should be good, because I'm still not sure you are attracted to me."

Talya sighed heavily and rolled her eyes up at him. "Do you want to hear this or not? You know I'll lose my nerve if you keep teasing me."

"Okay, okay. You may speak uninterrupted."

"Don't get me wrong when I say this. I think you are a very handsome man."

"How could I take that wrong?"

"Shh. What I find the sexiest about you is your voice. It reminds me of syrup. It's sweet and thick and if you're not careful, you'll get stuck—caught all up in it. Get it?" Talya poked his ribs.

Meridian used his best Barry White impersonation to answer. "Thank you, baby."

Talya poked him in his ribs with her elbow again.

"That's enough of that." Meridian sat up suddenly, causing Talya to fall back on the bed. He straddled her and tickled her all over until she could not speak.

CHAPTER FOURTEEN

Talya pulled her address book from her dresser. Darkness discarded her mother's phone number long ago. Her stepfather answered the phone. Not recognizing her voice, he dropped the phone without making small talk and called her mother.

"Mom, the police came here last night. They said that you called them."

"I did. Jason called me frantic about where you were and if you were okay. He said you ran away again and that he believed someone might be keeping you against your will."

Totally believable. Her mother was as gullible to his lies and deception as she herself had once been. His southern gentlemanly ways won her mother over immediately. Her mother's beliefs about relationships were old-fashioned and outdated. She identified with Jason's ways of thinking and supported him in all their arguments. The first time Talya tried to run away from Jason, she went to her mother's home in Tennessee. By morning, Jason sat in the living room waiting for her to wake up so he could take her home. "He'll settle down some once you're married." Her mother offered words of encouragement as Jason had escorted Talya to his car. Before reaching the end of the dark paved driveway, Jason smacked her with the back of his hand.

"Mom, the only one who ever kept me anywhere against my will is Jason. I ran away from him because I couldn't take it anymore. Did he tell you what he did to me to make me leave me home without telling him?"

"He told me you had a spat."

"A 'spat'? Mom, he beat me up."

"Now Talya, Jason told me everything. You have a tendency to exaggerate sometimes. I've told you many times before that men like women who know their place. You're supposed to support Jason and make things easier for him. When he comes home at the end of his day you should be there to comfort him."

Talya listened to the southern accent of her mother drone on about her duties to Jason. This advice made her stay many years trying to fix her relationship with Jason. Her mother had been raised in a home that was full of values and stereotypes. She passed these lessons on to her only child. This way of being might have worked with a man who was caring and considerate, but not with a selfish and insecure man like Jason. Now that Talya had met a man who treated her with value, she could never live that way again.

"Where are you? I'll send Jason to pick you up. He told me to let you know that he's not mad at you; he's worried about you."

"Jason came to my job, Mom."

"He told me that. He says it's the only way he can contact you. He also told me that he apologized to you and offered you as much time as you needed to clear your head. Is that right?"

"Yes, it's right." Talya became exasperated as she tried to explain. "That's what he said, but you had to be there to know how he said it. He told me not to run again."

"He's right. It's not safe for you to be out in the world without your family."

"You don't understand what Jason is like when we're alone. He comes across as being sweet, but he's a monster. I can't live like that anymore. I don't want him to know where I am so I won't tell you either."

"You're being ridiculous."

Hurt and anger brought tears to her eyes. Her mother never validated her fears. "You have no idea what I go through with Jason." Her voice was rising. "You never want to hear it. You automatically take his side because he's a man. You take his side against your own daughter."

"Don't talk to me like that." Her mother matched her tone. "I'm your mother."

"Then why don't you act like it? For once, why don't you consider that I might be telling the truth about Jason?"

"That's enough, young lady." Her stepfather's voice came across the telephone line. "I will not have you shouting at your mother. You call her back when you calm down and learn how to show her the respect she is due."

Talya gripped the receiver and listened to the dial tone buzz in her ear. Again, Jason had won. Her mother thought of him as incapable of doing any wrong and Talya as the ungrateful brat from hell. She would never be able to return home. Her mother and an aunt she barely knew on her father's side were her only remaining family. She was completely alone in the world. Meridian tapped on the bedroom door. She slumped down on the bed before replacing the receiver on its cradle.

Meridian tapped again. "Talya? Are you al right in there?"

"I'm fine." She wiped away the tears threatening to fall.

"Are you done talking with your mother?" The tenderness in his voice proved he knew the conversation hadn't gone well.

"Yes."

"How'd it go?" He asked from the other side of the door.

"Fine," she lied. How much drama would be too much for him to stand?

He paused and then spoke in a chipper voice. "Well, hurry up so that we can get to the skating rink."

Talya crossed the room and opened the door allowing him admittance into his own bedroom. "You won't let me fall, will you?"

"Never. You have my pledge of honor." He retrieved a pair of Roller Blades from the top of his walk-in closet.

"I've never skated before."

Meridian sat on the edge of his bed while he slipped on his shoes. "I know, you told me, and I still can't believe it. Stick with me, and you'll do many things you've never done before." He looked up at her with an intensity that gave his words another meaning. "If you put your trust in me, you'll see I can teach you many things. I would never stand by and watch you fall without giving myself first."

"Mom, listen, don't worry about it." Jason flipped several pages of the body-building magazine he was reading. "I'll take care of everything."

"I know you will. Talya's really upset me with some of the things she said." Her voice wavered.

"I'm sorry you had to go through that. I promise that I'll bring her back home and that everything will be okay. I'll have her call you and apologize once she gets here."

"You're a good man to put up with her stunts all these years."

"No, I just love her."

Jason's fist remained clenched until he hung up the phone. He jumped up from the sofa and paced the living room like a wild dog. He was sure that Talya's mother could talk some sense into her. She had so many times before.

The rules of the game had changed without Talya telling him. Now he would have to come up with a new strategy. He would be going on the body-building competition circuit with Rizzo soon. He wanted everything settled before then.

"Why didn't you snatch her when you had the chance?" Rizzo pulled his baseball cap over his eyes and sank down in the seat. "We've sat out front of this building for three days now. And you're paying the parking ticket you got on my car yesterday. I say the minute we see her girlfriend's car, we go in and get her. I'm not going to keep coming here every day."

"Will you shut up?" Jason snapped at him never taking his eyes off the entrance of the parking structure. "I told you Talya has to come back on her own. Otherwise, as soon as I get her home, she'll run again."

"Jason, she's not going to come back on her own. This is our third day sitting here," Rizzo complained.

"There she is!" Jason checked the traffic before he swung his door open.

"You want me to come with you?"

"No, wait here."

Jason ran through the parking structure. He found the car as the girlfriend stepped onto the elevator. He smiled and joined her. He exited the elevator one floor after the girlfriend. He jogged down the stairwell and watched the girlfriend go into her apartment. His first thought was that Talya might be her roommate. He casually strolled down the corridor and read the name engraved on the door knocker. Jennifer. His skin crawled. Mission accomplished, he strolled back toward the elevator. The people living in this building must have tall dollars, he thought as he read the name plates on the doors as he passed. The fancy downtown apartment building carried a heavy. Everything worked his way that day! The very next door displayed Stevenson in script writing.

Jason stood outside her door contemplating his next move. She avoided his calls at work. She admitted being involved with someone else. He checked both directions of the corridor before ringing the doorbell.

"Hi, Tae." He walked past her into the apartment.

"Jason, what are you doing here?" Talya stood holding the door open. "How did you find me?"

CHAPTER FIFTEEN

The city passed the necessary ordinances to begin construction of three casino sites. Brokers were scrambling to find connections to the project that would bring in millions of dollars in revenue every year. Meridian happened to be holding vacant property in the downtown area near the proposed casinos. He and Robert immediately put their heads together and came up with ideas to develop the land.

"Mrs. Braden, I asked not to be disturbed." Blueprints were spread across Meridian's conference table as they discussed the details of the plan.

"I understand, sir, but there's a young lady on the phone by the name of Jennifer who says it's urgent that she speak to you. She demanded that I interrupt your meeting."

Robert looked up from the sketches in front of him.

He pushed his black-rimmed glasses back on his nose and listened to the architect while watching Meridian.

Meridian started putting on his suit jacket before he hung up the phone. He apologized to the young architect leaving Robert in charge of the meeting.

Robert rushed after him, "What's going on?"

Meridian disappeared down the corridor.

"Get rid of her." Jason demanded through gritted teeth from behind the door.

"I have the Dating Adventure with the reverend of all times to tell you about."

Talya, with pleading eyes, cut Jennifer off before she could finish her anecdote. "I can't talk right now. I'll stop by later."

"Can I come in for a minute?"

"Talya, shut the door," Jason demanded.

Jennifer's eyes narrowed with puzzled questioning.

"I have to go." Talya's voice quivered.

Jason followed Talya around the room. He caught up with her in front of the sofa and wrapped his arms around her waist. "I love you." He kissed her cheek. "I want us to pick up where we left off and work everything out."

"Jason," Talya spoke very calmly, although she felt an incredible urge to run to the bathroom. "I'm doing my own thing now. I think it's better if we leave each other alone. That way we won't have to fight all the time."

"I don't think that's best. I want you back with me. I want you back home. I know that I'm not the easiest man to live with, but I'm better now. I promise you that I won't ever put my hands on you again." He kissed her forehead. "You believe me, don't you?"

"I believe you, but I always make you so crazy. It's not you; it's me." She had learned the right words to calm him down a long time ago. "Why would you want me home when I don't want to be there?"

"Because I want you there." Jason pressed his lips against Talya's and forced his tongue inside her mouth.

Talya brought her arms up between them. "Jason, please, leave me alone. I'm with someone else now."

Jason released her and started to walk around the living room checking everything out. He sat in a chair, letting his legs dangle over the side. "What did you do with my money? Is that how you moved into this fancy place? Two thousand dollars, I think it was."

"Most of that money came from my salary. I only took enough to get on my feet."

"Listen, what's done is done." He reached out to Talya. She didn't move until she saw the familiar flaring of his straight nose. He helped her down into his lap. He slowly examined Talya with his brown, almost black, eyes. He started at the top of her head and moved his hands down her body. He lifted her blouse and searched for the brand he had given her.

The phone rang.

"Just let the machine pick up, we have a lot to talk about."

The machine picked up, but the ringing soon started again.

"If I don't pick up, he'll come over." Talya fought her terror to stay calm. She would have to leave again. When her life was beginning to have meaning, when she found true friends and a wonderful man, she would have to leave. This time she would go further away. The last time she left, she was unemployed with only two thousand dollars and the clothes on her back. This time she had work experience and a suitcase hiding in her bedroom closet with enough money to get her another apartment far away.

Jason raised his voice. "I don't give a damn about him coming over here. Let him. I need to have a little talk with him anyway. Let him know that things are changing around here."

"Okay, I'll come home if you give me time to talk to him." Jason wouldn't get anywhere near Meridian. If she could get Jason out of the apartment, she'd leave town and he'd never find her again.

Jason smiled. "That's my girl."

Talya felt her skin crawl under Jason's fingers. He massaged his brand.

"But I want you home now. This guy will figure it out when you're not around anymore. You remember who you belong to." His fingers stroked her back.

"If you could give me a little time to clear things up, pack all my things—"

"Did he see this?" Jason ignored her request and focused his attention on the markings branding her back.

"No," Talya lied. It was a trick question—a test to see if she had slept with Meridian. He pulled her by her collar down next to him. "Does he have your name tattooed on his chest like I do?"

Talya shook her head. Her body shuddered. There was a day in time when he presented the tattoo on his muscled chest as a tribute to her while he competed. It had come to mean something entirely different after he lost the competition.

The knocking at the door made Jason release her.

"Talya," Jennifer called through the closed door, "if you don't open up, I'm going to call the police."

"I better get going." Jason had an uncanny fear of the police. He turned to Talya with darkening eyes as he tried to save face. "I want you to take care of that little problem you have. I'll be back to see you soon. Understand?"

"Understood," Talya said, remembering not to make eye contact with him. That's the way he liked her to answer him. One wrong move, and his fist would connect with her eye.

Jason kissed her forehead. "Don't run."

Jason gave Jennifer a pointed grimace as he passed by: This girlfriend would not become a problem. Talya would see to that.

Talya paced the length of the room. How did he find her? He had her phone number at work and knew where she lived. She would not be able to shake him now. She bought herself some time by telling him she would break up with Meridian, but Jason would return soon. What should she do? She refused to suffer Jason's abuse again. The beatings and the torture. The only viable solution shone as clear as the North Star: she had to leave.

Talya scrambled to her bedroom and lugged her survival suitcase from the closet. Jason feared being arrested; he wouldn't be back tonight. That gave her time to pack more clothes to start her third life. She began to throw her clothes into a travel bag. She would leave right now, before Jason came back. He would be there every day until she went back to him. She was sure of that. She knew him well enough.

Talya jumped when the doorbell rang. Her body froze, but her hands kept moving until her mind synchronized her actions. Jason had changed his mind and had returned to take her with him now. Time ticked away as she packed. She continued throwing her clothes into her suitcase. Jason would get tired of ringing the doorbell and go away thinking she had left, and that's when she would leave.

Calling the police would be useless. They would come and ask the same questions as before. Then they would make Jason promise to keep the noise down, and they would leave. Jason would chase her into the closet and wait outside until she had to come out to use the bathroom. Talya could wait him out most times. He'd fall asleep or pass out drunk; then she would sneak by him. Or he would pretend to be asleep until she came out so he could beat her until she lay slumped on the floor. Or Talya would be so afraid that she would stay in the closet for up to two days. She would use the bathroom right where she sat. It was better than the things Jason was promising to do to her when she opened the door.

"Talya, what are you doing?" Meridian walked into the bedroom, followed by Jennifer.

"Are you okay? I called Meridian." Seeing the narrow slits covering Jason's black eyes was enough to shake Jennifer. "I used my spare key to get in. I was worried about you, so I called Meridian to come over."

Meridian walked up to Talya and tried to touch her face.

Talya flinched and backed away. "I have to leave."

"Where are you going?" Jennifer asked.

"I can't tell you. I have to get out of here before he comes back."

Meridian asked Jennifer to leave them alone. She hugged her friend and told her not to go anywhere without talking to her first. She and the reverend could help. Talya agreed, knowing that she would not keep that promise. She couldn't place her friend in danger.

Talya pushed Meridian away. Holding her would not help.

"Talya," he coaxed, "put down the clothes and sit down." He pried the clothing from her grasp, steering her to sit down. He lowered himself down on the ottoman in front of her chair. "Who was here? Who scared you?" He took her trembling hands in his.

"Jason." She choked out.

"What did Jason want?"

Talya looked away while chewing on her bottom lip. She wanted to stay strong. She didn't want Meridian to see her crying.

"What happened? Tell me everything he said to you."

Talya held back her tears and told Meridian everything. "He will hurt me. I know that. He'll hurt you; I know that too."

"You're afraid he'll hurt you so you're running away? I don't understand. You told me you ended it between you two. You told me that you never have contact with him."

"I don't have contact with him anymore."

"Then why did he come here demanding that you come back to him?"

Talya had omitted a key portion of her history with Jason. "I didn't tell you everything about Jason and me."

Meridian wasn't surprised. The more time he spent with her, the more secrets he found. He braced himself to learn more.

"I ran away from Jason one day while he was at work. I took all the money I could find in the house and ran. None of my old friends would take me in because he had threatened them when they helped me in the past. I ended up at a shelter for abused women for three months."

Meridian was stunned. "What are you telling me?" He had no idea what he had gotten himself into. "Jason is after you?"

Talya saw the flicker of regret cross Meridian's face. She learned to recognize the demurring expression her friends gave her when she begged for their help. Her situation was too contorted and dangerous. No one wanted to voluntarily become involved in the conflict between her and Jason.

Talya gained control of her sobs before she attempted to answer. "Yes. He's after me. He's always after me. That's why I have to get away from here. He's coming back for me. I have to be out of town before he gets here."

"Calm down. I'll protect you from Jason." He squeezed her hands. "What about me? Are you going to run away from me too?"

Talya blinked. "If I stay, I put everyone I care about in danger. I don't want to leave you, but it's the only way."

"Why don't you run to me? We're together now. I'm not going to let Jason touch you again." Meridian leaned forward and kissed Talya's brow.

"There's no limit to what he'll do to get me to come home."

"There's no limit to what I'll do to protect you."

Talya laid back in the chair. Meridian's words soothed her. She felt safe with him.

"Talya, I want you to promise me that you won't take off and leave me."

She searched Meridian's eyes for any signs of doubt. Hurt lurked behind the intensity of his gaze.

Meridian pulled her up into his arms. "Do you trust me to take care of you?"

Talya nodded. "I do trust you, Meridian."

Meridian gave her a tight squeeze. He needed to hear those words. He had been too close to losing her. In a fleeting moment, Talya could have walked away without any explanation, leaving him to wonder.

CHAPTER SIXTEEN

Meridian planted his elbow on the shiny wood-grain desktop and propped his chin against his fist. The words on the page in front of him blurred. It would be the easiest thing to do: walk away. What Talya had shared with him was mind-blowing. No one would blame him; he had walked into the relationship without knowing all of the facts. Would he have pursued her if he had known about her past boyfriend? He remembered their first meeting and the feel of the smallness of her hand in his.

Mr. Martin came into his home office and set a tray of food on the corner of his desk. He listened without hearing as Mr. Martin told him good night. The sandwich was stacked high with ham and cheese. The aroma of sliced pickles wafted over to him. The tray of food appealed to all of his senses. He pushed the papers away from him and pulled the tray within reach.

Perhaps this was what having a real relationship meant. Accepting someone for not only their good qualities, but loving them for their bad ones. Robert had given him knowledge, as he always did, and told him that Talya was still the same person he loved the day before he found out about Jason. They were the same age, but Robert acted as if he were fifty. As he mentally examined his own relationship history, Meridian realized that he, too, carried baggage. Talya had never once inquired about the comments the wives and girlfriends made at the monthly get-togethers. She accepted him for what he was without question.

Robert's statement brought up another crucial point for Meridian. Talya had never told him that she loved him. He would stand by her as she handled her situation with Jason; he had given in to that fact. He couldn't let her go. But what would be the ultimate outcome of their time together? He lifted the sandwich and took a bite. Relationships were new to him, but he was very sure Talya should have reciprocated when he confessed his love for her. He didn't want to push her. He demonstrated his patience by waiting. It had been so many months now, didn't he have the right to know?

Meridian brushed his hands together, removing the crumbs from the bread before he lifted the phone to his ear. "Meridian Weston."

"Hi, are you busy?"

"Busy thinking about you."

"Can I drive out to see you?"

The jolt stunned his limbs. "I have two conditions. One, you have to be here before dark. And two, you must bring a bag and stay for the weekend."

"Hmmm." Talya hesitated. "I guess I can live with those conditions. See you soon."

"Talya," Meridian called before she hung up the phone. "Yes?"

"Never mind, we'll talk when you get here."

No, he could deny her nothing. All the hesitancy he was experiencing just moments earlier seemed silly to him now. His life would never go back to being the same. The past months he spent with Talya were about real emotion. It was what life was supposed to be about. He smiled in anticipation of her arrival.

CHAPTER SEVENTEEN

The temperate weather and the bright rising moon made a perfect night to sit on the patio outside of Meridian's bedroom. It took only a few minutes before he helped Talya into his lap on the lounge chair. They tore at each other's clothing as they made their way back inside to his king-size bed. The night wind blew a gentle breeze over their nude, perspiration-covered bodies. Meridian's urgency was outdone by the hunger of Talya's gyrating hips. Perspiration dropped down onto Talya's face as Meridian struggled to match her intensity. Her uninhibited display of need fueled his response. Their lovemaking was quick, but more vehement than either could remember.

Meridian pulled Talya against his smooth chest. "What's bothering you?"

"Nothing." She closed her eyes.

"You made love to me like you were leaving and never going to see me again." The implications disturbed him.

"Sometimes that's how I feel." Talya rolled away from him as she choked back her tears.

"Well, I love you, and I'm not going anywhere. I couldn't have said that with such conviction a few hours ago, but now I'm positive about where I want to be." He waited for Talya to give him verbal confirmation of her feelings for him. None came. He reminded himself that he wouldn't push her into a corner. "Are you where you want to be?"

"More than you know."

Silence muscled its way into the room, bringing with it quiet tranquillity they shared. He fit his body to hers and kissed her neck before drifting off to sleep.

Meridian woke in the middle of the night his stomach rumbling from hunger. He slid out of bed unnoticed by Talya and headed for the kitchen. He loved fresh fruit and Mr. Martin always kept whatever was in season in the refrigerator. Oranges would do. He sliced three oranges and placed them in a bowl.

Knowing that Talya slept safely in his bedroom comforted him. If he wanted to press his nose up against her hair and smell the baby powder, he could. He could go to her if he wanted to and kiss the freckles that defined her character. If he wanted to look into Talya's sultry brown eyes, he could. If he needed someone to talk to or laugh with, she was down the hall. He could touch her body erotically or hold her lovingly. Unbelievable, only hours ago he was considering walking away from the best thing that had ever happened to him in his blessed life. Meridian laughed at his musings; the real thing was better than any fantasy.

"Where were you?" Talya shielded her eyes from the light in the hallway.

"I was hungry. Do you want something?"

Talya sat up and watched Meridian move around the partially lit room. His caramel-colored lean legs and smooth, muscular chest were bare. "No."

Meridian tossed back the sheets and jumped into bed. "What should we do tomorrow? I want to do something special for you."

Talya climbed on top of him. "You smell like oranges." Her fingertips kneaded his narrow chest. The muscles in his abdomen rippled. He quivered when she kissed his navel. "Is there something you need to tell me?" Meridian asked, watching Talya's eyes, which had transported her miles away.

She shook her head, not breaking the stride of her hands raking his chest.

"You're not yourself at all tonight. You've been an animal one minute and preoccupied the next."

"Do you think it would be all right for me to work in your garden sometimes?"

Meridian's four-year-old French Rambler ranch-style home boasted grounds that were perfect. A pebble walkway surrounded the brown brick exterior that met the L-shaped driveway. Rare trees only seen in horticulture books shaded the property. There were flower gardens and islands of bushes of every variety splattered around the grounds. During their tour of the grounds, Meridian showed Talya where he and Robert spent time playing basketball on his private court. Next, he took her to his most special place. His mother insisted that he build an area outside that brought peace and quiet when he was stressed. He didn't see the need at first, but later he was glad he followed her advice.

The redwood deck hid behind a masterfully planned overgrowth of wild greenery. Once you walked through the greenery, you were hit with color bursts of different shapes and sizes. Talya roamed through the garden stopping to identify some rare plant or flower and smelling its fragrance. She followed a narrow gravel walkway three or four feet to the most spectacular man-made pond ever seen. She named for Meridian the different rocks and plants she observed in the pond. Meridian smiled at her excitement when he told her the pond was stocked with exotic fish in the summer.

Meridian pulled Talya up to him. "My garden?" He smacked his lips together, frustrated that she avoided answering his question. "You can work in my garden anytime that you want, if it makes you happy."

Talya kissed him.

"Why are you so preoccupied?" He attempted to steer the conversation back onto its original course.

"You smell like oranges, but——" she smiled down at him—"do you taste like oranges?"

The distraction caused by Talya's question made him forget what he asked. She leaned down and kissed him once quickly. She ran her finger across the fullness of his lips and traced their shape with the tip of her tongue. When he opened his mouth to receive her, she backed away until he closed his lips again. Meridian closed his eyes while Talya tasted his lips and caressed his face. He felt her breasts pass over his chest as she moved up to kiss each of his eyelids. Her breath was hot in his ear. Her gestures exploded with supple eroticism.

"Do you always have to avoid my questions?"

"Only the hard ones." Talya kissed his heart shaped lips as she ran her hands through his soft, curly hair. She touched his beard and traced his mustache with her finger.

Meridian pulled her face down to meet his for a deep kiss. He grabbed her around the waist. She removed his hands and placed them back at his side before carefully pinching his erect nipples. She savored the taste of coconut oil on his hairless chest and stomach with her tongue. Meridian tried to maneuver her body so that he could take her, but she moved to pull off his underwear and threw it off the foot of the bed.

"Talya," he moaned. What is she doing to me? he asked himself, already knowing the answer. He had finally found a way to control the urgency and now Talya was introducing it all over again in another way.

He grabbed her head and moved his body to parallel hers. He felt her hands move underneath his body and cradle him. The urgency to move inside of her mouth overcame him. He thrust his hips up and down while trying to steady her head. His arms spread out the length of the bed, his hips moved faster with more force and his moans grew louder. Talya's hands massaged him, his body tensed, he howled from the pleasure.

Meridian collapsed covered in a sheen of perspiration. He inhaled deeply trying to catch his breath.

Talya moved up next to him. His tongue was inside of her mouth sharing the flavor with her before their lips met. The urgency had returned.

Meridian started to move down in the bed to give Talya the opportunity to experience the same joy, but she stopped him.

"Just hold me."

Meridian pulled the sheets over them and put his arms around her. He pressed his head to hers. He had no words. He still reeled from the jerky sensations rocking his body.

"You are very intense," Talya told him. "It's like you're trying to take me inside of you."

"I feel like I need you inside of me." Meridian stroked her back. "What you did only makes it worse."

"Should I not do it again?"

"Not on your life. I'm spoiled now. You're going to have to do it more often."

Talya closed her eyes and let a smile fill her face.

"My intensity bothers you?"

She shrugged her shoulders. "It's overwhelming sometimes."

"And with your past history, it upsets you."

Talya opened her eyes to be met by his serious but apologetic face. "It makes me guarded sometimes."

How could he explain the jolt of electric energy that flowed through his veins when he was near her without sounding like a lunatic? He didn't understand it himself. He couldn't describe it to another person, especially the person unknowingly responsible for shutting down his system.

"I don't want to ever make you feel uncomfortable with me." Meridian kissed Talya's freckles one at a time. He looked deep into her eyes, "I love you."

"The world won't come to an end. The ceiling won't fall in on you. I won't leave you. Just say it." He kissed her lips. "I love you."

Talya closed her eyes.

Meridian kissed the tip of her nose. "Uh-huh, don't do that. Don't pull away from me and don't ignore me. I love you, Talya Stevenson."

Talya looked into his eyes.

"I can see it right here." He kissed each of her eyelids. "If it's true, tell me. I need to hear it." He lifted her chin with his hand. "I love you."

She swallowed a deep breath. "I love you."

Meridian held her head against his chest. Relief eased his body. He felt Talya's hot tears on his chest but he didn't let go, and he didn't ask her what was wrong. He held her as closely as he could and let her cry out all the fear and hurt. He wanted Talya to come to him ready to receive all he had to offer—and he had a lot to offer.

CHAPTER EIGHTEEN

"I know that this is the worst possible time for you to have to leave town," Robert apologized. "If Rena and I weren't having such a hard time—"

Meridian broke in. "Three days should be enough to check the progress of the Chicago housing venture. From there I'll fly to Atlanta and meet with the company that has an interest in purchasing houses for its employees to live in while they travel on business." The company often sent employees for on-site management training that required them to stay several months in one place. "My mother is in Atlanta for a few weeks, so I'll drop in on her and then get right back here."

"Rena and I will keep a close eye on Talya. I'll stop by the bank every day. We'll have her over for dinner."

"Robert," Meridian said, forcing a smile, "I wouldn't trust anyone but you to keep an eye on her. You know how she is, so don't let her tell you that you're invading her privacy or something like that. This Jason hasn't made any contact with her for weeks, but you never know what someone like that is capable of doing."

"Don't worry."

"That's what Talya told me."

Meridian reluctantly boarded the plane. Although Talya downplayed the danger Jason posed, he feared for her safety. Why would she have to run from him and virtually be living in hiding if Jason wasn't a serious threat? He blew out a puff of air. Until she came to him and said differently, he'd have to trust in her assessment of the situation. Robert would take good care of her. He smiled when he thought of Jason going up against Rena. He'd have his hands full.

"How much longer are you going to be staying with Auntie?" Meridian asked as he sat on the patio with his mother.

"I'm not sure, maybe another week or two."

Meridian nodded, surveying the grounds and watching the gardeners. He imagined Talya working in his own flower garden. She spent most of her time there.

"Is something bothering you? You've been deep in thought since you've been here."

Meridian leaned forward in his chair. "I've met someone that's very special to me."

His mother smiled over the rim of her glass of iced tea. "My son has met someone special? I don't believe it. By special, do you mean that you've gone out with her twice?"

Meridian dropped back and crossed his legs at the ankle. "I mean I'm in love with her."

The glass of iced tea made a clinking sound against the glass patio table. "Who is this girl that has captured your heart? Tell me everything."

Meridian beamed as he described Talya to his mother. He always imagined he would have this conversation with his father, but his mother made a perfect substitute. She had the same reservations any mother would have about her only son's first love. Meridian watched curious expressions cross his mother's face while he told her about Talya's extraordinary effect on his life.

"I don't understand the problem. You've told me nothing but how wonderful this girl is. Why are you sitting here with such a look of turmoil on your face? Does she feel the same way about you?"

Meridian adjusted his sunglasses. "I believe she does. The problem is, I don't know where I want my relationship with Talya to go. I really care for her, and I know I want more from her. I just don't know how much. I don't know what she wants from me."

"Are you thinking the M word, or is it getting stuck in your throat?" She chuckled as she reached out and swatted at his arm.

"M word?"

His mother tossed her head back and laughed harder. "You don't even know what the word is—marriage—I'm talking about marriage. Are you considering marrying Talya?"

Meridian blinked away his surprise. That would be the logical next step. He never wanted to let Talya go; he couldn't even fathom that reality. But a permanent future? There were many things to consider. He and Talya had never discussed their future. Every day he learned something new about her. He joined in his mother's laughter. He needed to do a lot of thinking.

Meridian stretched his weary body across the length of the bed. He held the phone on top of his chest as he waited for Talya to answer.

"I'm glad you're still at my house." She would be safer there than at her apartment without him around.

"I'm on my way back to the city now. Jennifer and I are going to meet for lunch. How's your visit with your family going?"

"Good. I told my mother all about you, and she can't wait to meet you." Meridian paused and continued on with a more serious tone. "I miss you."

"I miss you too."

"Are you going to spend the night at your place?"

"I'll be fine. Jennifer is right next door. Besides, I haven't heard anything from Jason. Maybe he's finally gotten the message."

"Okay, but if there is any trouble at all, I want you to call Robert first and then call me on my cell phone. I told Robert that I wanted him to look out for you while I'm away. He's very sensible, he'll know how to handle any problems that arise."

"Meridian," Talya said, cutting him off, "I'll be fine. Don't worry so much."

"I can't help but worry about you. You just remember that you promised me you'd stay at my place if there's any sign of trouble."

"I remember."

❖

Meridian spent the last day with his mother going over strategies to acquire new property. The situation with Mr. Percy made him start to think about economically challenged communities and what he could do to help. His father also said, "Son, you have to give back to the black community because they were the ones to support me when I was starting out. Always reach back and take someone with you as you walk down the road to success."

Adding an addendum to the plan he and Robert were putting together to present to the city council about his property near the proposed casino sites would be easy to do. He could buy up a block of old, worn down, vacant houses near downtown and rebuild them for low-income families. While the city was building the two new stadiums and the three casinos, Meridian would make the surrounding downtown areas more appealing to tourists.

"The idea sounds like it will work, but do we have the capital to pull it off?" his mother wanted to know.

"I'll have to meet with Robert and the bank about that to be sure. I'll ask Talya to put together some numbers for me. Then I'll have to locate the best area to build...." Meridian's mind trailed off at the mention of Talya. He wanted to get home and check on her.

"I'm sorry, Ms. Stevenson, but I have no choice but to ask you to take an indefinite leave of absence."

Talya couldn't believe what she heard. "Sir, is there anything else I can do to rectify the situation?"

"I'm afraid not. This decision came from above my head. The bank feels it can't take the chance of being liable if one of your coworkers were to be hurt. I tried everything I could to keep you on. I know you're doing excellent work and you still haven't met your full potential."

Talya stood and held her head high with dignity. "I know that you did all you could, thank you. I'll clean out my office immediately."

Talya went into her office under the watchful eyes of her coworkers. She closed the door behind her and fell to her knees in tears. Everything she worked for was gone in a matter of minutes. She pulled herself together and threw all of her personal belongings into a box. Everything she built over the past eighteen months fit into one compact, recycled box.

"I don't understand, what do you mean Ms. Stevenson is no longer with the bank? Where is she? Who is handling the Weston Realty account?" Robert was visibly upset. He didn't need one more problem. He knew that Meridian would find some way to blame this on him. He was so crazy over Talya.

The manager took Robert into his office. "Ms. Stevenson is on a leave of absence, but we do not expect her to return. I have assigned your account to a very experienced accountant that I'm sure you will enjoy working with."

"I don't think that will be acceptable. I will have to speak with Mr. Weston and get back to you."

"Weston Realty has been a valued customer here at Brunstown Bank for many years, and I'll personally do anything I can to make sure you're happy. If there is anything I can do, please let me know."

Robert shook the manager's hand. You better get

Talya back before Meridian returns from his business trip, he thought. Oh, boy. Meridian was irrational when it came to Talya. Somehow he would turn this into Robert's problem. He was supposed to be watching out for her while Meridian was away. He'd have to understand that Robert could not handle his own love life right now, let alone Meridian's.

Robert stood outside Talya's door waiting for her to answer. If there were trouble with her ex-boyfriend, a physical confrontation, what could he do? Robert wished that he was taller and built larger, but it wasn't in his genes. He worked out with Meridian at least three times a week at the club, he was in good shape, but he could never bulk up like the other men walking around the gym. He gave in to the idea that he was born to be a nerd for the rest of his life.

"Are you all right? I stopped by Brunstown for our appointment and your manager told me you left the bank." It was obvious to Robert that Talya had been crying. Her eyes were red and puffy.

"I'm fine, but I'm out of a job."

"What happened?"

"Jason came by the bank yesterday threatening my coworkers. He hasn't been able to contact me here since I've been staying at Meridian's house all week, so he must've gone there looking for me. My manager told me that he made such a scene, they called the police. He scared everybody half to death."

"It's not fair to let you go because of Jason's stupidity. Meridian will be back this evening, maybe he can help get your job back."

Talya shook her head. "The bank can't be liable if Jason hurts one of its employees." She turned her back to him to wipe away a tear. "This has happened before. Even if I had been at home, Jason would have eventually gotten around to getting me fired. It's the best way to control me." She faced Robert. "I don't want Meridian to know about what Jason did."

"How are you going to explain the fact that you don't work at the bank anymore?"

"He doesn't have to know that either for a while. I'll tell him after I find another job."

"I can't keep this from him. I couldn't do that as a friend or as his employee. He's bound to find out. It would be better to hear it from you. Why would you want to keep it from him anyway?"

"The more Meridian travels, the more he insists that I stay at his house when he's away. Imagine what he'll say when he finds out I'm not working? I understand that he only has my safety in mind, but I'm not ready to give up my independence to another man. You know how determined he gets about something when he puts his mind to it."

Robert knew that he was missing essential pieces of the puzzle. "Please, don't stick me in the middle of this. If Meridian found out that I knew something this important and didn't tell him—"

"He'd be upset with you."

"Exactly. This can't wait until you find another job, tell him as soon as you see him tonight. Not only because he loves you, but because it affects Weston Realty. You owe it to him to be honest with him."

CHAPTER NINETEEN

Jason looked over at his four-year-old son sitting next to him in the front seat of the car. His chest swelled with pride as he studied how handsome he'd become. Smart, too, and tough. Jason went to talk to his teacher many times because of the fights he initiated. Jason would talk to his son about that—tell him to settle down. The day care threatened to put him out if it happened again. Then his mother would be hard-pressed to keep her job.

Little Jason's mother could never take as good of care of their son as Talya could have. The day he brought little Jason home Talya fell in love with him. He told Talya that he would be staying with them for a few days. She didn't even question who the little boy was until she put him to bed for the night.

"Who does he belong to?" she had asked when they got into bed.

Jason found no reason to lie. "He's my son."

Talya lost her mind. Crying and demanding answers. They were definitely living together when the child was conceived. He couldn't deny that fact. Then Talya started demanding to know the name of the mother. Too tired to prolong the argument, he told the truth. He was seeing one of Talya's coworkers behind her back, and she got pregnant.

A minor traffic accident would keep her in the hospital for a few days. Little Jason would go home when she was released and could take care of him again.

Talya really lost it then. She was friendly with the girl every day at work. She went to the girl's baby shower. Talya cried and cursed him. He listened to it for a while, but quickly grew tired of her disrespect. He beat her bad that night, but he had to. Jason remembered how his heart beat so fast when she passed out. But he had to do it. He had to make sure Talya knew she would be taking care of Little Jason and that she better not do anything to hurt his son.

Talya begged him to let her quit her job; he agreed. He didn't want any trouble between the two women that would bring Little Jason's mother down on him. Shortly after that beating he came home and found that Talya had disappeared.

Jason didn't know why he never got Talya pregnant. That would have settled her down. She wouldn't have run away as fast if she had his kid. She knew how he was about Little Jason. He would have worked harder to hunt her down and he would have made sure she never left again. He was trying to be nice when he went to her apartment, but she tried to play him like a fool, now he would have to take care of that. He got her fired from the bank, so it wouldn't be long before she had to come back to him. She would need him to take care of her, just like in college.

Jason looked over at his son again. "Little J?"

"Yeah, Daddy?"

"What do you do when your girl smart-mouths you?"

"I punch her in her damn mouth!" Little Jason said, proudly demonstrating the move with his small fist.

Jason laughed. "That's right." He reached over and rubbed the top of his head.

CHAPTER TWENTY

Meridian drove his corvette at top speed to Talya's apartment. He barely had enough time to get to her place and change before time for the game. He missed her more than he realized. The closer he got to her apartment, the more excited he became. He used his mobile phone to call the stadium. He wanted everything in his private suite prepared as he ordered. Robert and Rena would be there. Jennifer and her reverend were coming. He doubted that the women would be very interested in the basketball play-offs, but it gave him comfort to know Talya would be only feet away in the suite.

The flight home gave him time to think about what he wanted with Talya. His mother gave him plenty to consider. Marriage. He was attracted to a very specific type woman, and he now knew exactly what he wanted in a long term partner. Besides the obvious—beauty, grace, and intelligence—he wanted someone that would depend on him. He wanted a quiet, reserved woman who respected and needed his opinion on major issues. The independent, working woman should be commended, but wasn't his type. He wanted to make all the major decisions for his family. He wanted two children: a boy and a girl that his wife would stay home and care for. He and his children were to be the center of his wife's life. She would want to please him in every way.

Meridian took being the man in a relationship seriously. He'd provide everything his wife and children needed. He'd send his wife shopping and buy her lavish gifts after they argued. He pictured his family idolizing him. He would groom his son to take over the business, just as his father had groomed him. His daughter would take ballet and piano lessons. She would marry a wealthy, educated man that treated her like a queen.

Meridian stood in Talya's steam-filled bathroom wrapped in a towel. He opened the door and called to Talya.

"Yes?" Talya pulled a Detroit Pistons jersey over her head.

"Do you ever think about where we're going in the future?"

Talya froze momentarily. "I think more about what's happening between us right now."

Meridian poked his head into the bedroom. "What's happening between us right now?"

"We're having a good time getting to know each other."

Meridian returned to the bathroom mirror. He pulled a stiff-bristled brush across the soft waves of his faded hair cut. "You must think about our future sometimes. I do. I've never been involved with anyone as seriously as I am with you." He dropped the towel and stepped into his underwear. "I'm thinking we should consider living together. We could spend more time together if we eliminated the hour commute."

Talya's fingertips went cold. She willed the tingling sensation away and continued to tie her gym shoes.

"So, what do you think?" Meridian called as he stepped into his jeans and began to button his shirt. He walked in his bare feet across the bedroom carpet. "Well?" He sat next to her on the bed.

"Would you like me to fix you something to eat before we leave?"

Meridian craned his neck to look into Talya's face. "Do you always have to avoid my questions?"

"Only the hard ones."

"Why is that a hard question?"

Talya finished tying her shoes and planted them firmly into the carpet. "That's a very hard question for me right now."

"Why?" Meridian lined up his shoes and slipped his feet into them.

"I'm experiencing independence for the first time in my life. I don't want to give it up. Moving in together is a huge step. I'm not ready yet."

Meridian laced up his gym shoes and stood up from the bed. "Do you have any idea when you'll be ready to take that step with me?"

Talya stood with him. "We'd better be going. Everyone will be waiting for us."

Meridian lifted Talya's chin. "Do you always have to avoid my questions?"

Talya placed her arms snugly around his waist. "Only the hard ones."

Talya was going to tell Meridian that she lost her job, but it never came up. The next morning when Meridian got dressed for work he asked Talya if she had to go to work and she simply told him no. She didn't bother to explain. She made all kinds of excuses in her mind about why she should wait for the right time. Truthfully, she didn't want to explain Jason's behavior or justify why she couldn't give up her freedom and find herself trapped in another situation beyond her control.

"Don't forget that I'm counting on you this Saturday," Jennifer reminded Talya.

Talya took the broiled chicken out of the oven, placing the pan on the kitchen table. "I won't forget. You want me to talk to the people in your program about budgeting their money so that they can have enough to buy more nutritious foods versus whatever is cheap or on sale. It is a problem that has plagued our people since slavery…."

"Okay, okay." Jennifer laughed at Talya's impersonation of her.

"I'm nervous about speaking in front of a group of people."

"I don't think it will be a large crowd. The people in the program are really good folks. The reverend and I will take you out to lunch afterwards."

"How are things going between you two?" Talya spooned salad unto Jennifer's plate.

"Things are going really well." Jennifer scraped some of the food back onto the serving dishes. "We're officially dating now—I think."

Talya joined her at the kitchen table.

"Did Meridian and Robert like him? Did he fit in at the basketball game?"

Talya shrugged as she sliced her chicken. "Meridian didn't say anything specifically, but he acted as if they had a good time together."

Jennifer nodded as she pushed food around her plate. "He really is a normal guy. He's not one of those people that are always preaching to you, no matter the place or time."

"Well, I really like him. He's very nice, and he seems to be very attentive toward you."

Jennifer smiled across the table at her friend. "He's great. Enough about me and my reverend. Are you still having reservations about Meridian?"

Her face blossomed into a telling smile. "There are still some doubts in the corner of my mind, but I'm working through it." She added salt and pepper to her mashed potatoes. "He asked me about moving in with him."

"What?! You never mentioned that. When did this happen?"

"Yesterday, before the game. I told him I wasn't ready."

Jennifer stuck her fork into her chicken, waving it at her friend.

Talya explained. "After Jason, I want to be careful. It all started to fall apart when I moved in with him. Our perfect relationship turned into a controlling nightmare. I can't take the chance of that happening with Meridian. I really love him. I don't want anything to go wrong. If he knew I lost my job—"

"If he knew? You haven't told him you lost your job at the bank?"

Talya shook her head. "I started to last night, but he brought up us living together. I couldn't tell him at the game."

"What about after the game?"

Talya grinned as her face reddened. "We were busy after the game."

Jennifer snickered. "That was the perfect time to tell him. He wouldn't get too upset then."

Talya nodded in agreement.

"Seriously, you should tell him soon. He'll be upset if he hears someone else is handling his multimillion dollar account because his girlfriend was fired. And when he finds out you were fired because of Jason—watch out."

"That's part of the reason I haven't told him. He'll worry about Jason coming around and really push me to move in with him."

"Maybe that wouldn't be such a bad idea. Give Jason time to cool off and leave you alone."

"Hmmm." Talya nodded nonchalantly.

Jason would never simply give up and walk away. She still had many issues regarding commitments and relationships to work through, but she was stronger. She would never tolerate his abusive ways again. She would prove to him, herself and her mother that she could make it on her own. Thirty years old was too young to spend the rest of her life running from Jason. Meeting Meridian had helped her to realize that she was worthy of being loved. She liked the feeling he gave her and she didn't want to let it go. Jason may have believed that getting her fired would drive her back to him—he was wrong.

"Good afternoon, Ms. Stevenson," Mr. Martin said as he opened the door. He wiped his hands on his apron before shaking hers in greeting.

Talya playfully scolded the gray-haired man and insisted that he call her by her given name. He nodded in agreement but Talya doubted he would. He reminded her of Kathy, the most stubborn receptionist on earth.

"Is Meridian here?" The house was quiet and still.

"He worked in his office this morning. I believe he went into his bedroom after lunch."

"He works too much." Talya smiled at Mr. Martin.

"I've told him that many times. I have to admit that he's getting better since he started seeing you. I need to check on something in the kitchen."

Instead of going to Meridian's room, Talya followed the elderly gentleman into the kitchen. His aging, outwardly gruff exterior appealed to her in a fatherly way. He fulfilled Talya's fantasies of an adoring grandfather. Her own family life was filled with memories of harsh punishments and a coldness that chilled the house even in the middle of summer. Sitting and talking with Mr. Martin about his wife and grandchildren comforted her and endeared her to him. Before long she was standing side by side with Mr. Martin in the kitchen learning how to make a new pastry. Once dinner and dessert were completed, Talya walked Mr. Martin to the door before she scurried to Meridian's bedroom.

Meridian lay across his bed, fully clothed, snoring lightly. Air conditioning cooled the rooms of the expansive house, but he preferred the breeze coming in from the French doors of his private patio. The sheer white drapes blew gently in response to the tame wind. Talya kicked off her shoes and tipped quietly across the plush tan carpeting. She lowered herself down on top of Meridian's back and pasted soft kisses on the back of his neck until he stirred.

Meridian didn't open his eyes, but his face drowned in a wide grin. "Who is that?" "Guess, and you better say the right name." Talya ran her fingers across the softness of his faint beard and mustache.

Meridian chuckled. "What are you doing here?"

"I was sitting at home thinking about you, so I figured I'd drive out to see you." She rolled off his hard frame and lay next to him on the bed.

Meridian stretched his yawn. He turned to face her, opening his eyes for the first time. A smile pulled at his full lips.

"You don't mind, do you?"

"You're welcome here anytime you want." He noticed the sun beginning to go down. "I must have overslept. I planned on taking a quick nap before getting back to work."

Talya sat up and watched him disappear into his bathroom. She practiced the way she would tell him she lost her job. Robert stopped by before she drove out, and he insisted that she tell him by Monday or he would. A week had passed since she was fired, and Robert didn't like being put in the position of deceiving his best friend. It was unfair to force him into an uncomfortable situation. Her counselor's words came clear to her memory. *Even though you've been hurt, you cannot compromise your principles. You must begin any future relationships with the same honesty and caring that you'd expect in return.*

Meridian came back into the bedroom after changing out of his suit into a matching pair of black cargo shorts and a polo shirt.

"I lost my job last week," Talya blurted out.

Meridian draped his slacks over the back of a chair. "What do you mean you lost your job last week?"

"My manager had to let me go."

"Why? And why didn't you mention it before now?" He folded his long arms across his chest.

Talya scooted to the edge of the bed. "Jason made a scene at the bank and the management felt they had to give me a permanent leave of absence."

"What kind of scene? Jason came by the bank, and you kept it from me?"

"I wasn't there when he came by, but from what the manager says, he accused my coworkers of helping me to hide from him." That was stating it mildly.

Meridian watched her for a long moment. "I know you're trying to make it sound like no big deal. Whatever you're telling me should be multiplied to the tenth power. He must have been loud and disruptive if Brunstown fired you. I can't believe you didn't tell me."

"I knew you would worry about nothing."

"Nothing? How can you call this nothing? You should have come to me right away about this. I'm going to hire a bodyguard to look after you."

"A bodyguard? No way. This is why I didn't rush to tell you. I knew you would try to take over. I don't need a body-guard."

"Really? Why do you insist on acting like you can handle Jason alone?"

"I can."

"You haven't."

The words stung. "What do you mean by that?"

Meridian's face softened. "All I meant is that Jason is dangerous. It doesn't make you weak to need help."

"I can deal with Jason myself. I know him better than anyone. The more force I show, the more determined he'll become. Jason will meet someone at a body-building competition and then he'll forget about me. I need to ride this out."

"If that's what you believe, you're in denial. Jason isn't going away."

Talya went over to the French doors. "I don't want to talk about Jason anymore. The most important thing now is for me to find another job."

"You can work at Weston Realty. First thing Monday morning, Robert will get you started."

"Meridian——" she stopped him as he was walking away——"I appreciate what you're offering, but I'd rather find my own job. I have enough saved to tide me over for a while. I have some calls in with other banks in the area——"

"The independence thing again, right? It would be easier for you to work with me."

"Easier, true, but I need to be in——"

"Independent," he finished for her. "This doesn't have anything to do with your independence. You need a job, and I need you to keep managing my finances. If we weren't involved with each other and I offered you the job, would you take it?"

Talya approached him. "In a minute, but we are involved and that's what makes it a bad idea. I need to keep the two separate. After what I went through with Jason, I don't ever want to be completely dependent on anyone again. Not even you." She stood on tiptoe and planted a kiss on his tight jaw.

"One month——if in one month you don't have a new job, you'll work at Weston Realty. Deal?"

Talya nodded. "Deal."

"Now, back to Jason being a threat to you."

"He's had his tantrum, he'll leave me alone now." She didn't believe the words as she spoke them and doubted Meridian was fooled by her nonchalant attitude.

"Just the same, we should consider you moving in here again. I would never forgive myself if something happened to you. Something that I could have stopped."

"He's gotten me fired from my job. Now he'll expect me to come back to him because I need him to take care of me. When I don't, he'll give up."

Meridian walked up behind her and lifted the cotton T-shirt she wore. His fingertips seared her skin as they traced the markings on her right lower back. She spun around.

"The look in your eyes confirms my suspicions. This guy is more of a threat to you than you want to admit. I don't know if you're trying to convince me or yourself, but neither of us is buying it."

Talya moved away from him. "I don't like anyone to see what he did to me. The physical pain goes away relatively quickly, but the mental pain lingers forever. Every time I remember the scars on my back, I remember something that I was glad I'd lost."

"Maybe you shouldn't try to forget those scars. They'll help you to remember how dangerous this guy can be."

Talya wrapped her arms around her middle in a useless attempt to still her shivering body. The darkness was welcomed when it removed a piece of her memory associated with her time with Jason. Meridian's eyes seemed to look right through her into her mind, which made her shiver even more.

Meridian took long, slow steps over to her. He took her arms away from her chest and placed them at her side. His eyes never left hers as he began to lift her T-shirt over her head. He spun her around, dropped on his knees, and seared her skin where the scars were embedded with the warmth of his lips.

CHAPTER TWENTY-ONE

"Mom." Meridian hugged his mother. "What are you doing here? You didn't tell me you were coming to town."

"Do I have to give you my schedule? Who's the parent? Now, get my bags and pay the driver."

His mother rented a limo to come from the airport. What a waste of money when he would have been happy to pick her up. His mother enjoyed the luxuries she could afford. She always told Meridian that his father worked hard so that she could have the finer things in life. Meridian heard his father's voice: "When you fall in love, you'll see. You'll do anything to keep a woman happy because she'll do anything to keep you happy. So, if your mother wants to blow all my hard-earned money, well, what can I say?"

"Are you hungry?" Meridian asked his mother after taking her bags into the bedroom he used only for her visits.

"Why are you asking me that? You can't cook me anything if I am."

"Mom, I have food in the kitchen if you're hungry."

His mother dropped down on the sofa and kicked off her designer pumps.

"Why are you in town? How long are you staying?" He sat down and placed his head on his mother's shoulder. He missed her when she was away.

"I'm in town because I miss my big baby of a son. I'll only be able to stay two days because I have a benefit to host in Los Angeles. From there I think I'll go home and get some much-needed rest."

"That'll be good for you."

She draped her arm around Meridian. "How are things with the business?"

"Good, we're growing every day."

"Are things any smoother with you and Talya?"

He nodded. "It's a challenge sometimes, but Talya and I are getting along well."

"Give her some time, it'll all work out. With what she has been through, it's understandable that she's hesitant about getting involved in another relationship."

"What do you mean by that?" Meridian's invisible antennae began to lift. No signal could get by him. He had never told his mother the details about Talya's past relationship. He sat up and waited for his mother's confession.

She exhaled a long breath. "I had her checked out."

"Mother." Meridian sprung from the sofa.

She raised her voice to match Meridian's. "Mother? Don't Mother me, and don't take that tone with me."

"Sorry," Meridian mumbled, averting his eyes to the carpeting beneath his feet.

"Now sit back down." She waited until he did as instructed before continuing. "Of course I had her investigated. You come to Atlanta telling me that you're head over heels for some girl I've never met. I didn't know what her intentions were. You've never had the best taste in women from what I've seen in the past. I wanted to know what kind of person you were involved with. Your father worked hard for what we have."

"I know that, Mom. I would never jeopardize everything he worked for."

"Good, I'm glad to hear that." She cupped Meridian's chin and turned him to face her. "If there was anything I thought you should know, I would have already told you."

"I don't want to know about anything you found out by digging into Talya's past. We have an honest relationship—anything I need to know, I'll hear directly from her."

"Fair enough, but I do want to give you one piece of advice, since your father's not around." She captured his attention with her eyes. "It takes a strong person to walk away from the situation she was in. If you truly care about this girl, be supportive of her and very, very patient."

Meridian gave her small frame a tight squeeze. His mother's approval of Talya was a very important component needed for a strong future with her. He loved Talya too much to leave her if his mother didn't approve of their relationship, but it made things a lot easier for him to have it.

"I can't wait to meet her." His mother sighed. "The detective can't tell you everything. I hope she's not another anorexic—too—much—make-up—wearing—in—love—with—my—son's—money woman."

Meridian laughed. "Not this time, Mom. Talya is special. She's the complete opposite of what you'd expect."

"We'll see."

"She's out back working in the garden."

"You have this girl working around your house?"

"I love Talya. She's very shy, so go easy on her. I know you'll like her."

"Are we talking marriage?"

"Let's just say I can at least pronounce the M word now."

"I dare you to say it." She punched his arm.

"Well, I can almost pronounce the word."

Talya became a nervous wreck when Meridian came out to the garden and told her his mother had arrived unexpectedly. He wanted her to come inside and meet her. Talya looked a mess. She was dressed in a pair of old sweats working in the dirt. The hair from her ponytail flew in all directions, and she wore no makeup.

"You're beautiful," Meridian told her. "My mother is easygoing. She knows you're working in the garden today. She doesn't expect you to walk in the house wearing an evening gown. She'll be offended if you don't come right in to meet her."

Meridian introduced the women and left the den before they could say their hellos. He wanted them to talk without him present. They should get to know each other without his interference. Talya would be shy, but his mother would like that and make her feel at ease. He knew they would hit it off. His mother would make a colossal effort since she knew how he felt about Talya.

"How'd it go?" Meridian asked when Talya walked into the recreation room.

She held her hand to her chest, letting a breath of relief escape. "Very well."

"I told you not to worry."

"She asked me so many questions about myself. I felt like I was interviewing for a job."

"You were—my caretaker. She's glad to be rid of me."

"No wonder she became so excited when I told her I like to garden and cook."

"Did you discuss the benefit plan?" Meridian wrapped his arms around her and found his place in the hollow of her neck.

Talya giggled. "She didn't mention any specifics."

"I'd like to demonstrate one or two right now."

Meridian's mother was a refined and educated woman. She dressed in expensive suits. Educated at Spelman University, she became a homemaker when her late husband's business became successful. She never regretted giving up her career and taking care of her treasured son. A little spoiled, she confessed with a faraway gaze and faint smile, but a wonderful man. She had strong convictions and lived by her own moral code. Talya wished her relationship with her own mother were so relaxed, but it wasn't to be.

"Meridian, can you drive me home now?" Talya asked after they finished dinner.

"I thought you were staying?"

"I don't want to interfere with your time together." Talya spoke in a hushed voice. She glanced over at his mother.

"Honey," his mother said, "from what my son tells me, I should be getting to know you a little better."

Talya stayed.

Talya and Meridian stood outside of his bedroom debating about where Talya should sleep. Meridian insisted she sleep in his room as always. Talya didn't think that would be proper with his mother on the other side of the house.

Meridian's mother joined them in the hallway. "Honey," she directed to Talya, "I know my son has sex. Please sleep where you usually sleep when I'm not here."

Talya slept in Meridian's bedroom.

"Do you like my mother?" Meridian asked, pulling the sheets back for Talya to climb into bed.

"She's very nice and very nice to me. Are you close?"

Meridian turned off the lights. "Very." He moved in the darkness and molded his body to Talya's. "We have always been close. I respect her and love her, but most times it's like having a cool big sister more than a mother."

"I wish I had that with my mother."

"Do you think you can ever work it out with her?"

"No."

"It might be worth a try. It's important to have ties with your family."

The sound of Talya's counselor saturated the dark room. She had lectured Talya on that point many times. She also understood that Talya's well-being might be in jeopardy if her mother chose to take Jason's side again. As Meridian went on supposing, Talya's head released the reasons why she couldn't contact her mother again.

"I could go with you," Meridian was saying. "We should get on a plane and fly to Tennessee—"

"No." Talya said with conviction. "It's not the right time."

"Well, anytime you want to do it, we will. But for right now, how about I share my mom with you?"

Talya laughed. "You are so silly sometimes."

"Um-huh. Give me a kiss."

Meridian felt the urgency growing and wanted to end it before it flourished. One kiss didn't relieve the feeling. Two kisses made the urgency move to other parts of his body. He used his tongue as if trying to reach one specific area or he would lose his mind instantly. Uncontrolled desire. Before he knew it, Talya was calling his name.

"Meridian, you're so intense; where do you go? Or should I ask where you're trying to go?"

"One more kiss, and then we'll go to sleep," Meridian whispered into Talya's ear. Talya met his lips with hers. He opened his mouth wide and accepted her tongue. Talya enjoyed Meridian's passion, but he could overwhelm her. His kisses changed from polite to passionate to frenzied. She felt as if she were his parachute and he was falling too fast. Strange for her to be in such a position because, all her life, she had always been dependent upon someone else to save her.

"Meridian," Talya called him back again.

Meridian was breathing hard and rocking his hardness against her cavern as he kissed her neck. "Yeah?"

"Where are you?"

"I'm here." What else could he tell Talya? He didn't understand the urgency himself, he couldn't explain it to her. Their kisses weren't enough. Right now the urgency pushed him to end the throbbing pain in his groin.

"Meridian, we can't." Talya made a point of telling him the time of the month before she agreed to spend the night with him. He told her to come anyway, he wanted to spend time with her.

The urgency inside of Meridian grew and grew, and there was only one place that would stop the throbbing torture. He asked Talya some questions about her method of dealing with her monthly. She refused to discuss that with him. He knew she'd be too shy to talk openly. He fired the yes or no questions.

Talya tried to hear, answer Meridian's questions, and breathe all at the same time. His hands were everywhere on her body. His lips caressed her neck and sucked her earlobe. He massaged her breasts while he moved against her. He tried to take all of her inside of his body. She'd never experienced desire and arousal at the level he offered.

Meridian pressed his lips against her mouth and parted her lips with his tongue. He kissed her seductively. He kissed her again. He felt Talya's passion growing, and he kept the rhythm with his tongue. His hands moved between her thighs and pushed away any obstacles. Meridian filled her mouth again when she started to speak; he couldn't listen to her protest because the urgency whispered in his other ear telling him what to do to end the pain. His thighs separated hers. He kept Talya's mouth occupied until he was inside of her, pumping softly. The heat of friction spurred him to pump faster and faster, harder and harder. Somehow, Meridian knew his desperation would not go away until after he pleased Talya.

"Talya, I love you," he repeated over and over until Talya released herself to him. Then Meridian found the only place that could stop his pain and let him regain control.

Meridian held Talya in his arms when she returned from the shower. "I get so caught up in you. It's weird to be disciplined in every part of my life, but when it comes to making love to you, I'm completely out of control. There're some serious emotions running through me, but believe me, everything I do is the result of the love I feel for you." He kissed her forehead.

CHAPTER TWENTY-TWO

"Are you sure you don't mind going to church this morning?" Talya zipped her skirt as she stood in front of her bedroom mirror.

"No, I wouldn't have agreed to go if I didn't want to." Meridian draped his tie around his neck and moved beside her into the mirror.

"The reverend kinda roped you into it at dinner last weekend. I should call Robert and Rena and make sure they're all right with going."

"Would you stop? Robert and Rena take their little girl to church every Sunday. They don't mind coming to the reverend's church this week. The Rev is really cool. Robert, the Rev, and me all get along fine. We want to go, okay?" He started to twist and shape his tie. "We get along almost as well as Jennifer, Rena, and you. We were watching you three checking out Grant Hill and Gary Patton at the game a few weeks ago." He winked at her.

"We did hit it off right away. We're all going shopping one day next week."

"You'll get the guys mad at me now. They'll kill me for putting three compulsive shoppers together to spend all their money."

"Ha-ha." Talya moved over to the vanity table next to the dresser.

Meridian watched her carefully put makeup around her eyes. She spread a lightly tinted pink gloss across her lips. Talya's bedroom was spotless, everything in its place. Except for the vanity table that was cluttered and overcrowded with all kinds of makeup and creams and hair products. He walked over and stood behind her, taking the thingabob out of her hands.

"Why do you always cover your freckles?"

She shrugged.

"Then don't do it." He leaned down and kissed the freckles on her nose.

Jennifer sat quietly, continually straightening the imaginary wrinkles in her dress. "Talya, Dating Adventure with the Reverend number twenty-eight?"

Meridian looked in the rearview mirror giving Jennifer a curious glance.

Talya turned against the black leather seat of the BMW and looked back at her friend. "Have you gone out that many times already?"

Jennifer nodded. "We had our first argument last night after he dropped me off after dinner." She leaned toward Talya. "You know that I've cut my dating down a whole lot, right?"

Talya nodded.

Meridian's eyes moved from Jennifer in the mirror to Talya. She's seeing other men? I wonder if she has any influence over Talya? Birds of a feather flock together. But Robert is my best friend, and we're nothing alike. Anyway, I'll have to keep my eyes open.

Jennifer continued her latest dating adventure. "I wouldn't even be seeing anyone if he could come to grips with our relationship and stop thinking that he's going straight to hell for having impure thoughts about me. Anyway, the women in the church have been talking about the reverend spending a lot of time with one of the sisters in the church. I confronted him about it, and he didn't deny it. He told me they spend time working together, but he's not having relations with her. He's not having relations with me. So, what's the difference?"

Meridian spoke up before Talya could answer. "The difference, Jennifer, is that he wants to have relations with you."

Robert, Rena and their little girl were sitting in the middle of the church, halfway up the aisle. Talya, Meridian and Jennifer joined them. The service started soon after. Jennifer's spirits were doused when a substitute minister walked up on the podium.

"I'm embarrassed you came to church at the reverend's invitation and now he's not even here to speak."

Talya took her hand and whispered, "Everything is all right; don't worry. Church is church, and the purpose is the same no matter who the speaker."

Jennifer gave Talya's hand an extra squeeze when the reverend walked out and stood in the front of the church as the guest minister began dismissing the choir. He was dressed in a three piece black suit instead of his majestic African robe.

The reverend took the microphone handed to him from the guest minister, and using his booming voice, thanked the speaker and the choir. Then his voice softened to the one that Talya was familiar with hearing in social situations.

"I'd like to ask the congregation to give me five minutes before we leave the sanctuary."

Everyone settled down in their seats. They knew and loved their reverened, and he looked troubled. Speculation went from him leaving the church to a death in the family. The congregation took a collective breath and waited for him to continue.

"I have to apologize for not fulfilling my duty to you this morning, but my heart is heavy, and I needed to pray on some things. I did not feel I would be doing the congregation any good to come before you when my own house was in such disarray that my mind could not think straight."

He paused, looking around the room until he located Jennifer. Her presence seemed to give him the strength to continue. Talya's heart was beating fast enough to power an airplane for takeoff. She wondered how Jennifer could sit so still and look so confident.

The reverend moved his eyes back to the congregation. "The power of prayer cannot be measured."

Someone yelled, "Amen!"

"As the choir sang its final song, God answered my prayer and sent me the answer I was searching for." He seemed to be at a loss for the right words.

A man in the back said, "Take your time, say what's on your heart."

The reverend continued, "The answer is that I am a man. I am the leader of this church and my mission is to give you all the information I have about how to live a good and decent life that will please God. As the leader of the church, I have to be a shovel, and I also have to be a crutch." He referenced a previous sermon. "But congregation, sometimes as a plain ol' man, I need a crutch. And sometimes you don't even know you're leaning on a crutch until it gets knocked out from under you."

The reverend moved up the aisle to the middle of the church. "I need to ask the congregation's blessing on the decision I have made. But before I do that, I need to tell Sister Jennifer right here in front of God, my friends and the congregation that I love her and I want her to be my wife."

Jennifer grabbed her mouth and gasped. Rena and Talya hugged her from each side and encouraged her to stand and answer the reverend.

The entire church was stunned. Once they recovered, they quieted the whispers and waited for Jennifer to answer.

Jennifer stood up in the pew with a straight back, head held high. Her hands were shaking so badly that she had to grab the bench in front of the her to steady them. She said a loud, strong "Yes!"

The reverend came down the aisle to meet her. He took her in his arms and swung her around in a circle then he put her down and kissed her lips passionately. The church erupted into applause.

The applause died down, and Jason turned to his right to follow the other two contestants off the winner's platform. Third place in the body-building contest entitled him to a five-hundred-dollar cash prize and some other trinkets not worth mentioning. He deserved first prize, but his performance was off. He couldn't shake thoughts of Talya. She should have been there. This was an important contest. The first-prize winner posed with the winner of the women's competition on the front cover of a popular body-building magazine. In the past, that exposure had led to things like movie deals and product endorsements. Not to mention the five-thousand-dollar cash prize.

Jason handed his trophy to Rizzo backstage while he posed for pictures with the other winners of the contest. He turned so that the photographer was sure to capture the tattoo of Talya's name plastered across his chest. He smiled as he circulated among the crowd, shaking hands and answering the same questions over and over. Inside he seethed from anger. Outside he was as charming as ever. He had given Talya long enough to respond to his requests. So far, she had not done anything he asked her to do. All the things he usually did to get her to forgive him were not working. Her causing him to lose the competition was the last straw. He searched the room for Rizzo. He should have taken his suggestion the day they found her in the movie theater. It would have been much easier to grab her in the parking lot, throw her in the backseat of the car and take her home.

The reverend's proposal and Jennifer's tears of happiness set off an avalanche of emotions for both Talya and Meridian. The ride back to Talya's apartment in Meridian's BMW was relatively quiet. They were both contemplating their future together.

Meridian spoke as if Talya had been able to hear his private thoughts. "I want you to move in with me. Why are you fighting me on this so hard? You don't have a way of supporting yourself right now. Jason has demonstrated that it's not safe for you to stay at your apartment alone. Why won't you move in with me? I can support you, and I definitely can keep Jason away from you. What's the problem?"

Talya looked over at Meridian. "Can—"

"Don't avoid my question." Meridian stopped her. The answer to his question was not another question. "Don't you care for me like I care for you? Why don't you want to be with me like I want to be with you? This is tearing me up inside. Explain this to me, Talya. Am I wasting my time here? Do we have a future together or not?"

"I can't talk about this." Talya opened her door and started up to her apartment. Meridian's love was so strong that it made it hard for her to breathe. He wanted answers to questions that were too hard to answer.

Meridian followed Talya onto the elevator. "I have been very patient with you, but I want some answers. I can't keep doing this. Am I always going to be chasing you when you know that there is no chance of me catching you?"

"Meridian, don't push me."

Meridian followed Talya down the hallway. The urgency stayed with him. He had trouble sleeping when they were not together. She never left his mind. He was always doing something to prepare for when they were together. Robert explained that love could have that effect on a man. Meridian did not like it. He was jealous. He worried about Talya if she wasn't with him. He talked about her to anyone who would listen. At work, he found himself sitting behind his desk, daydreaming about their future together.

Why was he enduring such torment? He loved Talya. When they were together, it was wonderful. Her femininity called to him. She listened with concern. She nurtured him. She was everything he needed in life to be happy. Love was too hard. No wonder he never found any use in it before Talya.

Talya moved quickly around her bedroom. She changed out of her dress and into a pair of sweats.

"Sit down." Meridian pointed to the chair. Frustration made him want to scream.

He pulled the ottoman up to meet the chair Talya sat in. "I know you don't want me to pressure you, but I am. I'm going to put you in a corner, and you're going to have to deal with me and our relationship once and for all. I deserve to know what's going on between us. You never let me in; I have to fight for everything you give me. I'm starting to have a lot of doubts, and that's not good. Tell me what you want."

"You want me to move in with you, but I can't do that."

"Why not?"

"You have no idea what I had to do to get to this time in my life. You don't know the half of what I went through with Jason. I'm not blaming Jason one hundred percent; I've learned that I enabled him to do what he did. But see, I'm not as strong as you are; it took a lot out of me to run away from him and to start over. I painted my bedroom walls teal. I spent months saving my money and budgeting to afford furniture. I went from store to store shopping until I found the right curtains and blankets and rugs. I did that with my own money. I did it because I wanted to please myself.

"Do you know what it is like to have nothing and nobody? I do. That's the place I started. Now I have my own place where I don't have to live in fear or hide in a closet because someone who says he loves me had a bad day. I have friends who I love and who love me. I have worked so hard to get where I am in my life. I don't want to give that up."

Meridian sat quietly, trying to manage his words. "Where does that leave me? What do you want with me?"

"I love you."

"Okay, I love you too. I'm looking to have something permanent with you. I understand what you've told me but you don't understand that I love you."

"I know that."

"No, you don't." Meridian's agitation could be heard in his voice. He regained his composure before he went on. "What you went through with Jason had nothing to do with love. I know what you've gone through; I would never do anything to make you feel like you were in that type of situation again. People who love each other feed off each other and grow together. I don't want to gain control over you. I want you to move in because I love you. When you're not with me I think about you every second." Meridian paused. "I like to watch you in the garden. Sometimes I just like to know you're wandering around my house."

Talya reached for his hand.

"We're not getting anywhere, are we?"

"I'll think about it."

"That's something." Meridian smiled. "I'll let you bring all your candles."

"How about I light all the candles in here right now?"

"Only if you let me keep trying to convince you of how much I love you."

"Dating Adventure with the Reverend number thirty-seven." Jennifer joined Talya on the sofa with a bowl of popcorn.

"Go on." Talya grabbed a handful of popcorn.

"We picked out my engagement ring and wedding band. The reverend will pick it up for me next week. He has this romantic night planned for the two of us, and he says he'll give it to me then. I told him we can set the date that night. He wants to hurry up and say the vows so we can get to the honeymoon."

"I'm happy for you. Did you think you'd ever be a preacher's wife?"

"Are you kidding? No way. My mother still thinks I'm lying. We're flying down to Florida in a couple of weeks so he can meet my family."

"The wedding will be at the church, I take it."

Jennifer nodded, swallowing her popcorn. "The honeymoon we're still debating. I want to go to the Poconos or Mexico. Like I said, he doesn't care, he just wants to get there as soon as possible."

"Do you think you'll be able to hold out until the honeymoon? Sounds like the reverend might crack."

Jennifer laughed. "I'll hold out for the both of us. I have to admit that I'm nervous about it. I keep thinking crazy thoughts like God won't think I'm worthy enough to marry a holy man and a lightning bolt will strike our marital bed the first night."

Talya jumped around on the couch excitedly. "I've got a dating adventure for you. Dating adventure number—seven?—anyway, I was nervous the first time Meridian and

I, you know. He asked me a couple of times, and it got hot and heavy, but I kept putting him off because I was scared."

"Good?" Jennifer said grinning.

Talya nodded and hid behind her hands.

Jennifer hit her with the pillow from the corner of the sofa.

"Seriously—" Talya forced herself to stop laughing. "He is so passionate that it's like his mind leaves the room and he just—I can't even describe it. I feel like he thinks he has to conquer me or something. When I look at his face, he has this expression like if he doesn't do it just right he'll drop dead on the spot."

"I don't hear a problem." Jennifer giggled. "Sounds like he takes care of his business. Am I wrong?"

"No." Talya giggled, shielding her face again.

"I've got something to be freaked out about. I'm not exactly inexperienced, if you know what I'm saying, so I'm used to certain things. I'm going to have sex with a thirty-three year old virgin after I get married. If he's no good I'm stuck! I kinda know what equipment I have to work with from that one make-out session we had, but I don't know if he knows what to do with it."

They laughed so hard they fell off the sofa onto the floor. Tears ran down their faces as they ad-libbed possible scenarios of Jennifer's wedding night. Talya asked herself, as she had a million times since meeting Meridian, why she waited so long to break away from Jason.

CHAPTER TWENTY-THREE

Mr. Martin earned another night of overtime pay from Meridian. Tonight was his night to host the poker party. Mr. Martin prepared enough food to last the men the entire night, made sure the refrigerator was stocked with beer and the bar was full. He then rushed home to his wife and grandchildren.

Meridian looked around and wondered how he got stuck at the table with these guys. The Bragger, Bill, and thank God, Robert. Every poker night they rotated seats, but in his own house? He should have some say at what table he sat at. Meridian looked around the table and tried to figure out where his money had gone. It looked like Robert was lucky. Once the men began losing, the talking started.

"Lucky at cards, unlucky at love," Bill said to Robert. All the guys knew that he and Rena were going through an 'adjustment period,' as Robert called it.

Meridian watched Robert finger his glasses and wished he would stand up for himself with Bill.

"What about you, player?" Bill looked with squinted eyes past the smoke of his cigar across the table at Meridian. "You laying the pipe to Talya on the regular? She looked pretty restless at lunch the other day."

"When did you see Talya?" Meridian threw two chips into the pot in the middle of the table.

"She didn't tell you I took her to lunch the other day?"

Meridian wanted to jump across the table and knock the smug expression off of his face.

Robert tried to change the subject. "Are you still seeing Mia?" he asked Bill.

"No, see, it seems she can't make up her mind what player she wants in her bed. Right, Meridian?"

Everyone at the table knew he was referring to the tennis match Meridian and Bill played with Mia. They also knew Mia was the catalyst that ended their friendship and further sparked their competitive relationship. Meridian didn't care; Bill had started that rivalry over Mia, now he had to deal with the results.

"That's how you got into her bed."

"Yeah, you're right. I'm thinking I need to change my ways. I need a sweet, pretty thing to share my bed with."

"Bill, this isn't a game. I'm warning you to stay away from Talya."

"It's always a game, player."

"Get out of my house." Meridian stood at the table.

Meridian never got mad, and he never put anyone out of his house, no matter how obnoxious. Robert intervened and asked everyone to call it a night. Meridian and Bill's relationship was strange, but this was different. Everybody suspected that Meridian was getting serious with Talya and knew that Bill had gone too far. Everyone left without too much complaint.

"Do you mind if I stay over?" Robert asked after everyone had gone.

"Rena not expecting you back?"

"She's hoping that I don't come back. I'm not sure we're going to be able to work out our problems."

Meridian saw the hurt buried deep in his friend's face. Bill hit a nerve with his comment earlier. "You know she loves you, and I know you love her. What's going on between you that you can't work out?"

"It's personal."

"Why don't you see a marriage counselor?"

"We're talking about it."

Meridian dropped the subject. He wouldn't pry into Robert's personal business. He would come to him if he needed advice. He hoped Robert and Rena could work out their problems; they were good together. Rena made Robert happy, and he settled her down. If they were a couple who could not work through their problems and survive, Meridian had little hope for his own future.

Meridian excused himself and went to his bedroom. Robert would be fine; he stayed at Meridian's house many times in the past. Right now he had something on his own mind. He took a quick shower and jumped into bed. He grabbed the phone next to his bed and hit the speed-dial button.

"Hello?" Talya's voice was heavy with the sultry accent of sleep.

"Hi, honey, it's me."

"Hi, the game over?"

Meridian rolled onto his back and looked up at the ceiling in the darkness. "The game is over, and your man is broke."

My man? The sound of those words tumbling from his lips made her stomach quiver. Was she dreaming? She turned on the lamp next to her bed, making the teal walls glow under the soft light.

"Is there anything I can do?"

Why did she say that in that voice? One part of his body stood at attention ready to give her the answer to her question. But that was not the reason he had called.

Meridian knew that Bill was going to continue to be trouble for him and Talya. He was trying hard to make his relationship with Talya work, and Bill was intent upon playing childish games. He was trying to keep his head with Bill, but it was getting harder. They had almost come to blows over Mia, and Meridian had no feelings for her. He knew that if Bill kept pushing him their friendship slash rivalry would end on a sour note.

"Bill was here, and he said something about taking you to lunch?"

"Yeah, I did see him Tuesday for lunch."

Meridian hesitated. He never doubted that Bill was lying. Why did it bothered him to hear Talya's confirmation? "You didn't mention it."

"Should I have? I didn't think it was important." Is he mad?

"It's important to me. I thought we weren't seeing any other people." She should not have even gone.

"It was business, not a date." She sat up in her bed.

"It's never business with Bill; I warned you about him."

"Are you're upset with me?"

"You shouldn't have gone," he snapped before he had a chance to stop himself. He didn't raise his voice. He made a declarative statement.

Talya turned quiet on the other end of the phone.

Meridian spoke in an extra-syrupy voice. "I'm not upset with you. I'm jealous."

"It was only business, really. I ran into him after an interview. We started talking in the lobby of the bank, and he offered to take me to lunch." Talya enjoyed talking with Bill. He was funny, and helped her to forget her lack of success in finding a job. The market was slow; companies were downsizing. She didn't confess that she didn't mention the lunch to him because it was one of the pieces of her memory that she lost that day.

"I'm sorry, Talya. He made it sound like more. And you have a habit of keeping things from me."

"Believe me, lunch was completely innocent."

CHAPTER TWENTY-FOUR

Meridian waved Robert into his office as he fiercely scribbled his signature onto the pile of documents on his desk. As usual, he was past the deadline given to him by the business office to return the legal papers. He spent most of the night reading the deeds and charters and needed only to sign and return them to Robert.

Robert looked at the watch on his wrist. "Are you going to make your flight?"

"Three hours—I should make it." Meridian double-checked his briefcase to make sure he had all the needed information for his trip. "Keep an eye on Talya while I'm gone."

When the flight attendant gave the all-clear over the intercom, Meridian pulled the telephone out of the back of the seat in front of him and dialed Talya's number.

"Are you in the air?"

"Look up, I'm flying over your apartment now."

"Then you're going the wrong way." Talya giggled into the phone. "You're silly."

Meridian refused the drink the flight attendant offered. "Any luck finding a job today?"

"None."

"My offer still stands. Weston Realty would love to have you as part of the team. Think of the long lunches we could take."

"It's the long lunches that scare me."

Meridian lowered his voice for privacy. "I miss you already. You be careful while I'm gone. If anything seems out of the normal—"

"Call Robert, and then you on your cell. Meridian, stop worrying about me."

"Never."

"I have to admit that it does feel good."

"I have to go. I'll call you from the hotel tonight. I love you."

"I love you, too, Meridian."

He never tired of hearing her croon her confession of love for him.

Jet lag set in as Meridian completed his work in New York and boarded a plane for Chicago. After checking in with Robert, Meridian learned that an opportunity presented itself with the Chicago project. The land developers he worked with previously wanted to make him an offer related to land they had recently purchased. The interest in the program continued to grow, so Meridian readily agreed to fly there right away.

Shortly after takeoff, Meridian called Talya. "You still sound down. I take it you haven't had any luck finding a job."

"No, not yet, but I have some leads. Are you on your way home?"

Meridian explained his change in plans. Talya became silent on the other end of the phone. "Are you still there?"

"Yeah."

"What's wrong?"

Talya tried to sound upbeat. "Nothing."

"Talya, tell me what's on your mind."

Talya hesitated. "I don't want you to go to Chicago. I want you to come home. I miss you."

Meridian felt his heart rip in two. "Talya, if I had known you needed me, I wouldn't have gone, but I'm already in the air."

"I know. Listen, I'm being selfish. I'll see you when you get back. Come straight here from the airport. I have to go."

"Wait." Meridian heard Talya hang up before he could say anything more.

Shameful, the guilt she had laid on Meridian's shoulders. He spent more time on planes than he did at home. Always calling her from someplace other than home. Their time together, when he was in town, couldn't be better. She wished there were more days that Meridian was at home rather than traveling. Not having work to occupy her days, she missed him terribly.

Talya opened the door to a tall man in a black overcoat. "Ms. Stevenson?"

"Yes."

He tipped his cap. "I have something for you." He handed Talya a large white envelope.

"Thank you." Talya started for her purse to offer the man a tip for his services.

"No thank you, Ms. Stevenson. The tip has been taken care of. I'm supposed to wait until you open the letter."

Talya eyed the man. His shoes were black patent leather that mirrored her reflection in their shine. He stood straight and stiff waiting for her to open the envelope.

Talya opened the envelope and a letter fell to the floor. She picked it up and read Meridian's message.

Meet me in Chicago. A driver will pick you up at the airport. Love you always. P.S. The driver can't leave unless you leave with him.

Talya looked at the man standing in the doorway watching her. "Is this a joke?"

"No, I can assure you it is not. I have been given very specific instructions to wait for you to pack and take you to the airport. I have your airline ticket in the limo."

Talya's mind raced.

"Please, ma'am, the flight leaves in ninety minutes."

Talya smiled all the way to the airport. She didn't like to take expensive gifts from Meridian, but she needed to get away. She couldn't remember the last time she'd been on a vacation. Meridian would still be working, but it would be fun for her to have the chance to be away from home. True, she missed Meridian more than she ever felt possible. She couldn't wait until he took her in his arms and held her. Having a rich boyfriend sure came with nice perks. Especially, a rich boyfriend that didn't treat you like a trophy or like you were indebted to him because of his kindness.

Meridian instructed the driver of the limo that picked Talya up at the airport in Chicago to help her check into the hotel. The driver gave her another envelope once she was inside of the limo. The note, with his company credit card, told her to go shopping and have dinner. He would return to the hotel as soon as he could.

Talya took a look around the suite on Lakeshore Drive with the view of the Lake Michigan. Small boats peppered the lake. The sun was beginning to go down, and the lights were beginning to illuminate the tall regal buildings. She decided to unpack hers and Meridian's things and then take a walk while she waited for him to return.

Talya held up each of Meridian's shirts and examined the softness of the fabric. The sleeves of each of his suit jackets were stuffed with tissue paper. The creases on his slacks were sharp and crisp. Each of his silk ties carried a designer name matching the rest of his clothing. He had more shoes in his bag than she owned. Talya wanted to have the opportunity to see his monthly clothing and cleaning bills. It was amazing that he wasn't bankrupt. Talya believed her first impression of him in her office was correct: One of his suits cost more than her entire wardrobe.

Meridian sat in the suite at the desk, reading business papers, when Talya returned from her walk. She ran over to him when he opened his arms to her. She kissed him passionately as his reward for his kindness.

"I'm glad you're here with me." Meridian held Talya around the waist. "I miss you when I'm away. You know I wouldn't go if I didn't have to, don't you?"

"I know, and I feel stupid for being such a baby about it."

"I like that you miss me." He kissed Talya and then went back to his work.

Talya watched the trepidation on Meridian's face. "How did it go today?" The stress lines crossing his forehead disappeared when he looked up at her standing over him, which made her smile.

"Good, all in all." He started to place the papers neatly into his briefcase. "You didn't have to unpack for me."

Talya stood behind him and started helping him off with his jacket. Then she massaged his shoulders. "Believe me, it was enlightening." She giggled.

Meridian looked at her over his shoulder. "Are you teasing me about my clothes?"

They went down to the lobby and found a bar to grab hamburgers. Meridian planned out the rest of their week. He wanted Talya to accompany him to some of the business meetings as his financial adviser. Talya didn't feel comfortable knowing the intimate details of his finances but

Meridian ignored her hesitation. He would spend time scouting for property, and, of course, she would ride along with him. He also needed to check on the property that was already nearing its final construction phase; he wanted her there for that too. Meridian promised they would have time together to see the city and have fun. Until then, he demanded that she go out and do whatever she wanted. He didn't want her sitting in the suite waiting for him all day while he was working.

When they returned to the room, the message light blinked. Robert called wanting an update and also to give Meridian information he needed for the next day's meetings.

Meridian reached for Talya as he talked to Robert on the phone. He pulled her down to sit in his lap in the winged chair in the office area of their suite. Talya wrapped her arms around his neck and made faces until he got off the phone.

"Do you want Robert to know you're sitting in my lap? You know how uptight he is. He would have a heart attack, and then we would have to fly home."

Talya kissed his forehead and then settled in his lap. "You love me?"

Meridian raised his eyebrows and studied Talya's face. "I could show you exactly how much I love you if you let me…." He whispered an obscene suggestion in her ear.

"Are you serious?" The look on Talya's face told Meridian it was definitely out of the question.

Meridian wrapped his arms around her hips. He nodded.

"Okay." Talya started to get up out of the chair.

Meridian tightened his grip on her hips. "But not if you don't want to." He leaned up and kissed her until he felt her relax into him. "If there was something you wanted to do—I would do it. If there was something you needed to do—I would do it."

"After what you just asked me to do, I doubt if there's anything exciting enough for me to come up with that would be new to you."

"Hey." He pinched her behind. He pulled Talya's face down to meet his in a kiss. "So, tell me."

"Tell you what?"

"What you need me to do. Don't shy away and avoid the question. Tell me who is going to do what you need but me? And I can't unless you share it with me." He ran his hands across her back.

"Have you ever made love before?"

Meridian chuckled. "I'm not exactly a virgin."

"No, I mean have you made love before?"

"Well, from the question I have to deduce that you don't think I have. Don't you like it between us?"

"When we are together, it's so profound—fierce really. Tonight, let's slow down and make love to each other."

Meridian knew Talya was alluding to the fact that he would become a lunatic and lose his mind whenever they were intimate. He still did not understand the transformation he felt inside of himself when he lay next to Talya and the urgency took possession of his mind and body. He didn't want to try to justify his actions because he didn't know how. He wished he could control himself when he felt the need begin to grow, but as of yet, he had not learned how.

"I'll make a conscious effort if you lead the way," Meridian whispered, locking his eyes with Talya's sultry browns.

Talya spent the next fifteen minutes sitting atop Meridian's lap kissing his lips, chasing his tongue and stroking his silky soft beard. When Meridian wanted easier access to Talya's body, he stood and carried her into the bedroom. They did not speak as he laid her on the bed and positioned himself beside her.

Meridian leaned over Talya and opened every button of her blouse. Seductively, he paused between each loop to kiss the newly exposed chocolate cocoa-colored skin. He helped her sit up while he slipped the blouse off her arms.

Meridian stood next to the bed while Talya slowly helped him remove all of his clothing. The sight of his tie in Talya's mouth ignited the urgency, but she doused the fire by sliding her tongue into his mouth. Every stitch removed, Meridian began to make love to the only woman he ever truly loved in his life.

Talya let Meridian place her on her stomach. His body moved over hers as he slid his hands underneath her and opened her jeans. His body hovered over hers as he slid the jeans off and onto the floor. Meridian used his teeth to open the clasp of her bra. Talya gasped when she felt the release. He moved up to her ear and tasted her with his tongue. She quivered every time she felt his teeth meet her skin as he gave her love bites from head to toe.

Meridian kneeled next to the bed in order to find the markings on her back. He examined them as if for the first time with his fingers. Then his lips. Then his tongue. Then he kissed the markings so passionately, Talya would never think of them negatively again.

Talya rolled over onto her back and reached out for Meridian, but he didn't want to come to her. He helped her over onto her stomach again, and Talya felt his fingers retrace the markings. When he believed he had given the markings another meaning for Talya, he joined her on the bed.

Meridian pushed Talya's thighs apart and sat between them. He opened her to examine the source of so much of his pleasure. He sensed Talya's arousal when he did this, so he heightened her enjoyment by stroking her gently. The warm feathery hair against his palms called him to peek inside. He parted Talya and rewarded her movements with the stroke of his finger. Her temperature rose, and her juices increased around his finger. He knew that he found the core of her pleasure when his finger circled the firm button, and Talya arched her back for him. He watched Talya's face as he teased the button with small circles. He waited until he needed for her to explode before he applied pressure. Talya shuddered under his hand, and he stroked her slowly until she settled back down on the bed.

Talya reached out for him, and he moaned when she massaged his already painfully throbbing manhood. He wanted to do this right, so he took her hand away. Meridian went to her and let her kiss the urgency away.

Meridian was beginning to realize the difference in what their intimate sessions had been and what he was feeling at that moment. He used his tongue to trace Talya's body. He followed with his hands. He found Talya's warm, wet area and let his lips massage the mound of black hair. Meridian's tongue tested the morsel his finger guided him to. He refused to stop until he tasted all there was to sample, even though Talya reached down and tried to guide him up to her lips. When she tried to move her hips away from him, he chased her all over the bed never losing his rhythm until he heard her groan and felt her body shake and rise off the bed.

Meridian lay next to Talya and listened as she tried to catch her breath. He stroked her hair. "Should I put some water in the Jacuzzi?"

Talya waited until her breathing was normal before she looked over at him and answered. "Have you ever been with a woman in a Jacuzzi?"

Meridian nodded, still stroking her hair. "Not in the shower."

They moved to the bathroom. Meridian stood in the doorway and watched as Talya adjusted the water to the correct temperature and pressure. He wanted to pick her up and carry her to the bed, if he could make it and end the pain in his groin. But he was liking this new way of being together and forced himself to wait it out.

Talya turned to him and held out her hand. "C'mon."

Talya stood facing him with her back to the water as she lathered a sponge with an exotic smelling fragrance and ran it all over Meridian's body. He stood paralyzed when she kneeled in front of him and took extra gentle care of his body. He knew that if he did not take her soon he would explode and then he would have to wait until he recovered before he could feel her tightness surround him.

Talya pressed her body against his and stood on her tiptoes to kiss his lips. She placed her lips against his. "You love me?"

Meridian could not spare the energy needed to speak, he nodded his answer.

"Make love to me."

Meridian took her into his mouth as he lifted her in the shower and lowered her onto his throbbing manhood. He felt relief as soon as he was fully inside of her. He moved her hips to his rhythm and kissed her neck seductively as she whispered into his ear how much she loved him and how good he felt inside of her. Meridian could have counted the strokes it took to make him explode because there were so few required. He never heard such a desperate, longing, painfully sweet sound come from inside of him as when he ruptured.

With Talya's guidance, Meridian walked back to the bedroom. He lay on the bed exhausted. Talya wrapped her body in a towel and then dried him head to toe. He fell asleep to the aroma of coconut as Talya oiled his body.

When Meridian woke two hours later, Talya lay next to him asleep without any clothes. He reached over her and retrieved the oil and began to gently caress her skin with the same smell of coconut. When she stirred, he pushed her onto her back and made love to her the old-fashioned way. This time she remembered the lack of the use of a condom, but Meridian whispered in her ear that he loved her and wanted to make love to her.

"Just let this happen," he said breathing into her ear. "Let me make love to you."

Minutes later, Talya was calling his name. Not because he was chasing the urgency and trying to consume her. Because he made her feel so good that she believed if she called his name over and over, he would not stop. Her body surprised her by its violent shaking and vibrations. Meridian held her face with his hands as she let her passion flow. He kissed her lips. This, too, was not the possessive kiss Talya had grown used to getting from Meridian. This kiss was full of tenderness and love. Emotions welled up inside her heart and overflowed as tears that ran down her face.

"What's wrong?" Meridian asked when the tears touched his hands. "Did I hurt you?" He reached over to turn on the light, but Talya gave him a squeeze that stopped him.

"You didn't hurt me." The tears kept rolling down her face. "I love you."

Meridian had never experienced anything near what happened between them that night. "Oh, my God," he whispered. He kissed her tears away and then moved his body on top of hers. He told her how much he loved her and how special she was to him until he could not speak any more words. He didn't know if it was his body or his heart that exploded.

CHAPTER TWENTY-FIVE

"Talya still hasn't called to come home, Jason. What's the big deal about her anyway? All of these women on the circuit are always trying to hit on you. Why don't you hook up with one of them?"

"I don't want those chasers. Talya is better than any two of them. I want her back."

"Hmm." Rizzo dropped the barbell to the mat. "I'm hitting the shower."

"You think I'm stupid, don't you?" Jason matched Rizzo's height.

"Man, I believe that there are more fish in the sea. If Talya doesn't want you, leave her alone."

"You'd understand if you'd ever been in love." Jason brushed past him in the direction of the locker room.

Rizzo sat next to him on the bench in front of the locker they shared. "Maybe you're right. I can't understand what it's like because I've never been in love, but this is tearing you up. You know you should have won that last competition. You would have won if you were concentrating."

Jason fussed with the Velcro securing his weight-lifting gloves.

"What are you going to do?"

Jason's shoulders slumped as he rested his elbows on his knees. "I don't know. I went by her place today. No one was there. I searched the parking lot for her girlfriend's car, but I couldn't find it." He straightened his back. "Rizzo, I'd never admit this to anyone but you. I don't know what I'll do if I lose Talya."

Rizzo placed a firm hand on his friend's shoulder. "Don't worry about that, man. I'll help you get her back. We'll put our heads together and come up with something."

CHAPTER TWENTY-SIX

"Ms. Stevenson, did you enjoy your breakfast?" The same driver that picked her up from the airport appeared at the door of their suite.

"Great, thank you." All the drivers for the limo company stood tall and stiff.

"I have another letter." He went inside his overcoat and produced an envelope.

Meridian's broad-stroked handwriting sloped to the right. Go shopping. Have the driver show you the city. I'll meet you at two for lunch. Love always. P.S. The driver cannot go unless you leave with him.

Talya peeked over the letter at the driver's stern expression.

"Mr. Weston gave me very specific instructions."

Talya grabbed her jacket and left with the driver. Meridian had given him very specific instructions. The driver took her to a lavish vertical mall and accompanied her to each store. After an hour of window shopping, the driver protested their lack of progress. "Ms. Stevenson, Mr. Weston instructed me not to drive you back to the hotel until you purchase something."

"Mr. Weston covered all the bases, didn't he?"

"Yes, ma'am."

A clown stood outside of FAO Schwartz drawing a crowd of excited children. "Let's go over there." The driver followed without protest. After watching the clown's antics, Talya browsed the aisles of the toy store. Children were something she hoped would be a part of her future, after she became financially and emotionally secure enough to be able to devote her time to them.

"Ms. Stevenson, this is very generous of you, but this is not what Mr. Weston had in mind. I could get into a great deal of trouble."

Talya handed the cashier Meridian's credit card. "No, you won't get into any trouble. This is my idea. Trust me, Mr. Weston would approve."

The cashier began to wrap the toys she selected for the driver's two children, three nieces, and six nephews.

"Still—"

"There's a flower shop next door, let's send your wife flowers at work."

She walked away as the driver gathered her toy purchases. To keep the driver from having a coronary, Talya went into a men's clothing shop and purchased a gray suit for Meridian. After selecting a tie, belt, shirt, and shoes, they returned to the limo. The driver helped her up to the suite with her packages just before two.

Meridian examined Talya's purchases when he returned for lunch.

"Are you mad? I spent a lot of money."

Meridian's mouth curled into a broad smile. "You didn't do what I told you to do. Why do you insist on being so hard headed? Do you know that any other woman wouldn't have come back with clothes and jewelry for days? I would have had to buy another airline ticket to get everything home." He scratched his head in disbelief. "I can't believe you spent all morning shopping for a total stranger and his family. Do you know how special this makes you in my book?"

"So, you're not mad?"

Meridian answered her with a kiss. "Let's go to lunch. I'm starving."

After lunch, Meridian instructed the driver to an exclusive clothing store where he purchased most of his suits.

"This time I'll shop for you," Meridian told Talya as he took a seat in a private shopping area.

"Why are we in this room?" Talya asked. Dark plums and greens covered the walls. The jade leather love seat sat positioned in front of a small elevated stage.

The owner of the clothing shop floated into the room. Her strawberry-blond hair flowed around her face in a mass of loose curls. "Mr. Weston, I didn't expect to see you again so soon."

Meridian stood to greet the slender older woman. "This time I'm shopping for a very special friend." He held out his hand to Talya. "I want to purchase several outfits for Talya: casual and dress."

The woman walked a circle around Talya's frame. "Anything special in mind?" she asked absently.

Meridian returned to the sofa where a bottle of wine waited along with a tray of fruit. "Anything she wants."

The woman and her assistant whisked Talya off to a dressing area and took her measurements. Minutes later, they returned with a rack of items for Talya to try. She put the suits on one by one and modeled them for Meridian. The price attached to the garments made Talya reject every outfit.

"Excuse us for a minute."

The assistant exited the room.

Meridian touched the fabric of the toffee-colored evening gown Talya modeled. "We've been at this for more than a hour, and you haven't liked one thing you've tried. Should we go somewhere else?"

"Yes, back to the suite. Meridian, I asked the assistant how much these dresses cost—I can't accept this."

Meridian exhaled an exasperated breath. "Didn't we go through this about the tennis bracelet?" He slipped his arms around her waist. "Stop being a financial adviser and be my woman. Your man wants to buy you something nice, let him." He ravished her mouth. "Okay?"

After that kiss, she couldn't deny him anything. "All right."

He motioned for the assistant to return. "I like the way you feel in my arms in this dress." He turned to the assistant, "We'll start with this one. I think you'll find Ms. Stevenson more cooperative now." He swatted her behind before returning to the sofa.

Meridian chose two formal gowns, three pairs of designer jeans, four blouses, a casual dress, and a bright sporty jacket. While Talya changed back into her clothes, he asked the owner to also include four very sexy nightgowns of various colors. He requested that the owner have Talya try on any shoes she carried with at least a three-inch heel. He examined every shoe Talya slipped on by placing her foot in his lap and stroking her calf with his long fingers. Meridian gave in to her pleading and let her escape with only one pair.

"Now," Meridian said to Talya once they returned to the limo, "the next time I tell you to go shopping, do what I say or you'll have to go with me again."

Talya settled back against the seat of the limo. She caught a glimpse of the driver smiling at her in the rearview mirror.

Meridian instructed the driver to drive them around the city before returning to the hotel. He held Talya against his chest and stroked her hair as they watched the people and the sights. Meridian asked to return to the hotel when Talya's eyelids began to flutter.

They spent the next day driving through the suburbs of Chicago looking for vacant land and houses. If anything caught Meridian's eye, they stopped to take a closer look. Talya admired his astute eye for potentially profitable property. He was very serious when he worked. He smiled only when he looked in her direction or when she took his hand. He made several calls to Robert from the limo and started the negotiations in motion. Robert gave Meridian addresses of homes he should see while in the city.

"This is the last place," Meridian assured Talya. "Are you bored?"

Talya shook her head. She was in awe of his knowledge. She loved every minute she got to spend with Meridian. She told him all of this, and he beamed from her admiration.

The last place turned out to be a condominium on Lakeshore Drive with a breathtaking view. Talya had never seen a home so fabulous in her life. The owner of the property was a plastic surgeon who recently relocated to the West Coast to start a new practice. He couldn't find a buyer before he left the city and needed to sell quickly.

Talya roamed through the condo. The walls, carpet and appliances were all white. The furniture was all black—every piece of it. There were four bedrooms, each with its own bathroom, and a kitchen with breakfast nook, den, dining room and a great room. Talya stood in the great room and looked out over the city. One entire wall was glass, and the sun shining in on the all-white interior made the room celestial.

Meridian walked up behind Talya and held her. "What do you think?"

"I can't believe people actually live this way. It's gorgeous."

The agent showing Meridian the condo appeared in the room. "This is truly a special place. It has the largest square footage of any condo in the building. If you need time to think it over…"

Meridian released Talya and stepped up to the agent. "If my wife likes it then I have to take it. Can I have the keys by this evening?"

The agent's mouth dropped, but not as quickly as Talya's.

"Miss?" Meridian asked, pulling out his cell phone and dialing Robert at the office.

The agent swallowed hard. The amount of commission she would receive from the sale must be huge, Talya thought. "Yes, sir, Mr. Weston, I can have the keys for you immediately."

"Good. I'll have you handle all the details with Mr. Uley. I'll meet you here tonight to pick up the keys and sign the contracts." Meridian talked briefly with Robert and then handed the phone to the realty agent.

Talya's mouth still hung open. "Just like that?" Talya whispered when Meridian rejoined her. "You're buying this place just like that?"

"You said you liked it."

Talya watched him, speechless. She had access to only a splattering of Meridian's accounts when she worked at the bank and knew he was quite wealthy, but she had no idea of his full net worth. Obviously, it was greater than she imagined.

Meridian kissed her lips. "Are you okay, Mrs. Weston?"

Talya nodded.

The agent returned the cell phone to Meridian. They returned to the limo and headed back to the hotel. They would pack their things and spend their last two nights in Chicago in the newly purchased condo.

The message light on the phone was blinking when they arrived at the room. Meridian knew before he called the front desk that it was Robert. He prepared to swallow his medicine with him as he called the office.

"Please correct me if I'm wrong," Robert said in a stern and disbelieving tone, "but did you purchase a million-dollar condo on a whim?"

"You're correct." Meridian watched Talya watching him from the sofa as he spoke.

"Why? For what purpose?"

"Because Talya liked it."

"I'm sure you've lost your mind over Talya now. What are you going to do with it? Are you planning to move to Chicago on a whim too? And what is Talya doing there anyway?"

"Talya is here because I wanted her here with me." His eyes never left Talya. "I brought the condo for a wedding present to Talya. The day we get married, it's hers. Until that day, I'll use it whenever I'm in Chicago."

"What?" Robert asked. "Should I freeze your access to your financial accounts until I can reach your mother?"

"Calm down, everything will be all right." Meridian laughed at his friend. "He wants to talk to you." Meridian handed Talya the receiver.

"Hi, Robert."

"Do you realize the magnitude of Meridian's purchase today? One million dollars is a large amount of money to spend on a whim. Please, whatever you do, don't tell him you like anything else until I can crunch these numbers."

One million dollars? And what was Meridian talking about marriage for?

"Talya, what is going on there?"

"I don't know."

"Do I need to fly to Chicago to bring my boss home before I end up on the unemployment line?"

"I think he's okay."

Meridian pulled Talya into his lap and took the phone. He laughed at Robert's worried voice. "I'm going to hang up now, Robert, so I can let Talya repay me for buying the condo. Bye." He hung up before Robert could say another word. "He keeps me grounded." Meridian smiled at Talya.

Meridian couldn't find a compelling reason to leave the condo over the next two days. They started out to a jazz club one night, but never made it. Talya stepped out of the bedroom wearing one of the dresses he purchased along with the pair of black heels he personally selected, instantly changing Meridian's mind about them going out. Instead, he removed the jacket of his suit and asked Talya to join him in the living room in front of the fireplace. The wind off the water made the August night cool enough for Meridian to start a fire. After that was done, he reached for Talya and removed every stitch of her clothing except her shoes. He took great care in kissing and caressing her calves. Then he laid Talya down on the floor in front of the fire where he made love to her.

"Today is our last day in Chicago; what do you want to do?" Meridian watched Talya at the stove cooking their breakfast.

"I'm afraid to say. You might go out and buy a museum or something."

Meridian chuckled. "You just want an excuse to stay here and seduce me all day. I can't believe you."

Talya sat next to Meridian at the kitchen table. "Why did you buy this place?"

"What I said to Robert was true. I brought it because you liked it, and I knew it would make you happy. And when we get married, it is yours. I'm holding it hostage until then."

Talya squeezed his hand. "I can't believe that you would do something like this for me. Everything that you've done for me this week is unbelievable."

"I love you. It's that simple."

"I feel like I should do something to repay you."

"Actually, I was thinking the same thing. If you could cook breakfast in only an apron and those heels…"

"You're a pervert." Talya covered her face.

"That is not what you were saying last night. If I remember correctly it was something like, Meridian, don't stop. Please, don't stop. Give it to me, Daddy. Give it all to me, Daddy."

They laughed together.

"I did not." Talya swatted at him.

"Well, what's wrong with you then? Let's go." Meridian grabbed Talya by the hand and led her to one of the bedrooms they had not christened yet.

Talya held Meridian's head against her breasts as he slept. She looked out the window at the clouds. She did not want to return to the harsh realities of home. Everything was so magical while they were in Chicago. The two of them alone and all the fun they could think of to have together. No insecurities or doubts were allowed into her heart during their vacation. She began to appreciate Meridian's special qualities even more. He gave her so much. Not the material things, but the greatest gift of all: love. One day she would make him as happy.

Meridian stirred. He kissed Talya's breasts softly before he sat upright. "How long before we land?"

"A few minutes."

"Did you have a good time this week?"

"This was the best time of my life. No one has ever been as nice to me."

Meridian secured his seat belt and then Talya's. His lean arm unfolded around her shoulders. He moved in close to her ear. "Why did you stay so long? Six years is a long time to take such awful abuse."

A chill crossed Talya's body, and she stiffened in response. As the plane approached Detroit Metro Airport, reality came back into view. The last week had been like a dream, a fantasy. Meridian's inquiry was a cold reminder that life was not made of dreams, only hard reality.

Deep breath. "I stayed because I felt I had to. I was scared to stay, but scared to leave. I had no one to turn to. I was completely dependent on Jason. And I was afraid that he would follow through on his threats if he caught me before I got far enough away."

"But you did leave eventually. Why?"

Talya's eyes were locked on the back of the seat in front of her. She did not want to chance seeing disappointment in Meridian's eyes. "The last time he hit me, before I left him, I was afraid he wouldn't stop beating me until I was dead."

Meridian flinched from the reality of her words. Domestic abuse did not have many outcomes. Death was certainly a possibility. He pulled Talya closer and kissed the top of her head. He wanted to make everything right for her. He wanted to correct her past and make her future more wonderful than she could imagine. A prickling sensation scattered inside of his chest as he tried to picture a scene between Talya and Jason. He promised himself that he would make Talya happy every day of her life.

CHAPTER TWENTY-SEVEN

Another unsuccessful week of job hunting. She hadn't realized the banking network spread so far. Everywhere she went, she met excuse after excuse from recruiters. The initial interviews went well, but once the banks called Brunstown for a reference, everything fell apart. They were always gracious, but nevertheless she remained unemployed.

Talya had to dip into her savings to cover her August expenses. The way she calculated it she had until the end of the month to begin another job or else she would be financially wiped out. That time would not come because Meridian kept reminding her of their agreement. The thought of losing her independence stifled her. Meridian kept offering to pay her expenses until she started a new job. If she took him up on his offer there would be strings attached. Living with Meridian did appeal to Talya. She loved him. She couldn't bring herself to pack up everything she worked for and incorporate her life into his. She did think about it as she promised, but she wasn't ready to make that commitment.

"Talya, I thought that I recognized you." Bill took her hand. "How have you been? I haven't seen you since our lunch."

She returned his greeting.

"Do you have time for lunch now? My treat. You look a little flustered." He put his arm around Talya's shoulder and gave her a squeeze.

"Actually, that would be nice." Talya enjoyed talking with Bill. Their conversations were always lively. He was very flirtatious, but he never crossed the line, so Talya found his behavior harmless. His sense of humor lifted her spirits.

Talya told Bill about her unsuccessful employment search.

"I assumed when I ran into you at the bank again that you were working there. Why doesn't Meridian hire you into his company?"

"He has offered me a position working there, but I don't want to mix our relationship with work."

"That can be hard." Bill snapped his fingers. "Why don't you come back to my office with me? I think I might have something that you'd be interested in doing."

"Thanks, but I don't want to take advantage of our friendship."

"I won't let you. I've heard nothing but praise for the work you've done with Weston Realty. I'd be a fool not to snatch you up to work in my office. My practice is not as large as what you're used to at the bank, but you'd be the only financial person working with us. You could develop your own job role. We'd work closely together, of course, until you were comfortable with realty law and what I expect you to deliver, but this could be a wonderful opportunity for you."

Talya spent the rest of the afternoon with Bill. He did not let the reason she was fired from the bank deter him; he made an attractive job offer. The salary he offered her was almost obscene, plus she had the opportunity to gain bonuses if she brought in new clients. The practice was small—only thirty employees. She would have a large office looking out over the heart of downtown, right across the hall from Bill's. She would have complete autonomy over her role in the company. The venture would benefit Bill because he would be able to counsel his clients both in the law and financing their business endeavors. Talya could not refuse Bill's offer.

"Aren't you worried about Rena getting mad if you go home toasted?" Meridian shared a booth with Robert at the corner bar after completing another hectic work week.

Robert downed his third drink and slammed the glass on the table. He went into his suit jacket and pulled out an envelope. He slid it across the table to Meridian before waving at the waitress, signaling an order for another drink.

Meridian opened the envelope and glanced over the papers. "Rena wants a legal separation? Have things gotten that bad?"

Robert nodded. "What am I going to do?"

"Is this what you want to do?" Meridian acknowledged the waitress's request to bring him another bottle of beer.

"Hell, no. I'll die if Rena takes my family away." He fumbled with the rim of his glasses. "What am I going to do?" he asked again.

"As your best friend, I'm going to tell you that there's no way in hell that I would sign these papers." Meridian replaced the papers and slid the envelope back to Robert. "A separation is not designed to save a marriage. The next logical step will be divorce, and I know that you would just let things deteriorate out of your control. The snowball effect." He took a long drink of beer.

"I can't refuse to sign the papers. Rena will leave even if I don't."

"Why don't you try to change her mind? Why is she wanting to leave you?"

Robert took off his glasses and laid them down on the table in front of him. He had suffered so much humiliation. He wasn't anxious to tell his friend about his problem. He wanted to save his marriage, though, and maybe his friend could offer him some insight. Meridian always seemed to do well with women. Robert rubbed his eyes as he felt the alcohol he consumed taking effect.

Robert lowered his voice and glanced around, making sure no one was near enough to hear them over the soft jazz music playing to the small afterwork crowd. "Rena says I don't satisfy her."

Meridian's eyes widened.

Robert clarified, "In bed."

Meridian still could not comprehend the situation. He chuckled. "Is it the size? Because there's no advice I can give you about that."

"Not funny."

Meridian took another drink from his beer in an attempt to hold back his laughter.

"Performance."

"And you're going to let your marriage end because of that? Are you crazy?"

Robert found the situation quite complicated. "What do you mean?"

"What did she say, exactly?"

Robert smoothed out the edges of his intimate conversations with his wife and confided the details to his best friend. It made him feel better to talk aloud about his own frustration with the situation. He had been carrying around the shame and guilt for so long that it became a part of his soul.

"I don't want to go to some therapist and discuss my performance with a stranger. What am I supposed to do? Read a book on how to please my wife?"

"Exactly. Why not? Why don't you go get some movies, some magazines, a couple of books, and go home and study."

"Not funny."

"I'm not trying to be. You told me before that you didn't date much before Rena. Right? Well, maybe you need to see what's out there and try something new. You said Rena told you that it was too routine? Maybe she needs some rated-X variety." Meridian had to grin at the thought.

"You're talking about my wife." Robert sat up straight and tense.

"No offense intended, but I'm making a point. One of the best things about being married is that all the restraints are lifted. No more inhibitions and, thank God, no more condoms." He lifted his beer bottle in a salute. "You can try everything, and do anything you want with Rena. That's the beauty of it. Nothing is off-limits for you to experiment with. Some stuff you'll like, some stuff you won't, but you have the opportunity to try them all. You better get busy. Do some research and start practicing. You want to blow her mind in bed? Switch it up on her and do something completely out of character."

"You are really sick, you know that, don't you? Is this what you do with Talya?" Robert felt his stomach churning, but picked up his drink anyway. He wasn't sure if it was from Meridian's graphic descriptions or the alcohol.

"No, Talya and I aren't married. But you better believe that when we do take that step, I've got some things floating around in my mind that I'd like to try. I'm not saying force Rena into anything she doesn't want to do, but how do you know what she wants to do if you aren't trying to find out? Robert, you better loosen up, and stop being so uptight about sex. Let me tell you, what you won't do, some other brother will. Remember when Rena was talking about singing for Bill?"

Meridian called the waitress over and paid their tab. He drank down the last of his beer. "Let's go."

"Where are we going?"

"I know this store that'll have everything you need."

Robert lost his balance when he stood up and grabbed the table to steady himself.

"I'll drive."

Meridian hoped that he had allowed enough time for Talya and Jennifer to return home. They were at a bridal shop being fitted for their dresses for the wedding. One of his friends was facing divorce while the other was planning a wedding. It was strange how fast love could swing from one extreme to the other. He and Talya were on a steady path and very happy together, even Jason seemed to have disappeared in thin air, but he could not stop wondering about their future.

The weekends were their time together. Meridian picked Talya up after he finished at the office and drove her to his place. His home, once off-limits to all females, was being slowly transformed before his eyes. The vanity table in his master bath held bottles of cold cream and perfumes. Talya kept a change of clothes in his closet. She had chased the grounds people out of the garden after they accidentally chopped down a rare type of flower. A domestic future suited him, and he hoped that Talya was beginning to surrender to the idea.

Meridian held Talya against his chest in the early-morning hours. They had awakened hours ago and found themselves making love until the sun began to rise. "Let's go see that new movie today."

"Um-huh." Talya snuggled up against his chest and pulled the sheets up to her shoulder. "I found a job yesterday."

Meridian gave her a squeeze. "Good for you. Where?"

Meridian listened intently as Talya explained her new job role. He was happy and full of pride at her upcoming success. Until she told him the job was with Bill.

He sat up in bed and peered down at her. "Let me get this right. You took a job with Bill? Bill Ritter?"

"Yes." She sat up and faced him in the bed.

"You're not going to take the job," he said definitively.

"I have already taken the job. We spent all afternoon Friday working out the details. What's wrong?"

"Why didn't you let me give you a job at my office like I wanted to?"

"I explained that to you."

"I know. You never let me do anything to help you. How could you take a job with Bill?"

Talya asked Meridian why he had such a problem with her relationship with Bill. Anytime she mentioned Bill's name Meridian got that stressed look on his face. She knew that he had the idea that Bill was trying to pursue her, but it wasn't true. Bill was a flirt. As best as she could tell he was a flirt with every woman.

"You can't seriously be that naive? Don't you know he only hired you because he's been trying to sleep with you?"

"What are you talking about? He's never approached me like that. Are you saying that I'm not good enough at what I do for him to hire me because I'll do a good job?" Meridian's insinuations hurt.

"No." He reached out and stroked her face. "I know Bill. He's told me what his intentions are with you. It's a game to him."

"Meridian, I already agreed to take the job, and besides, I want the job. It's an excellent opportunity for me. You're going to have to trust me. I'm not going to get involved with him."

"What if I put my foot down?"

"Down where?"

They stared each other down until they started to giggle.

"This whole independence thing with you really sucks."

"Only a man as secure as you could handle it." Talya kissed his lips. "I love you. I'm not thinking about Bill Ritter."

Sunday night, Meridian drove Talya home so that she could prepare for her first day at work with Bill Ritter. Meridian decided he would stay the night at her place and go to the office from there. They could have breakfast together, then he would see her off to her first day of work. He wanted to speak to Bill, make sure he knew the revised rules of the game.

"C'mon, man." Jason slapped Rizzo on the back. "Hurry up before someone comes out into the hallway. Her girl-friend lives right next door."

"I'm working as fast as I can." Rizzo looked up from his place on his knees outside of Talya's door. The top lock was giving him some trouble. He instructed Jason to retrieve a kit out of his gym bag. A few minutes more, and Rizzo was smiling at the familiar clicking sound that meant he'd been successful. Jason handed him a flat card and they were inside.

CHAPTER TWENTY-EIGHT

Meridian followed Talya inside with one of their overnight bags in each hand. She flipped on the lamp and froze immediately. The darkness moved over her and shattered her memories before it swept them away. Her eyes darted around the living room, trying to make sense of the damage.

"Wait here." Meridian dropped their bags where he stood and moved quietly through the apartment, searching for those responsible.

Talya couldn't move. Debris was everywhere. Her sofa and chairs had been shredded and stuffing covered the entire room. Broken glass crunched under Meridian's feet as she listened to him move from room to room. Papers were thrown about. Food from the kitchen was spilled around the room, over the furniture and smeared on the walls. Nothing was left untouched. She took a silent inventory. "Nothing's missing."

"No one's here." Meridian traced the cord to the phone, but it had been cut. He went into the pocket of his jacket and dialed the police on his cell phone. "They'll be here shortly."

For the first time, Meridian noticed that Talya was still standing in the same spot since their arrival. He approached her, but she moved away.

"The bedroom is in even worse shape." He tried to prepare her before she entered the room.

The overturned mattress impeded her entrance into the bedroom. Everything was smashed or ripped. Clothes were strewn around the room. A message in soap awaited her on the bathroom mirror. "I'll be back."

She looked at Meridian's reflection in the mirror. "Call the police and stop them from coming." Her words were measured carefully, and she spoke as if in a hypnotic trance.

"What are you talking about?"

"Stop them." One slice of her memory returned. The night after she called the police to stop Jason from trying to strangle her. The memory was so vivid she touched her neck and glanced in the mirror to see if the bruising was still there. "Stop them from coming!" She swung around and screamed at Meridian.

"I know you're scared, but the police can help. They'll put that maniac behind bars where he belongs."

"You don't understand." Talya pushed past him out of the bathroom in search of a working phone.

Meridian followed her. He watched as she frantically searched through the rubble for a phone that had not been destroyed.

"If Jason finds out I called the police, he'll come after me."

"No one is coming after you." Meridian grabbed Talya by the shoulders, lifting her from the floor and out of the broken glass. "I'm here to protect you. I'm not going to let Jason near you."

Talya looked up into Meridian's dark eyes, letting his syrupy voice wash over her.

"Are you okay now?" Meridian asked before releasing her.

Talya nodded. She straightened her clothes and regained her survey of the damage. She turned to look at Meridian, who was trailing her every movement. "I have nothing left." She held her arms out from her body and turned slowly in a full circle. "I worked so hard to find a job and get my own place. I budgeted and saved for every piece of furniture in this apartment." Her arms dropped to her sides. The water welling up inside of her lids began to tumble down her face. "I don't even have any clothing to put on my back."

The horrible truth struck her. She was right back where she started when she left Jason. She literally had nothing. Most of her savings were depleted while looking for work. All of her clothes and furniture would have to be thrown out. Nothing was salvageable. Jason made sure of that. The only thing she had with her now was her fear of him. For a short while, she thought she was beyond being scared of a coward that would hit a woman to control her. The fancy clothes, elegant gifts, wonderful lovemaking, and spontaneous trips to Chicago had fooled her into thinking she was safe.

Meridian rushed to her, catching her before she collapsed. He eased her onto the floor and held her head against her chest, as she cried. He could control his painful emotions because the anger would not let them escape. His heart broke as he held the woman he loved. The loss devastated her. Not that she was a material person, because he knew well she was not. The desolate look clouding her sultry brown eyes was due once again to her loss of independence. She had worked so hard to get to this place in her life, and now it was all selfishly taken away.

The police dusted for fingerprints at Meridian's demand, but they weren't hopeful about catching the vandals who invaded Talya's home. Meridian told them his suspicions, but he had no proof to substantiate his claim. Talya listened to the exchange between Meridian and the policemen. She had heard all the speeches before.

The darkness of night unwound in front of Meridian as quickly as the two-lane asphalt highway. He was driving his Navigator too fast, but the day and night had been too long. A sideways glance at Talya dabbing away her tears made him grab the steering wheel even tighter. "There are two useless emotions in this world, son," his father told him after being suspended from school for fighting, "anger and jealousy. They make you do crazy things that you regret when you find your mind and get smart again. You learned a hard lesson today. Never, ever show the world these emotions. Bury them inside and transform them into something more useful—like hard work." Meridian wished his father were alive for him to ask precisely how you bury two emotions so strong they made your body physically weak with grief.

His knuckles were now beginning to turn white, and his fingertips were cold. The jazz music spilling from the eight surround-sound speakers couldn't drown out the vision of Talya's shoulders lifting up and down with each sob. He hoped that the crying would stop once they were outside of the city, away from the damage to her apartment, but he was wrong. It irked him. The whole situation was out of control. He was standing on unsteady ground with Talya's past and their future. The uncertainty stressed him. Emotional instability did not suit him. He was a planner. He liked to know what the obstacles were and have a plan formulated to overcome them. He was completely off-kilter with Talya.

He reached out and clicked off the radio. "Stop crying." His words were harsher than he intended.

Talya's red, swollen eyes widened as much as the puffiness would allow. She lowered the tissue from her face and entangled her fingers together in her lap. Meridian could never understand where she was in her life and how long it had taken her to get there. He was wealthy by inheritance. She was poor by circumstance. Seeing her apartment torn to shreds weakened her reserves, and she began to cry. Once she started, it all poured out. All the helplessness, vulnerability and fear she tried to ignore, crashed into her chest knocking her heart to the right enough to activate her brain's response to her pain.

Meridian glanced sideways again. Talya's shoulders were still, her hands in her lap, but the tears were still rolling down her cheeks onto her lap. He was mad, mad, mad. He gripped the steering wheel and turned sharply to the right, bringing the Navigator onto the dirt and gravel shoulder of the road. He slammed the gearshift into park and depressed the hazard-light button. "I asked you to stop crying." His words were tight and harsher still.

Talya looked over at him confused. "I'm trying. What do you want me to do?"

The opening he was waiting for. "I want you to do better than try. I want it to stop right now. I'm tired of watching my girlfriend cry over another man."

"I'm not crying over Jason." Talya fired back.

"Then why are you crying? I'm taking you back to my place to stay for a while. I'll send a cleaning company to your apartment to clear up the mess. I'll take you shopping to replace your furniture and clothing. What is wrong with you?"

Talya watched the change come over Meridian's face. His normally relaxed, fun-loving demeanor was replaced by expressions that were foreign to Talya in connection with Meridian. He was angry with her; the tightness of his jaw confirmed her beliefs.

"Do you think that's all you have to do to fix my life? Do you think that you can give me pat solutions with half-planned ideas and I'm not supposed to hurt anymore?"

"No." Meridian looked ahead on the dark road, then back to Talya. "You never let me give you anything and," he added sarcastically, "you give me even less."

The words hurt. The words were always more hurtful than the punches or slaps because they lasted longer. Much longer. It had taken a long time to learn that Jason's words were not truthful, with the help of Meridian, but if he was going to start tearing her down, she could leave him behind too. She stared at Meridian in the partially darkened compartment of the Navigator. She blinked back the pain of his words, she was good at storing them away so that she could survive the immediate danger. Without thinking, she grabbed the door handle and jumped out of the sports utility vehicle.

"Damn." Meridian slammed his fist on the dashboard in front of him, cut the engine and ran after Talya.

The dust of the dirt and gravel made a small cloud under Talya's feet as she walked as fast as she could in the opposite direction of Meridian's truck.

"Talya, wait," Meridian called after her. When she did not stop, he ran to catch up to her.

The darkness frightened Talya, but she was determined to walk all the way back into town. No way. No way, she would stay in a relationship that might sour on her. Jason was determined to make life miserable for her. She had to find a way to break free of him and get him off her back. She could not deal with the emotional upheaval of losing the man she had grown to love and trust. She would tuck away her emotions and move on with her life. This time she wouldn't make the mistake of thinking that another man and another relationship would be different. She ignored Meridian's pleading for her to stop and get back into his truck.

Meridian stopped. His breathing was heavy. "You run away," Meridian yelled at Talya's back. "You can't stand to hear the truth. You want to live in the past, where it's safe, and hold on to all your fear." Meridian raised his hand and pointed his forefinger with every word. "I thought it took a lot of strength to leave Jason, but I was wrong. You are weak, and you still haven't left him."

The dust stopped clouding under Talya's feet. She spun around to see Meridian panting and pointing at her. The crickets in the nearby field stopped chirping. The only sound Talya could hear were Meridian's shouts of condemnation.

"That's right. You still belong to him. You can't give me a commitment. He comes into your apartment and destroys everything you own, and you won't even press charges against him. He owns the part of you that counts. He owns your mind."

Meridian knew he should regret his words, but he didn't. They needed to be said. He needed to say them, and Talya needed to hear them. He watched the shock make her sultry browns blink. He hoped the truth would shake her. He stood watching her, waiting for a reply.

Talya crossed the distance between them before she realized she was near him. Her arms flew up, and she shoved his tall, slender frame with all of her pent-up anger. His step faltered for only a second, but it gave Talya time to respond to his accusations.

"How dare you talk to me like that?" she screamed at him. "You have no idea what I had to do to survive. You have no idea what every day was like for me. Don't you dare tell me I liked it, and don't tell me I deserved it."

"I didn't mean—"

"You meant I have no right to be scared of Jason. You meant that what's important to me is insignificant. You think just because everything has always come easy for you, that I should accept your small trinkets of caring and shut up! Well, I built everything I have on my own, and I don't need you throwing me a bone and expecting me to grovel and fetch."

Now it was Meridian's turn to be shaken by Talya's words. He opened his mouth to defend his arrogance, but Talya was not finished.

"You act like I'm wrong for being upset over everything I had being gone. I guess that's because you can buy everything I owned in one afternoon and never even miss the money. I can't do that. I struggled for what I had, and it hurts me that it's gone. If you can't understand that, then to hell with you."

Talya paused for emphasis. She spun away from Meridian and started back down the road.

"Don't you run away from me!" Meridian yelled. The absence of his deep syrupy voice made her stop in her tracks. "This is exactly what I'm talking about. You have nothing left. What about me? I've been here suffering because of Jason's actions since the first day I met you. There has not been one time that you considered me before him."

"What—"

"Not one time!"

A car flashed its headlights over them as it passed down the deserted road. They stood only a few feet away from each other on the side of the road, but they both felt they were worlds apart. One could not understand the anguish the other suffered. All brought on by Jason, who was in a bar getting a lap dance from a stripper. An animal sound in the brush caught Talya's attention.

"I'm here, right now." Meridian's voice yielded to the hurt he internalized. "I'm here, where are you?"

Talya's voice softened. "When I pull away from you, it's because I am considering you. I can't commit to you when Jason is still terrorizing my life. I don't want to put you in any danger. I can't open my heart to you freely when I'm scared the past will repeat itself. I'm sorry. I should have never gotten involved with you. My feelings were so strong—I thought I could handle it."

Meridian moved closer so that he could clearly see her face. "I don't regret one second that we've been together. I want more." He wiped away a drying tear with his thumb. "I didn't mean to hurt you with what I said. I'm in a scary position. I don't feel assured that you would stay with me if things ever got rough between us. I would never hurt you, and it kills me deep inside to see you crying from the pain of another man."

"I can't change my past."

"I know." Meridian looked away at another passing car.

"Maybe you were right. Jason does still have possession of my mind." She vowed silently to call her counselor in the morning.

"I was angry—" Meridian tried to offer an apology.

"You were right." Talya took his hands in hers. "You have to give me the benefit of your understanding. My time with Jason was very bad and occurred during what were supposed be the best years of my life. It's going to take some time before I get over it all."

"You have my understanding and my love." Meridian pulled her into him and held her tightly against his chest. "I'm sorry for making a scene out here in the middle of the night. I try to control my anger better than this. It all hit me at once."

"I'm sorry I jumped out of your car." She looked up at Meridian and smiled. "One of Jennifer's dating adventures."

Meridian tossed his head back and laughed. "Let's go home."

No bell rings in the atmosphere and signals when it's time to take control of your life. If there were, it would have rung with the loudness of the Liberty Bell when Meridian stood in the darkness on the side of the road telling Talya that Jason still owned her. His harsh words were enough to trigger late-night soul searching. She stopped crying and finally got mad at Jason. She turned the body-trembling fear into fist-shaking mettle aimed at Jason.

Despite Meridian's concern, Talya started her new job with Bill as scheduled. She allowed Meridian to hire the company that cleaned his house to bring some order to the shambles left behind by Jason. She also allowed him to buy her clothes and other needed essentials although she kept track of every penny he spent with the promise that she would pay him back as soon as she could. When the cleaning company removed the bulk of the mess, Talya returned home and began trying to sort through what was left of her important documents. Jason found the survival suitcase tucked away in the back of her closet and cut every sheet of paper into slivers. She didn't fret. She took a deep breath and started to replace what she could.

The new job and the new attitude made her feel as if she were flying above the clouds. Having a handsome man that loved her also helped to fuel her flight. It was true that she had physically removed herself from Jason a year ago, but until recently, she was still his prisoner.

CHAPTER TWENTY-NINE

"It's this new guy she's seeing, Mom. He's got some kind of control over her," Jason whined. "I tried to call her the other night, but she wasn't there and hasn't returned my call." She studied Jason intently.

He had driven by her place, banged on the door, and she never answered. Whoever she was seeing had to be influencing her. She had nothing—no job, not even clothing. If his plan had worked, she would have come home weeks ago. Instead, he couldn't find her anywhere.

Visiting her mother proved his desperation. What could she do in Tennessee? Nothing. He considered asking her to come back with him. Taking her to Talya and having her talk some sense into her might work. It was a stretch, but he had no more options. He should have known her husband would never allow her out of his sight for more than two minutes. She wouldn't be making the trip up north. The only thing she could do for him now was to provide him the comfort he craved from a mother's arms.

"I don't know what to do. I've lost her for good this time." His head hung over the breakfast she had prepared for him.

"My daughter can be strong willed, you've seen that. I can guarantee you that once she realizes what she's missing being with you, she'll run back home."

"Mom." He rested his head on her shoulder, relishing the warmth of her hug.

He refused to be this miserable every day. He wanted Talya's forgiveness, but it was clear he wouldn't have it. If that's the way she wanted it, then that's the way it would be. Her not forgiving him didn't mean she could walk away like he never existed. No. Talya would be home before the holidays.

"Now, it's important that you don't give up. The only reason I haven't lost my mind with worry is because I know you're keeping an eye out for her safety."

Jason sat upright and steered the fork through his food. "This is so hard."

"I know, son."

Talya thought long and hard about what to get Meridian for his thirty-sixth birthday. She wanted something special. She baked a cake from scratch—sifted the floor and everything. The cake was his favorite, vanilla with white icing. He liked the icing piled on thick and that's how Talya made it for him.

Talya wandered in and out of the downtown shops on her lunch break. The vintage record shop gave her ideas. She purchased a rare original recording by Ella Fitzgerald, the greatest jazz singer ever, according to Meridian. He would appreciate the recording. The record took several hundred dollars from her budget, but with the obscene amount Bill was paying her, she didn't worry. She wanted things to be special for Meridian. He made things so special for her all of the time.

Meridian sat across the table staring at Talya beyond the two long stemmed white candles. "Thank you for making my birthday so nice." He leaned around the candles to kiss her.

"Did you like the record?"

"I love the record."

The waiter appeared with the check. Talya settled the debate over who would pay the bill by handing the waiter her newly acquired credit card. She smiled as she wrote in the tip; she was becoming financially independent.

"Are you ready to leave?"

"Yeah, in a minute."

"What is it?" Talya noticed that Meridian was quieter than usual the entire evening.

Meridian held her hand across the table. "I want to ask you for one thing for my birthday."

"Okay." Talya smiled. "Do I know what that is?"

Meridian chuckled. "That goes without saying."

Talya waited for him to continue.

Meridian had no words. He did not want to have the same discussion they always had because it never led anywhere. They always dead-ended with him wanting something that he never received: a solid commitment. Meridian went into his jacket and found the burgundy box.

He placed it on the table slowly and pushed it with one finger to Talya.

"You're not supposed to give me presents on your birthday."

"Believe me, this is a present for me." He nodded at her, prompting her to open the box.

Talya took the box in her hands, looking at him before she lifted the velvety soft lid. Inside there were two keys on a small, gold, square key ring with her name engraved on it. Talya took them out of the box and held them up in front of her.

"The keys to my house." he said, answering her unspoken question.

They sat in the restaurant staring at each other. Meridian tried to let the soft music in the background grab the beating of his heart and slow it down. Talya looked into Meridian's face and saw the same look he had when they made love and he got lost in his thoughts. She knew she would hurt him if she gave him back the keys, but he couldn't understand that she wasn't ready. They had plenty of time together before they had to take such a big step.

"Meridian, I don't know what to say."

"You don't have to say anything. Put the keys in your purse, and I'll have my answer."

"We have talked about this so many times."

Meridian nodded. "I've been thinking about what you said. If I understand, you love me enough to accept my offer, it's just that you don't want to give up your independence, which is rooted in your work and having your own place. Am I correct?"

"Pretty much." Talya was still dangling the keys in front of her.

"From what I can see, you have job security with Bill."

Talya nodded, the keys clinking together in her hand.

"Keep your apartment and still move in with me. Keep your apartment until you feel comfortable enough to give it up. That way, we'll both have what we need."

Talya looked at the keys.

"It's what I want for my birthday."

Talya placed the keys in her purse.

Meridian's mood lightened drastically after Talya gave in to him. It took him weeks of convincing to get her to agree to move in with him. He was elated.

Talya sat on the sofa next to Meridian with her legs tucked up under her, facing him. She held a piece of cake in her hand and cut through it with a fork. Meridian closed his eyes as he took the cake in his mouth.

"Well?" Talya asked nervously. She spent so much time trying to get it just right.

Meridian waited until he swallowed the cake before he opened his eyes. He gave her a big smile. "It's great."

Talya smiled from relief. She put another piece of cake in his mouth.

Meridian took the plate from her and used two fingers to scoop up the icing. "I like the sweet stuff."

He held his hand up to Talya's mouth after scooping his fingers back into the icing. She licked his fingers clean.

Meridian dipped his fingers again, and this time let them find their way inside Talya's mouth. He moved his fingers in and out suggestively, and Talya helped him simulate the gesture. She smiled, overdramatizing her role with the flick of her tongue as she used her hand to steady his. Meridian felt the growth in his pants as he undid the zipper as best he could with the use of only one hand.

CHAPTER THIRTY

"Dating Adventure with the Reverend number forty-three." Jennifer said as soon as Talya picked up the phone.

Talya dropped down next to Meridian on the sofa in the den. "You're back!"

"Yeah, it's over."

"It couldn't have been that bad."

Jennifer giggled. "Actually, it was fun. My family loves the reverend. The crazy thing is that I think he likes them too. He was right at home after my mother gave him the once-over."

"Did you finally set the date?"

"Date set."

"Well?"

"I want a Christmas wedding, so the reverend agreed to December 22. It's a Saturday."

"That doesn't give us much time to plan—only four months."

Talya and Bill sat together on the sofa with papers covering the antique oak chest, the only piece of original furniture not completely destroyed by Jason's rampage, as they ate Chinese take-out. Developing a financial program was tiresome, but she enjoyed every moment of the planning. It helped to work for someone as easygoing and knowledgeable as Bill. They worked closely together, learning what they needed from each other. The lunch and late nights they spent working together helped them form a friendship.

There was much work to do before Talya started seeing clients. Most of her time was consumed training with Bill and working with the systems guy to get up a computerized financial program that she and Bill could agree upon. She needed to decide on the furniture she wanted for her office. Bill insisted that she hire a secretary to help with some of the phone calls and paperwork. He wanted her to focus on her work, and not the mundane details that could be handled by someone else.

Talya also needed to market her new skills and find new clients. She had never had to do anything like that in her previous job. The clients were all assigned by the manager. Now she would have to build her own client base. Some clients would come from Bill, but he was counting on her to bring in new business. Meridian was very personable with his business associates; she could get some pointers from him.

Talya picked up the phone in her apartment.

"What are you doing? It's getting late; why aren't you on the way home?" Meridian's irritation sounded in his voice.

"We're still working. I'll stay here tonight."

"Bill is there with you?" This was becoming the norm for Bill and Talya, and he didn't like it. "Why are you working at your apartment alone with Bill?"

"C'mon, Meridian." Talya had this same discussion with Meridian more than once.

"If you're not home in an hour, I'm coming to get you."

"I said I'll stay here for the night. I'll come home tomorrow after work."

Meridian maintained his even temperament. "Don't talk to me about our personal business in front of Bill."

"I have to get back to work. I'll call you when we finish."

"No." Meridian was stern. "You go in the other room and get on the phone."

"Hold on." Talya laid the phone down and went into the bedroom.

Bill waited for Talya's signal before he returned the phone to the cradle.

"I want you home tonight, Talya. You need to wrap up whatever you're doing and leave right now, before it gets any later."

"I can't. We're working. How can I tell my boss that my boyfriend said I have to come home now?"

"You tell him just like that. Bill knows the hours you've been keeping aren't reasonable. You work more hours than I do, and I own my business."

Talya held the phone. Arguing with Meridian was useless once he set his mind on something.

Meridian broke the silence. "Come home now. If you're not here in one hour I will come and get you."

Meridian hung up the phone. Serious relationships were new to him, but he knew there definitely were problems between him and Talya. First of all, he wanted to yell and scream at her sometimes but felt he couldn't. They never yelled at each other. They discussed their problems. They discussed their problems, and Meridian gave in to Talya's wishes. He worried Talya would equate him with Jason, so he remained calm and levelheaded no matter what he felt. When Meridian suppressed his anger, he wasn't being real with Talya. Couples were supposed to argue with each other sometimes. It showed that they care and are passionate about their relationship. That's what Meridian believed. They left too much unsaid.

Meridian was in the bedroom putting on his shoes when he heard Talya come home. He returned his shoes to the closet and found her sitting in the living room.

"You made it," Meridian said dryly.

"Just as ordered."

"What does that mean?"

"I don't want to fight with you." Talya walked away toward the bedroom.

They didn't speak much during the rest of the evening. Meridian was asleep by the time Talya came to bed. When he woke in the morning, Talya was already up and dressing for work. Meridian looked at the clock next to the bed: not even seven o'clock.

"Are you going to work this early?" Meridian followed Talya into the kitchen.

"I have to finish the work you interrupted last night."

"This is going to stop."

Talya sat down at the kitchen table and waited for Meridian to begin the same argument they had every day.

"I want you to tell Bill that I said you need to work regular hours. If you don't, I'll call him and tell him myself."

Talya could not believe her ears. "I'm not in school, and you're not my father calling the teacher to complain about a grade. You can't call my boss and tell him something absurd like that."

"The hell I can't."

"This is why I didn't want to move in with you. It's happening all over again. You think that because I live in your house you can control me." Talya rushed from the room.

Damn, Meridian thought. He followed Talya, finding her in their bedroom. He sat down with her on the bed and apologized for his arrogance. "I didn't mean to upset you." He gave in to her again, but there was nothing else he could do.

"I've got to get going." Talya stroked his beard and planted a kiss on his cheek before walking away.

They were supposed to be living together, but Talya behaved like an overnight guest who visited every now and then. She didn't have any clothes in his closet. She stopped by her apartment every week to do her wash and pick up new clothes. When Talya did spend the night, she showed up so late Meridian was already asleep. There'd be reasonable rationale for her late arrival. Mostly, she had to work late with Bill.

Meridian really wanted to blow up about that situation, but he didn't. All night Talya would toss in the bed. Sleeping soundly would end in her having a nightmare, and Meridian shaking her awake. After that she'd stay up watching TV or working until it was time to leave in the morning. If it wasn't the nightmares, it was the headaches. Talya never complained about them, but Meridian observed her taking something to cure them every four hours, like clockwork. Every four hours, even during the night, Talya went to the medicine cabinet and swallowed a Tylenol, Excedrin or whatever he had stocked on the shelf.

On the weekends, there was no excuse for Talya not being at Meridian's house. She'd spend most of her time out in the garden working. There wasn't that much dirt to move in the world. Especially since he hired a lawn service that came by once a week. Even if she was inside with Meridian she was busy catching up on work. If they had uninterrupted time together Talya lapsed into quiet shyness. She was more inhibited now than when they first started dating. Her thoughts were scattered, and she forgot things easily. She forgot everything. Simple things. Food in the oven, the water running in the bathroom. She even lost her car in the mini-mall parking lot while at the grocery store. It took her twenty minutes and the help of security to find it.

"Why is it hard for you to remember things?"

Talya shrugged, not giving him her full attention. "I get this way when I'm under a lot of stress."

"What stress are you under?" he asked.

"All kinds." She never looked up from her work.

Meridian grabbed his basketball and headed for his private court.

Affection vanished from their relationship. She maintained a distance when they were alone. They couldn't make love, she was too tired or not there. When they were intimate, Talya tensed beneath him. She went through the motions, but his touch didn't make her smile anymore.

All the tension, along with Talya distancing herself from Meridian, made the urgency grow. Meridian's mind focused on his movements as he tried to ease the pain and desperation that threatened the stability of his relationship. Her body didn't tense and release underneath him. His concentration wasn't focused on her body's needs; his emotions were too great. He didn't comprehend the weight of his inconsideration until he found Talya in the shower after their lovemaking.

Talya stood under the hot water, trying to steady her thoughts. Meridian's intensity finally crossed the threshold of her being and possessed her. She had been trying over the past several weeks to maintain her identity and keep Meridian from incorporating her into him. Meridian climbed on top of her body, entered her and coiled through her insides until he reached her will and broke it in two. The last time this happened, she found herself chained to Jason, accepting years of his abuse. The possibility of it happening again, paralyzed her emotionally. As much as she loved Meridian, she feared him. She feared his dominance of her heart and mind.

"Talya, are you still in the shower?" She'd been there when he dozed off. He slid the glass shower doors apart. "The water's turning cold."

"I'm losing myself here."

Meridian turned off the water and handed her a towel. "Come out before you catch a cold."

Talya stepped out, wrapping herself in the bath sheet.

Meridian handed her another towel for her hair. "I love you." He closed the door on his way out.

The next morning, Talya was gone when he awoke. She couldn't be working on Sunday. He dressed and went out to the garden. Talya sat on the ground next to the pond, running her hand through the water.

"Good morning." Meridian sat next to her on the ground.

She forced a smile.

Meridian watched the pain covering Talya's face. "This isn't working." He hoped that she would protest and say that they could work everything out.

"I know, it's my fault."

"I don't know what to do." Meridian stroked her hair. "I want to be the soldier during the Civil War who rides in on the stallion and rescues the mistreated slave."

Talya smiled at his fantasy.

"You won't let me do that." He retraced her path through the water with his finger. "Why were you crying in the shower last night? What does it mean, you're losing yourself here? Did I do something wrong?"

Talya shook her head, holding back the tears. "You want to rescue me and take me back to your castle and lock me in. The thought of that terrifies me. Last night I almost gave in. My will broke, and I couldn't save any of me for myself."

"I'm in this for the long haul. From the first time I saw you at the bank I was in love with you. I knew it was what I was feeling although I tried to deny it. Now that I've come this far, I can't go back to being just your boyfriend."

"Are you saying that you don't want to be with me if I don't stay here?"

Meridian nodded. "I can't keep loving you unevenly. You're not into this relationship."

Talya looked at him as the water from her eyes fell onto her legs. "I want to be with you, it's just that I can't give up—"

"You can't open up. After all this time, everything we've been to each other, you're still pulling away from me. I've been so into making you love me as much as I love you that I didn't realize I wasn't happy. I always feel desperate to keep you."

"I can't stay here."

"I know." Meridian stood and walked away.

CHAPTER THIRTY-ONE

Robert closed the door to Meridian's office behind him. He crossed the large room halfway to where Meridian was staring out over the snow-covered city. "Mr. Percy had to go into the hospital over the weekend, but he's back at work today."

Meridian started at his presence. He turned to look at his friend.

"The new insurance company has agreed to cover him, despite his illnesses and their cause. Our lawyers are working on recouping his past medical expenses."

Meridian nodded and turned back to the window. He locked his hands behind his back. "I'll go down and see Mr. Percy tomorrow—welcome him back."

They walked over to the conference table. "He'll appreciate that." Robert cleared his throat.

Meridian looked over at him. "What?"

"Are you coming tonight? Rena really wants to see you." It was Robert's turn to sponsor the monthly get-together for the poker group and their wives.

"I have a lot of work to do." Meridian shuffled the photos of new homes he was reviewing. Robert watched him. Meridian put down his pen. "So things are going well between you two?"

Robert tried to hide his devilish smile. "Things are going really well. We're thinking about having a baby."

Meridian slapped Robert on the back. "Great. I'll be an uncle again."

Robert nodded. "How about tonight? You didn't say if you'd be able to come."

"Will Talya be there?"

"Rena invited her."

"No, I won't be able to make it." Meridian went back to the photos. "Bill has probably made his move on Talya by now, and she'll be his date."

"Talya's coming alone."

Meridian pushed the photos away. "I think I'll pass."

"Do you think it's over for good between you and Talya?"

Meridian nodded. "It's over."

"Maybe if you talk to her—"

Meridian looked up at Robert, who was pushing his glasses back on his nose. "I want it to be over. It was my choice."

"Your choice? It's what you want?" Robert raised his eyebrow.

Meridian nodded, knowing that Robert was about to start with the lectures. "I have received love's education, and it was a hard lesson to learn."

"Talya is a very good woman. A rare type of woman."

Meridian placed his pen down squarely in front of him. He watched Robert squirm under his icy gaze, but that didn't stop him from going on.

"Sometimes things that come easily for some can be a struggle for others."

"Do you think that anything having to do with Talya has been easy for me? She's the first woman I ever loved. I didn't know how to handle the whole Jason thing. It left her with scars I thought I could heal, but I couldn't." Meridian pushed his chair back and walked over to the bar. He lifted the glass decanter and poured himself a drink, straight. "I tried my best, but it wasn't good enough." He took a gulp from the glass.

"Talya has to heal her own scars. She needs you to love her and understand that she's in the middle of an internal conflict. If you give her time, she'll come around."

"You sound like a woman." A fifty year old woman, at that. Meridian came back to the conference table. "I suppose this advice comes to me, from Rena, straight out of your mouth."

"I know you're hurting, so I'll ignore that remark."

Meridian was uncharacteristically venomous. "You do that, and I'll ignore your advice. Let's not talk about Talya anymore—ever."

"One more thing," Robert said. "There has been some interest in the condo in Chicago. The offers have been very good; I guess I should take one."

"I don't want to sell it," Meridian snapped.

"I see." Robert pushed his glasses up on his nose.

"Don't you have some work to do?"

"What brings you back to the shelter? You disappeared off the face of the Earth."

Talya sat down in the counselor's office. "I'm doing much better financially, thanks to your help. I'd like make a donation to the shelter for Thanksgiving."

Talya handed the counselor an envelope containing a check. She also brought several boxes of food, blankets, baby clothes and toiletries, the things she remembered that were scarce when she was a resident at the shelter. One of the volunteers relieved her of the boxes before the counselor showed Talya into her office.

"Enough about your job. How are you doing since leaving us?"

"I'm doing all right. Jason found me several months ago, but he hasn't made contact with me since."

"Did he threaten you when he found you?"

Talya shook her head. "Never directly. He caused a scene at my job and got me fired. I also believe he broke into my apartment and trashed everything, but I couldn't prove it. I haven't heard anything from him since then. Maybe he got the hint, or found someone else to torment."

The counselor explained the benefits of having an Order of Protection. Talya promised to investigate the possibility the following week. The counselor was familiar with the indecision the women faced when taking tangible legal action against their abusers. She pulled the necessary papers from her desk and they completed them together. The new laws in Michigan to deter domestic abuse and stalking made it easy for a woman to complete the needed papers without an attorney.

"Have you renewed your relationship with your mother?"

Talya shook her head. "I don't think I'll ever be able to repair that relationship. She still believes I should stay with Jason and tolerate his behavior." Talya couldn't relive the betrayal she felt from her mother.

"Have you developed any new relationships? It is important to have support systems in place."

Talya told the counselor about her strong friendship with Jennifer. The reverend was also very kind to her, but she needed to work out her problems with God and the church before she could completely accept his compassion and friendship. Talking about Jennifer led to a discussion of Jennifer's upcoming wedding.

"Have you developed any personal relationships? It's important to be able to maintain a loving relationship with a man. You should not be focusing on it, but you should also not be intentionally avoiding it."

Talya related her brief, but serious, relationship with Meridian.

"What was this man like? What kind of personality traits did he have?"

"He's handsome. Quiet spoken. Generous and patient. Very intelligent. Loving."

"I don't understand why you ended the relationship."

"He's also very intense."

"Intense?"

"He needed too much from me. He wanted me to surrender myself to him. It's like he couldn't love me unless—"

"Unless you loved him in return? Unless you trusted him?"

Talya looked away from the counselor, not wanting to admit what she knew to be true.

"Did something about this man remind you of Jason?"

Talya thought about the question before she answered. "I loved them both, and they both hurt me."

The counselor shook her head. "This man didn't intentionally hurt you, did he? From what you've told me he wanted a real relationship, and you told him you couldn't give him that. Is it fair to ask him to compromise what he needs to be happy? If you loved him, why was it so difficult to commit to him?"

"He made me feel like he couldn't love me unless I relinquished myself to him. When we were—intimate—he would get lost inside of me. He loved me too much, totally and completely. He had to take over my heart and my will in order to love me."

"When did he tell you this?"

"He didn't tell me directly."

"What actions did he take that led you to believe this? Was he controlling? Was he abusive physically or emotionally?"

Talya looked out the window again. "No," she admitted, "he was never anything but kind to me."

"In other words, it's what you perceived. Did he ever treat you like a possession or try to control you through his words or actions?"

"Not really."

"Do you see how you transposed your past relationship and fears with Jason to this man?"

Talya tried to understand the analogy. Did the blame of the failure of their relationship fall on her shoulders? It was easier to see Meridian as uncompromising. It hurt less when she thought about him. It made it easier for Talya to go on with her life.

"Are there any feelings left for this man in your heart? Is there any chance of talking with him? Even if you cannot mend your relationship, it would be helpful to speak to him and have an honest conversation to put a closure to the situation."

"He doesn't want to see me. He wanted a clean break."

"How do you feel about this man? Right now—today. How do you feel about him?"

A noise outside of the door caught Talya's attention. When all was quiet, the counselor waited for an answer. "I love him more than anything in the world. I miss him. I want to be with him. I just can't."

CHAPTER THIRTY-TWO

Rena spent the entire day cooking Thanksgiving dinner. She shooed Robert out of the kitchen when he grabbed her and tried to pin her against the counter. She smiled at the sexual monster her frustration created. After they were married, Rena figured things would get better. Month after month went by, and things became more routine between them. Finally, she let her frustration pour out in her tears and confessed her unhappiness to her husband. It was a hard thing to do—as hard as it was for him to hear. But she loved her husband and knew that everything would work out; they would resolve their problem or their marriage would end. She was overjoyed that Robert's dam broke, and he let his passions flow through their marital bed.

"You told me Talya wasn't going to be here. Do you realize how awkward this is? Not only for me, but for her?" Meridian tried to keep his voice down, but did a bad job of it.

"I couldn't let her be alone for Thanksgiving. Talya is a friend to Rena and me. I know it's a little awkward, but we are all adults here. Sit down to dinner and be polite."

"I'm going to stay for Rena's sake. That's all. I can't believe you would do this, Robert."

Talya's hands turned cold as she listened to Meridian and Robert argue in the foyer. She knew Meridian might be there, but she came anyway, because Rena insisted. She hadn't seen Meridian in months, and thought she would be able to handle the situation with dignity. She would treat him as she would any of her friends. Obviously, the dinner was going to be stressful to everyone. Talya decided that she should leave them to their friendship and go home. Robert and Rena were friends to Meridian long before she came into the picture, and she didn't want to be the cause of any animosity between them.

"Rena—" Talya appeared in the kitchen with her winter coat fastened tightly against the chill inside Rena's house— "I'm sorry, but I'm going to leave."

"No," Rena said, rushing to her, "don't leave. Robert will calm Meridian down and then we'll have a nice dinner together."

"I don't want to have dinner with someone who has to be calmed down in order to sit at the same table with me."

"Honey, you know what this is all about—the male ego. Meridian will get over it."

"It's too uncomfortable for everyone. I shouldn't have agreed to come. Make my apologies." Talya rushed out the kitchen door before Rena tried to stop her. Listening to the deep syrupy voice shake the walls with hostility was already more than she could handle.

Rena stomped into the foyer and interrupted the men and their debate. "I have never been so embarrassed in my life! Meridian, how could you come into my house at Thanksgiving and make my guest feel unwanted?"

Meridian felt his stomach tingle from shame at Rena's words. His mother would be just as upset if he acted that way in her house. "I'm sorry. I didn't realize that you could hear me."

"I don't want your apology. You need to get Talya back in here before she leaves."

Robert peeked into the dining room "Where did she go?"

"She left by the kitchen door. Meridian made her feel so bad that she didn't even want to leave by my front door." She turned to Meridian. "She left here out the back door like Jim Crow had been reinstated. I'm disgusted with you right now." Rena turned around on her heels and marched back into the kitchen.

Meridian hurried out the front door. Talya sat in the driveway, waiting for the heat of the car to melt the frost on the windows. He walked around to the passenger side of the car and tapped on the window. When he heard the sound of the locks being popped, he opened the door and got inside the car.

Meridian sat with his hands shoved in his pockets, looking straight ahead. He took his time to gather his thoughts before he spoke. "I'm sorry about what I said."

"Don't be. I shouldn't have come."

"I didn't mean what I said. I wasn't prepared to see you....It's been a long time since we talked."

Talya watched his full lips. The quality of his voice was more seductive than she remembered.

"How have you been?" Meridian watched the ice begin to disappear and knew that his time with Talya was fading as quickly.

"Good. You?"

Meridian nodded.

Nervousness made Talya circle the steering wheel with her gloved hands. The ice disappeared from the rear window. "You better go in. Rena's probably holding dinner."

Meridian ran his hand across the dashboard. "Are you coming back in?"

Talya shook her head, returning her gaze to the front window. She chanted in her head for the window to clear so that she could leave the driveway before their conversation became even more strained.

"Rena is really upset with me. She's going to kill me if I don't get you to come back inside."

Talya caught Meridian's eyes and did not look away. "Is that the only reason you're asking me to come back inside? Because Rena wants it?"

Meridian was caught off guard by the explosion in his head when his eyes met Talya's sexy browns. He studied her face, trying to find the freckles he spent so many hours kissing. They were covered under her makeup. He wanted to remove all of the camouflage with his lips and tongue. He regained his composure and tucked his heart away. "Rena is not someone to mess with."

Talya wanted Meridian to say anything other than that. She wanted to have the opportunity to spend some time with him. She wanted to watch his lips as they talked. She wanted to reach over as he spoke and stroke his beard and mustache. The devilish grin waited for an answer. "I'll call her and apologize tomorrow."

Meridian glanced at the windshield in time to see the last of the ice melt away and slide down and to the side of the glass. "Where are you going to go? Are you going to spend Thanksgiving alone?"

"I've got some work I can catch up on. I'd better go."

"Is there anything I can say to make you stay?" Meridian wanted Talya to come back inside. Even if they couldn't be together, he could enjoy searching for her freckles one last time. They ended so abruptly that there were still emotions that he found hard to suppress.

"I better get going."

"Do you always have to avoid my questions?"

Talya's heartbeat sped up at the remembrance of Meridian's words. The rush of emotions she was feeling made her empty stomach feel nauseous. "Only the hard ones." Talya whispered as their eyes locked again.

"Why is that so hard to answer?" Meridian asked, matching her whispered tone with his syrupy voice.

"What do you want?"

"You know what I want, Talya." Meridian spoke before he could restrain himself. "I want you."

Talya blinked, not really expecting him to be so forthright. "Then why did you let me go?"

"I want you, but I don't want to be in a relationship with you until you can give yourself to me one hundred percent."

Talya looked down at the steering wheel.

Meridian wanted Talya to declare her love for him, grab him around his neck and smother him with kisses. He pictured driving off in her car, going back to her apartment and reuniting with each other all night. Instead, Talya looked down at the steering wheel without a word.

"Good night." He jumped out of the car and crossed the lawn without looking back. Talya had initiated the conversation and, when he spoke freely about his feelings, she was silent. He felt foolish; his pride was injured. No matter how much he denied it, he still loved Talya.

Talya thought about turning off the engine and running after Meridian but he disappeared inside the house so quickly that it gave her an excuse to lose her nerve. Better to leave everything as it was. She wanted to be with Meridian, but she couldn't give him what he wanted, and he wouldn't be happy in the long term. Talya turned on the radio and drove home to be alone.

"I tried to get Talya to stay, Rena. I was very nice to her." Meridian had been defending himself all through dinner and dessert.

"Did you apologize?" Rena demanded.

Robert watched the exchange quietly. He looked over at his stepdaughter, whose eyes were getting heavy.

"I apologized."

"Uncle," their little girl said, "why don't you like Ms. Talya—" She opened her mouth to a yawn before completing her question.

"Yeah, I'd like to know the answer to that question myself." Rena glared at him.

"I'll put her to bed." Robert picked up his stepdaughter and carried her away from the table.

Rena glared at Meridian, waiting for an answer.

"It's complicated." Meridian put a piece of pumpkin pie in his mouth, thinking Robert was a coward for leaving him alone with Rena. She seemed determined to make him suffer for Talya's leaving.

"I'm smart—try me."

Meridian slouched over the plate holding his piece of pie. "She doesn't love me as much as I love her."

"I don't understand. How can you measure how much Talya loves you?"

"I wanted something serious, and she wasn't ready."

"And you dumped her? For what? Do you have something serious with someone now? Or could you have just waited until Talya was ready?"

Meridian's head snapped up. Rena continued to glare at him.

"I guess you're much happier now that you don't have to wait until Talya is ready to be more serious," Rena said sarcastically. "You look pretty lost without her to me. But what do I know?" Rena stood to go check on Robert. "You should go and talk to Talya."

Jason crossed the room to Talya and stroked her chin.

She turned away. "You're wrong. It's different this time. I'm completely over you. I will never go back to that house." Talya stood stiff and straight, her courage building. "I'm a different person. I have a good job and my own place to live. I would never freely come back to that abusive situation."

Jason's fist balled at his side. He remained calm. "I'm finished touring the circuit for the year, and the holidays are coming; it's time to stop all this silliness and come home. It's been long enough. I'm not taking any excuses. Get your stuff and let's be getting home."

"I said I'm not going, now leave my apartment before I call the police."

Jason stepped up close enough to press his nose against Talya's forehead. "You think you're something just because you've got a job and this fancy apartment?" His voice started to rise. He noticed the new furniture as soon as he stepped through the door. He couldn't comment on it because it would have tipped Talya's hand that he was the one who broke in and destroyed everything.

Talya didn't yield her space. She was too close to focus on Jason's face, but she knew from experience that his eyes were narrowing and his straight nose was flaring. "You think I'm nothing because I made the mistake of loving you? You've always punished me because I did what you were too lazy to do: get an education."

"Don't you disrespect me!" Jason screamed, spraying saliva into her face.

Talya refused to back down. "I lost all respect for you a long time ago."

The blow came so fast Talya was sprawled on the floor before she realized she had been hit. The toe of Jason's gym shoe struck her abdomen before she protected herself. She doubled over in pain that was intensified by uncontrolled coughing.

"Now, shut your mouth and get your stuff together." He picked her up by the hair and dragged her by the roots into the bedroom.

CHAPTER THIRTY-THREE

The long and tedious drive back to Meridian's house left him exhausted after the disaster of Thanksgiving dinner. He pulled into his driveway almost two hours after leaving Robert's house. Whenever the weather was bad in the city, it was twice as bad in the rural area where he lived. The three inches of new snow covered the unplowed roads, and underneath laid a fresh sheet of ice. The traffic on the streets was worse than normal because of the slow pace of driving. He originally planned to stay overnight at Robert's house, but decided against it when Rena kept nagging him about Talya.

Meridian had apologized as best he could. He couldn't be blamed because Talya wouldn't return to dinner. The guilt bit at him as he shared dinner with Robert's family. He kept thinking of her alone—no family to share the Thanksgiving holiday. He should have conducted himself better when he found out Talya was in the dining room, but it caught him off guard.

Meridian stripped out of his suit and got into bed. Rena and Robert went on all evening about him going to talk to Talya. They wanted them to work things out. There wasn't much hope of that. They had gone as far as they could go together. There was no way for him to force Talya to trust in him. The wall erected between them had been of Talya's construction, and she never hinted at tearing it down. Her past with Jason blocked the love he wanted to give her. There was nothing he could do to remove her pain from the past. He had tried everything he knew to do.

Meridian drifted off into a fitful sleep of distorted images.

The dream was so realistic that Meridian could feel the cold of the snow freezing his feet. He couldn't recall the dialogue. The emotions left after Meridian awoke were distinctive. He could feel Talya's fear and loneliness. The dream consisted of only one scene. Meridian sat out in his snow-covered garden when he saw Talya run away from his house out onto the grounds. Although it was a cold winter day, she wore only a T-shirt and jeans; no shoes or coat. He stood and watched her run away as if someone chased her. He called after her, but no sounds came. She kept running and running until she disappeared. Her running away brought incredible distress to Meridian. He could feel the anguish and anxiety grow as she ran farther away from him. And then he woke up.

Meridian carried the torment of the dream with him the next day. He worked out in his gym trying to rid himself of the feelings without success. He tried to review real estate scouting reports, but he couldn't concentrate. Whenever his mind trailed off, the anguished memories of the dream would return. He didn't believe dreams held spiritual meaning, and he didn't know why this one remained so vivid in his memory. As the day went on, Meridian felt he needed to see Talya. He told himself he needed to make sure that she was all right after abruptly leaving Robert and Rena's house the night before. He could have called, but that wouldn't have satisfied him. He jumped in his Navigator and drove into the city.

The closer Meridian got to Talya's apartment, the more he realized the impulse to see her was being driven by the emptiness occupying his heart. After the failure of their conversation the previous night, what could he say to her to make her understand? Everything in the world he wanted was no more than a phone call away; his father had left a legacy to assure that fact. But he needed Talya. All of his days were spent imagining her in his arms, him kissing every one of her freckles. He wanted to tease her and make her laugh. He missed her smile. By the time Meridian pulled into Talya's parking structure, he knew exactly what he would say to her.

Meridian heard strange noises as he approached the door to Talya's apartment. He rang the doorbell, but no one answered. He stepped next door and rang Jennifer's bell. Her apartment was quiet and dark. He went back to Talya's apartment and rang the bell again.

He put his ear to the door and heard a loud noise that sounded like something falling to the floor. He jumped at the next unexpected thump.

"Talya?" He knocked on the door while jingling the doorknob. To his surprise, the door opened. His instincts kicked in, and he knew that there was a problem. Talya wasn't in the habit of leaving her door unlocked.

Confusion overcame him when he stepped inside the apartment. The neat and orderly rooms he remembered were in disarray. The new furniture was tousled, and a lamp lay on the floor giving enough light for Meridian to see broken glass and candles covering the floor. Before his mind could register and make sense of the disarray, he heard shouting and screaming come from Talya's bedroom. Without hesitation, he followed the sounds.

"What the hell is going on?" Meridian asked when he walked into Talya's bedroom.

The bedroom was in worse condition than the living-room. Talya's clothes were thrown all over the floor. The drawers to the dresser were partially opened or lying on the floor. The contents of the usually crowded vanity table were broken and scattered all over the room. Meridian was struck by an overpowering aroma of perfume that would have smelled sensuous in the right dose, but choked him with its full-strength potency.

Meridian was shocked into reality, and everything became clear to him when his eyes met the eyes of the man who straddled Talya's waist as she lay on the floor. He could not see Talya's face, but he heard her pleas for the man to leave her alone.

The man jumped up and faced Meridian. He was several inches shorter than Meridian's six plus feet, but much larger in stature.

"What the hell do you want?" he shouted at Meridian.

Talya took the opportunity to move away from Jason. She scooted to the head of the bed, hiding between the bed and the bedside table. She drew her legs up and wrapped her arms around herself. The blood beginning to run into her eyes blurred her vision.

"Who the hell are you?" Meridian shouted back.

"Meridian?" Talya couldn't see clearly through the blood in her eyes or the obstructed view around Jason's legs.

"Shut up!" Jason yelled over his shoulder at her.

"What the hell is going on? What are you doing to her?" Meridian took a step toward Talya, but Jason moved to block his path.

"This is between me and my girlfriend. You can leave before you get hurt."

Meridian had already assumed that the man in front of him was Jason. The scene fit his MO. Had she resurrected her relationship with him? He'd heard stories of women who could never break away from their abusers. "Talya," he called to her, not taking his eyes off Jason, "do you want him here?"

"No," she managed through her sobs, "he won't leave."

Jason turned to her. "I told you to shut up."

Before Jason could turn back around, Meridian started toward Talya. He caught a glimpse of her hiding at the head of the bed. A heavy stream of blood flowed down her face. Her hair hung loose, disheveled. It was obvious that she had suffered a severe beating.

Jason intercepted Meridian before he could reach her. Talya watched helplessly as they started fighting. She wanted to do something to help Meridian, but fear paralyzed her. If she interfered, and Jason won out, Jason would beat her with more severity than he had just done. From what she could see in the partial darkness, Meridian had Jason pinned to the bed, beating his body without mercy. The sound of flesh pounding flesh pierced Talya's soul as she relived the pain she related to the sound of Jason's punches slamming into her face. Meridian's fierce beating of Jason scared her. It wasn't in his nature to be so savage. He was out of control; his fist kept coming down on Jason.

"Meridian, stop!" Talya covered her ears to the sounds of yielding flesh. "Meridian!"

The punches kept coming.

All the times Meridian explored the markings on Talya's back he envisioned being able to do this to Jason. He heard the deafening noise, but didn't know what caused the sound. Then he felt an indescribable burning in his gut. All the strength in his body disappeared simultaneously. Jason pushed him aside onto the bed and ran from the room.

Talya rushed to him. "Meridian?"

The scream from her mouth made Meridian's ears crack. When he saw the redness on her hands, he searched with his own hands in the places on his body that she touched. He lifted his hands in front of his face and saw what he knew had to be blood.

Talya held Meridian's body against hers. "Help! Somebody help us! Please, somebody help!" She was going to lose him before she could apologize for being too stupid to love him totally.

Talya wanted to turn back the clock to the first time she kissed him. She would have treated his kindness and caring with more respect. Now it was being taken away from her. All the daydreams of how she wanted to caress him would be reality. Everything would be different for them if she could go back in time a few months. Please God, one more chance.

Meridian was so stunned by the pain that he felt no fear. Talya was squeezing him tightly, crying, and telling him how sorry she was for everything. He knew what had to be done, and he told Talya in a slow, calming voice. "Just call for an ambulance. Pick up the phone and call 911." He wanted to do it himself, but he did not have the energy to sit up. "Go ahead, Talya. Call for help. I need some help."

Talya gathered herself enough to find the phone and call for help. She ignored the operator's request for her to stay on the line and returned to Meridian. She held his head in her lap. She stroked his perfectly manicured beard and mustache. "I love you, Meridian." Her sobs crippled her words. "I love you. You're too special to leave me alone. Don't leave me, Meridian."

Meridian listened to Talya's confessions of love and commitment. He wished he could take her in his arms and hold her. He wanted to kiss her; make love to her like in the suite in Chicago. But he was too weak. The pain was unbearable. He could feel the wetness running through his fingers. Meridian remembered one more important thing. "Where's Jason? Did he leave the apartment?" He had to ask several times before Talya answered.

"I don't know." Talya's voice was shaking. "I don't know where he is." She couldn't see well enough to know if Jason was still in the apartment with them.

The blood from Meridian's torso gushed through her fingers. "Help! Somebody help us!"

Meridian didn't want Talya to search the apartment and take the chance that Jason might be there. He also worried that Jason might have left but would return before the police arrived. He knew he would survive, and he wanted Talya there when it was all over. If Jason got hold of her again there would be nothing he could do in his present condition.

"Talya, listen to me. Stop crying." He couldn't speak without pausing in between words to catch his breath or fight off the pain.

"I'm here, Meridian." Talya stroked his beard.

"Go to your closet and stay there in case he comes back."

Talya shook her head violently. "No, I'm not going to leave you alone. You don't leave me, I won't leave you."

"Talya, if you love me, do it. I'm not strong enough to argue with you. Please."

Talya searched Meridian's face. "No, Meridian."

"I love you. Now go before Jason comes back. Hurry up!" He seemed to be in more pain when he pleaded with her to do as he instructed.

"Meridian—"

"Go!"

She kissed his forehead and hid in the closet like she did many times before. The difference this time was that the

most important person in her life lay on the other side of
the door dying.

CHAPTER THIRTY-FOUR

Talya opened her eyes and worked at focusing in order to make out her surroundings. The right side of her view was completely blacked out. She raised her right hand and touched a bulky bandage that stretched from her right eye up to the middle of her forehead. When she replaced her arm to its original position, the IV tubing hit the siderail of the bed. A strange itchy-burning sensation irritated the left side of her mouth. She tried to use her left hand to investigate the feeling, but found she couldn't lift her arm. She looked down and focused her vision on a yellowish fiberglass cast held securely in place across her abdomen by a dark blue sling. The white strap of the sling encircled her neck and when she moved, it scratched an already sensitive area on her shoulder. Talya squinted from the burning sensation the sunshine caused when it hit her left eye. The curtains were drawn at the window, butthe sun was still very bright. The TV at the foot of her bed was suspended near the ceiling on a platform. She realized that she had to be in a hospital, but how did she get there? Talya sat up and was met with the sensation of a brick hitting her in the back of the head and a flash of blinding light in front of her left eye. The pain throbbed with every beat of her heart. The pain was so deleterious that Talya fell back onto the pillow.

Talya felt a strong touch rest on the back of her right hand while another gripped her right thigh. "Are you awake, Tae?"

Talya's body froze at the recognition of the sad, humble voice. Jason came around to the other side of the bed so that Talya could see him. "You are awake. How do you feel?"

"Where am I?"

"You're in the hospital. You've been out of it for two days."

The smell penetrating the room was a mixture of body fluids and antiseptics. The television suspended from the ceiling confirmed the information Jason had given her. But Talya didn't remember how she came to be in the hospital. All of the years they were together, she had never needed to spend two days hospitalized. She tried to remember why Jason's love had driven him to beat her this time.

"Why am I here?" she asked the only person who truly knew the answer.

Jason's broad, muscled chest lifted and then relaxed. He blew out a long breath. "You pushed me so far." His eyes roamed about the hospital room as he spoke. "All I want— all I need—is for you to love me for who I am, but you're always looking down on me like I'm nothing."

When Jason shifted his body weight onto his right foot, the bright light from the window traveled past him and blinded Talya. Her only uncovered eye was unusually sensitive to the light. She flinched, taking in a deep breath. Jason scurried quickly to pull the green and cream netted dividing curtain to the left side of the bed so that it shielded the annoying light. Talya watched his body move quickly, but meekly, to please her.

This was their normal pattern. Jason's rage would build over days or weeks. The signs were clear: belittling comments, brushing past her in the kitchen, the sulking, angry sex. He took great care in nurturing his rage until it grew and festered and exploded over the littlest nothing. She knew those signs too: the flaring of his small, straight nose and the narrowing of the darkest eyes she had ever seen. She wished she could remember why the explosion had occurred this time. They were now at the good part, the aftermath, of it all. He was sorry. He would apologize. He would love her beyond her greatest fantasies of being loved. It was starting now, as he lowered the siderail nearest her and sat next to her on the bed, his hand closed around hers.

"Why am I here?" Talya asked again. She kept her tone low so as not to offend him. He demanded her respect.

"We had an argument." He offered as little explanation as possible. His head hung in shame.

Normally, his evasive answer would have been enough for Talya, and she would wait until the missing sliver of her memory returned on its own. She had enough memories of beatings from Jason to last her long beyond her burial day; she wouldn't search for more to add to the hidden vault in the corner of her mind. But something was different. The entire scene with his sitting on her bed seemed strange. She pushed on.

"Jason, why did you hit me?"

"You pushed me into a corner." His eyes met her only open eye.

"How did I push you into a corner?" Her tone was more authoritative than she usually used with Jason, but something didn't seem right to her.

"I told you to come home. Your own mother told you to come back to me. You," his voice was no longer subdued and humble, it rang sharp with warning, "would not listen to what you were told to do."

A bat of Talya's eye brought darkness that disappeared before she could adjust to it. Boom! A slice of the past came to her. She remembered the sound of her front door slamming against the wall at Jason's forced entry into her apartment. Every bat of her eye and every word of justification Jason supplied fueled her mental motor. Scenes flashed in front of her. The confusion made the brick slam against the back of her head again. Was that a dream or was this a dream? Had she been brave enough to leave Jason and start her life again? Or was it something she dreamed as she lay unconscious, probably on the bathroom floor?

Talya flinched when Jason stroked her face. She remembered Jason tossing her clothing around the bedroom. No, that was from the past. She had gone away from him. He should not be near her. One droplet of sweat moved from his temple down past his cheek and off his jawbone. He was rambling now. He was scared. Talya could sense that, but still didn't understand what had transpired between them that made him beat her so badly that she had to be hospitalized.

Jason was still explaining his right to hit Talya when she heard the words that made her head erupt with memories. "…that was our business. I don't know who he thought he was barging into your apartment trying to take charge of the situation. He should have backed off and left, but he thought you were his business. Mr. Suit and Tie." His thoughts were speeding away from him, and he began to confess too much. "I've seen him come to your place before in his new Corvette." His narrowing eyes darkened as they turned on Talya. "I guess that's why you think you're better than me. Now that you're seeing Mr. Rich."

Before Jason's nose became small, and his nostrils flared, signaling the moment of explosion, Talya remembered. Gunfire sounded in her ears, blocking a portion of his confession. She touched her swollen fingers together to see if she could still fell the stickiness of dried blood. Meridian's blood.

"Get away from me." Talya's eyes darted to the other side of the room, finding a vacant bed between hers and the door. She used her left eye to search her bed for the nursing call light. It was on the bed next to her disabled left hand, which forced her to reach for it with her right hand.

Jason grabbed her hand and pinned it down on the bed. "What are you doing?" He moved closer to her face so that he could use the tone in his voice instead of volume to reflect his anger.

"Somebody help me," Talya tried to yell at the top of her voice, but the dryness of her throat did not cooperate. Her call for help was too muffled for anyone passing by to hear.

Jason took his other hand and pressed it against Talya's mouth. "Shut up. What are you doing? Do you think that I'm going to hurt you?"

The pain Jason's hand caused as it pressed against Talya's injured mouth made her stop struggling.

"You better not tell anyone what happened the other night. The police are waiting to talk to you, and if you say anything I'll make you wish you didn't. Understand?" Jason applied more pressure to Talya's mouth and right wrist.

Talya nodded. The tears were contained behind the bandage of her right eye, but flowed freely from her left.

"I don't give a damn about Mr. Suit and Tie. If you tell anyone what happened in that apartment, I'll come back and finish what I started."

The threat held a string of hope for Talya when she reasoned that he could only kill Meridian if he were still alive.

"Now—" Jason removed his hand from her mouth only—"I have told these people that you left me and were messing around with Mr. Suit and Tie and that's all I know. You can tell them whatever else you want as long as you don't tell them that I was anywhere near your apartment that night. Understand?"

Talya nodded slowly. Her mind was losing its memories again. This time the good memories of her time with Meridian were fading. But that was best. She would have to forget she ever knew him if she was to save him from Jason's threats.

"See what you made me do? I wanted to be here when you woke up so that I could take care of you, and you ruined everything." He released Talya's wrist. "Just like the other night. None of that would have happened if you would act like you're supposed to."

Bang! The sound of the gun again, and the sight of Jason running from her disheveled bedroom.

"What did you do?" Talya whimpered.

"I did what I had to do to protect what's mine. No one is ever going to come between us. I hope you realize that now." Jason kissed Talya's cheek. "I'm going to leave before the police come back. I'll see you later today." He placed his lips next to her ear. "Remember what I told you." Jason strolled from the room. The humble man had disappeared and was replaced by the cocky one that kept her in fear of his violence.

All the memories of Talya's last night of consciousness flooded in on her as soon as the door swung shut. Her last meeting with Meridian made her so upset that she wasn't thinking when she opened her front door without checking the peephole. She assumed it could only be Jennifer ringing her doorbell. Jason pushed through the door and slammed it behind him. He was ranting at her about not being around for the last several weeks. He expected her back home soon after he had gotten her fired from the bank. A chunk of memories were gone.

Talya remembered running for the bedroom door, and Jason grabbing her from behind. Then it was only memories of Jason yelling and beating her into submission. He destroyed her apartment. He drug her around the bedroom, flinging her newly replaced clothes out of the closet and dresser. He demanded that she start picking up the clothes and packing so that they could leave. Talya again protested, and Jason began his assault to her body. That was when Meridian walked in.

When Talya heard Meridian's voice she had thought she was dreaming. She was so glad that she was wrong. She was relieved that he had come to save her. And then everything happened too fast. So much blood. The darkness of the closet. Meridian's moans of pain. The last thing she remembered hearing was the calls of the policemen when they entered her apartment. Then she woke up with Jason at her bedside.

As soon as the hospital room door closed, Talya grabbed the call light and pushed the button frantically. The nurse didn't come soon enough, so Talya tried to climb over the siderails surrounding the perimeter of the bed. Her panic, coupled with the extreme pain she felt covering her body, made her unable to accomplish her goal. The nurse found her stuck between the siderails—half in the bed and half on the floor. The IV had become dislodged and blood dripped onto the bed. Talya spotted the small puddle of blood and her mind reeled, pulling her back two nights ago when she held Meridian's injured body against her own.

"Ms. Stevenson, calm down."

"I have to get out of here!"

The nurse struggled to untangle her from the rails. "You're in no condition to go anywhere right now." The nurse solicited help to return Talya back to bed.

"Where's Meridian?"

A man dressed in green entered the room with a syringe in hand, ready to administer an injection that would quiet Talya's ranting.

"I don't need that." Talya appealed to the man in green not to administer the medication. "I'm fine now." She settled down as promised and asked about Meridian's condition.

When they couldn't tell her, the frantic movements began again. She needed to get to him. The man in green swiped her arm with a small white pad saturated with what smelled like rubbing alcohol. Talya fought against those holding her down. The needle dove into her arm, and she knew she had lost. She would be asleep soon. The more she thrashed around on the bed, the more energy she used. Her reserves were soon depleted and the medication made her drop down onto the bed like a lead beam. Her only open eye fluttered and then closed against her will.

CHAPTER THIRTY FIVE

It wasn't until Monday that Bill began to worry about Talya. She wasn't at work when he arrived. He asked his secretary to call her home, but there was no answer. They were supposed to meet first thing in the morning. He talked with her last the Friday after Thanksgiving to confirm. The next day he boarded a plane with Mia, headed to New York. She was modeling over the weekend, and he decided to join her to celebrate the holiday.

Bill received the call from Robert. There was no use coming to the hospital because Talya's family restricted her visitors. Talya, being a close friend, would need support. He ignored Robert's warning, canceled his appointments for the day, and drove to the hospital.

Talya confided in him that she was estranged from her only family, her mother. Why would they restrict her visits from her close friends? There was more going on than Robert knew. He'd get to the bottom of everything; he associated with people in the administrative offices at the hospital. He called them directly and asked for favors that he would gladly repay later.

"Bill, please," Talya pleaded, holding his hand tightly, "please tell me where Meridian is. No one will tell me what's going on with him. Is he okay? Is he—"

Bill put his arm around her. "I'll find out where he is." Her speech was slurred, and the nurses had already warned him that she became violently upset when she asked about Meridian. "I'll find out where he is. You try to get some rest so that you can get out of here."

"They won't let me leave my room. I have to know where Meridian is." Talya's left eye was fluttering again, and her words were slow and hard to understand. "Bill, I really love him more than anything in the world. Please. Please, help me find him."

Bill waited until Talya drifted into a restless sleep before leaving her room to fulfill her request. It took only a couple of phone calls before a hospital employee led him to the intensive care unit. Bill talked with Robert and Rena and introduced himself to Meridian's mother. He took Robert to Talya's room.

Robert pulled his chair next to Talya's bed and waited for her to wake up from her medically induced sleep. "He's not doing too well. He's been to surgery three times in two days. The doctors are having trouble controlling his bleeding. They tried to take him off the respirator this morning, but he started having trouble breathing again. The doctors had to put him back on. They say that if they can control the bleeding his breathing should get better, and he'll make it through. They say that since he's so young and healthy they're hopeful he'll make a full recovery."

Talya looked away from Robert toward the window. The tears burned her face. "This is all my fault. If he dies…"

"He won't die," Robert sternly corrected her. "The police don't understand what happened in your apartment. They found no gun. Your place was a mess."

Talya's head throbbed as she formulated another lie to cover Jason's behavior. She was comfortable about it with strangers, but Robert was her friend as much as Meridian's.

"The police will probably question you soon." Robert rested his hand on top of her swollen fingers. "What happened, Talya?"

She turned toward the empty bed. Just hours before, Jason sat there, warning her to cover for him like she always did.

"The police told us that Meridian said Jason was there. That's all he was able to say before he lost consciousness and the paramedics took over."

Talya welcomed the fleeting darkness. "I can't remember." She quickly asked, "Can I see him?"

Robert shook his head. "You're not in any condition to see him. Besides, only his mother is allowed in the intensive care unit. Once they move him to another floor, Rena and I will be able to see him."

Tears ran down Talya's face. She didn't have the heart to look in Robert's face. She knew when Jason found her there would be trouble. She should have run like she started to when he first resurfaced in her life. Meridian was caught in the middle of a situation that had nothing to do with him. He would hate her for the rest of his life.

"Do you know why Meridian was coming to see you?"

Talya looked up into his soothing face.

He pushed his glasses past the bridge of his nose. "He was coming to see you because he wanted to talk to you about what happened Thanksgiving night. You know he still loves you, right?"

"He'll hate me after this."

"It's not your fault. He won't blame you for this." Robert handed her a tissue to wipe her face free of tears. "Do you still love him?"

"More than anything. I messed things up so badly between us and now—" This time the tears were accompanied by uncontrollable sobs.

Robert hugged her close to him. When Talya's sobbing stopped, he held her away from him. "You promise me that when you see Meridian you won't let him see you crying like this. You know how he is. It'll only make him feel bad to know that you're hurting this much."

Talya nodded at his request.

"One more thing?"

Talya patted her eyes with the tissue.

"I want you to tell my best friend how you really feel about him the first chance you get. He loves you so much, but doesn't know that you love him just as much. Promise?"

Talya nodded. That was one promise Jason would be sure she would not get the chance to keep. Robert stood when the nurse entered the room with a new IV bottle. He kissed Talya's forehead and assured her he would be back soon with Rena.

Jennifer entered the hospital room with the reverend in tow. She placed a vase filled with colorful flowers next to Talya's bed. The reverend talked with Talya and offered a prayer while Jennifer occupied herself outside the room. She would believe in God and go to church every Sunday, Talya prayed, if only He would let Meridian live and not hate her for everything that had happened.

The reverend was going to Meridian's room next. As a minister, he was allowed to visit with Meridian every day to pray with him and his mother. Talya started to send a message to Meridian, but what could she say to make up for all of the tragedy she had brought into his life?

The reverend looked down into Talya's troubled face and spoke with the soothing voice of knowledge that had persuaded her to make changes in her life with his soul-stirring sermons.

"People ask me all the time why God lets good people suffer. You're probably doubting Him and wondering how He could let this happen." He paused for a response but when he did not receive one, he went on. "God has supplied us with the rules of the world and told us the consequences if we do not follow them. We all govern our own behavior. Sometimes we don't use good judgment or let our hearts guide us, and others, innocent people, get hurt. God can't monitor every single person's behavior who is walking this earth; He has more important things to do. But He does come right on time and make sure that something positive comes from every negative situation." He searched for understanding in

Talya's face. "That's what I believe. That's how I survive and go on every day of my life. If you can believe that also, start searching for the good in this situation and run wild with it."

The reverend gave a large, majestic smile that revealed his perfectly aligned, creamy pearl-like teeth. At that moment, Talya could understand why Jennifer loved him so much. He was a genuinely good man that still possessed hope. Despite all the cruelty exposed by the news media, and all the suffering he listened to in silent confidence, he believed things would always be a little better in a while.

"I'll send Jennifer in to see you."

"Thank you," Talya said to him as he turned to leave the room.

Jennifer pulled a chair up close to Talya's bed.

Talya mustered up a smile. "I've got the Dating Adventure to beat all now."

Jennifer laughed. "Yeah, you sure do. Do you remember anything?"

They all led with that question. Talya didn't want to lie to her best friend, her only friend. "Some." Telling her would only place her in danger. Talya turned away from her, too, although she wanted to confide in Jennifer and let her help.

"It'll all come back to you in time. Don't push yourself and don't let those detectives bully you. Do you know when you'll be released?"

"The doctor wants to run another test on my head, and if everything looks good, I'll be out in a couple of days."

Every day the reverend came to visit Talya and updated her on Meridian's condition. The reports were always hopeful but there was never much change. There was always some new development on the state of his oxygenation. Talya could tell by the worried expressions on the faces of her friends that Meridian's breathing was the problem that kept him in the ICU. They were positive as they spoke of what new thing Meridian was able to do or do without, but he was still in critical condition. And in danger of losing his life.

The day finally came for Talya's discharge. Robert and Rena insisted that Talya stay with them until she was completely healed. Meridian would have insisted upon it if he were conscious. She moved gingerly as she dressed in the clothes Bill brought for her to wear home. The constant influx of friends visiting her must have kept Jason away from the hospital room. Every time the door swung open, she held her breath anticipating his return. Her prayers were answered, and he never came.

Talya went to her apartment to pack her clothes. Although she knew what to expect, Talya was not fully prepared for the sight of Meridian's blood in her bedroom. Jennifer had come to the apartment and removed the mattress and her soiled clothing, but there was still blood in the carpet. Talya's legs collapsed underneath her. Rena and Jennifer had to help her back to the car. Rena would have Robert replace the carpet before Talya returned again.

Meridian's mother called before Talya left for church with Jennifer. Meridian was getting better. The doctor planned to move him from the ICU in the morning. Talya would be able to visit him. His mother would come for her the next day, early afternoon.

Jennifer exited the sanctuary and went to the vestibule of the church to help encourage participation in an upcoming nutrition program she would be running. Talya sat in the darkened church and watched the parishioners greet the reverend after his sermon. She didn't know how long she had been sitting there when he joined her in the pew.

"I hear that Meridian will be moved in the morning, and you can see him." The reverend tugged at the collar of his grand African motif robe.

Talya nodded, not taking her eyes off the large cross adorning the wall behind the podium at which the reverend had spoken. It was her focus point as she meditated on the roads her life had taken to bring her to this church, with these friends, at this time.

"Why aren't you overjoyed? It's been three weeks, and you haven't been able to visit him in all that time. I would think you would be happy and excited about seeing him."

"How do I move past this?" Talya turned first her eyes and then her whole body to face him in the pew. "I can't handle the guilt of Meridian lying in the hospital because of me."

"This is not your fault."

Talya shook her head as vehemently as she could. The friction from the strap of the sling burned her neck. "You don't know." Talya thought back to how Meridian lay on her bed bleeding and in pain. All he could do was worry about Jason coming back into the apartment to harm her. "You just don't know."

"I don't know what?" He paused. "I suspected it before; now I'm sure. Are you keeping something inside?"

Only crucial information about what happened the night Meridian was shot. "If I tell you, Meridian will be hurt." Her head dropped in defeat and, before the reverend could ask her anymore, she stood and left the pew.

CHAPTER THIRTY-SIX

"My son will want to see you alone." Mrs. Weston said when they approached the waiting area. "Are you sure this is all right with Meridian?"

"Meridian asked for you when he was still in the intensive care unit. He really wants to see you. If he didn't, I wouldn't allow you to be here."

"Mrs. Weston—"

"Meridian can be a handful sometimes. I know that his father and I are responsible for that, but he's a good man. I couldn't be more proud of what he's done with Weston Realty. He's turned out to be a better man than I ever imagined. He's chosen you to be in his life. I respect that; besides, I'm fond of you too. So, please, get in there and talk to him."

Talya took a deep breath and pushed open the swinging doors leading to the hallway of rooms where patients lay recovering from their injuries. Several family members doted over their loved ones. Buzzers sounded. Bells rang. The complexity of the operations being performed by the staff overwhelmed her. She found the correct room number, took another deep breath, and entered. She would finally see for herself that Meridian was alive.

The nurse finished her work with Meridian before she smiled at Talya and left the room.

Meridian's helpless appearance shocked Talya. She knew from daily reports that he was still weak, but he looked almost as battered as she did. The pole standing next to the bed held several machines that blinked as they delivered medications from hanging IV bags. A disturbing rhythmic beep came from a screen suspended above the head of the bed. The blankets on Meridian's bed were folded down to his waist, exposing the bandages on his stomach. His chest was still muscular, but his frame seemed somewhat smaller than she remembered.

Talya walked over to the bed and leaned against the siderail nearest his face. "I'm sorry. I don't know what to say."

"I know you can't possibly be blaming yourself for this. It's not your fault."

"Do you remember what happened?" Talya held a tense breath. He wouldn't keep silent to protect Jason, which would put his life in danger again.

"I remember coming to see you, the police arriving and waking up here. The rest is still fuzzy. My mother told me you can't recall much either."

Relieved, and afraid she might trigger a memory, she changed the subject. "Is there anything I can do?"

Meridian patted a space on the bed beside him. Talya fumbled with the siderail and then joined him on the bed. She took Meridian's hand in hers. His fingernails were longer than he usually allowed, his skin not as soft.

Meridian touched her face, and Talya instantly remembered how bad she looked. The bandage over her right eye had been reduced to cover the cut above her eye, but the many tiny cuts and scrapes still remained. The doctors told her that the scarring there would be permanent. Several blood vessels burst when Jason hit her in her right eye, and it remained red and misshapen.

"I wish I could have gotten to you sooner." Meridian glanced down at the swollen, multicolored fingers extending past the cast on her left hand.

Talya averted her eyes to Meridian's hand. He held her hand tightly spreading warmth and security throughout her body. She wanted to say something. What were the right words to thank him for sacrificing his body for hers?

"Your beard has grown in."

Meridian grinned at her. "I must look awful. I haven't seen a mirror in a long time."

Talya returned his smile as she stroked his beard. "No, you look great." A solemn thought weighed heavily on her. "I'm just happy that you're here."

"Me too." He captured her hand as she stroked his face. "I'm happy that you're here."

The silence moved between them. Meridian shifted his position in the bed to get more comfortable. His eyes were at half-mast. "The nurse gave me something for pain."

Talya stood up. "I'll let you get some rest."

"I don't want you to leave."

The weight of Talya's guilt multiplied when Meridian recoiled from a pain moving through his body. She had the opportunity to run several times, but she never took them.

Her selfishness kept her there, greedily consuming all of the love he offered. What he had given her over the last year could never truly be measured. All he ever asked in return was an equal commitment, and she had never reciprocated.

"Our relationship never had a chance of surviving. I never gave it one."

Meridian's eyes fluttered. "I didn't help by pushing you when you kept telling me you weren't ready."

"I've made so many mistakes…."

Meridian's eyelids slipped slowly over his faltering gaze.

Talya pulled a chair next to his bedside and rested her hand on his arm. As she watched him breathe, she imagined what it must have been like for him not to be able to breathe without the assistance of a machine. She tried to focus on a happier time. The nights when he slept with his arms around her waist snoring lightly in her ear. The sound would rock her to sleep. He never knew how much he comforted her at night while he slept.

"I love you, Meridian. More than anything."

A slight smile came to Meridian's lips. Soon he was asleep, making the comforting noise that Talya missed at night.

Talya rose to kiss his forehead. "You never knew it, I never showed it, but you had me one hundred percent all the time," she whispered to him, remembering his request as they sat in her car outside of Robert's house on Thanksgiving night.

Meridian deliberately turned his head to face her. His eyes fought to open. "What did you say?"

"Get some rest."

Meridian closed his eyes again. "Do you always have to avoid my questions?"

Talya smiled and whispered, "Only the hard ones."

CHAPTER THIRTY-SEVEN

God answered Talya's prayers; she kept her promise to Him. She went to church every Sunday with Jennifer. She listened to the reverend's words and found her own understanding of them. A meaning that she could believe and understand. One that could provide her with faith and security. Jennifer smiled. The reverend waited—letting her know that he was there if she needed to talk—as her minister and as her friend. Talya smiled.

The cast on Talya's left arm loitered under her dress when she walked down the aisle as Jennifer's maid of honor. The scarring remained above her right eye. As she listened to the wedding ceremony, she doubted her worthiness of the title. There was no honor in assisting the man who almost killed your one true love to go free. The shame ate away at her every time she visited Meridian's hospital room. She tried to view her silence as protecting Meridian, but deep down inside, as she watched Jennifer and the reverend seal their future with a kiss, she knew she was deceiving herself.

Jason must be panicked. Not sure if she would reveal what she remembered to the police or if she would keep quiet. Over a month later, he would be wallowing in self-pleasure at what he had gotten away with. In another couple of weeks, once Talya returned to her own apartment, he would come for her. There was no doubt in her mind that he would. And if she refused, he would threaten Meridian again. She resigned herself to the fact that she would have to go back to Jason or run away—far away—again.

The wedding and reception made for a long day. Talya promised Meridian she would see him the next day. She had made a habit of visiting him every day, sitting beside him, tending to his needs, until the nurses made her leave for the night. Mrs. Weston was glad to be relieved. She had been at his bedside every single day and night for the three weeks when only family was allowed to visit.

Talya pushed past the metal wall plate near the entrance of the hospital ward where Meridian was now being cared for. She carried boxes of cookies, enough for all of the nurses and doctors that were taking such good care of Meridian. Her first stop was always at the nurse's desk to exchange greetings and receive an update on Meridian's progress. He was a natural charmer, and the staff became fond of him quickly. Talya was standing at the desk, talking with a nurse, when the doctor rushed from Meridian's room bellowing orders that might as well have been in a foreign language.

Talya asked the people running past her, pushing medical equipment into Meridian's room, what the doctor's words all meant. None of them had the time to answer. The staff moved with precision. Their pleasant and cheerful demeanors replaced with intense words and looks of concentration. Talya floundered at the desk trying to gain someone's attention. Fear made her walk slowly, although her head kept screaming at her to run. When she slipped by the medical personnel into Meridian's room, she released a scream muffled only by her hands clasped over her mouth.

A nurse noticed her and ushered her by the shoulders into a private lounge. Talya's hands were shaking, a piece of her memory slipped away. The doctors and nurses swarmed around Meridian's bed. Blood from a procedure they were performing at his neck area ran like water from a fountain down onto the white hospital sheets. Meridian was too relaxed. His eyes were closed, and his head held back, neck extended, while the doctor inserted a tube into his throat with the help of an odd-shaped metal instrument.

A lanky man dressed in white ran past the waiting room with a ventilator. She recalled the reports of Meridian's lung being damaged by the bullet. And the failed attempts to breathe unassisted. Talya cried as she told his mother to come right away.

"Talya, you should come home with us and get some rest. When Meridian is able to have visitors again, you'll be too exhausted to see him." Robert stood over her while Rena tried again to convince her to leave the hospital.

Mrs. Weston crossed the room and stood next to Robert. "Take her home." Her tired eyes focused on Talya. "I'll call you if there's any change, but I want you to leave now. He's going to need you when he wakes up."

Talya let Robert and Rena take her back to their apartment. As she lay in the lavishly decorated guest bedroom of their condo, her brain flooded with memories she had enjoyed forgetting. The cycle of violence was so reliable, more reliable than any of the people who should have believed her. The anticipation of the explosion was worse than the abuse itself. Talya subconsciously did things she knew would provoke Jason into a rage in order to get it all over with. Then they could move on to the concern and caring that followed. She rolled over on her side facing the aqua-colored walls with the flowered border dissecting it at its middle. She was weak and more confused in her own mind about what love should be than Jason had been.

Running away from Jason had been hard—emotionally and financially. But she had made it. Made it on her own, despite his repeated warnings that if she ever left him she would die. "Because," he screamed, "you're too stupid to take care of yourself." For a fleeting moment, pride moved across her chest. Shame and remorse replaced the pride as quickly as it appeared. She had worked too hard and come too far to allow Jason to shatter her world again.

Meridian was the most important person in the world to her. She loved him and that should mean something. His love for her meant he was willing to risk his life for her. She would do no less than the same for him. But what she needed to do would risk his life. That wasn't her decision to make. Still, she had to do something. If she let Jason control her one more time, after such a serious, life-threatening incident, she would perish at his hands for sure. Too many nights she lay next to Jason afraid to go to sleep.

Talya pulled the extra blanket up to her chin; her body was cold and exhausted. Rena had stared at her when she asked for it. She offered to turn up the thermostat for the furnace, but Talya knew the coldness only surrounded her body. She vowed that when she woke up from the much-needed sleep, she would know the answer; she prayed for it before she drifted off to sleep. Her belief in religion was still shaky, but she knew she needed something divine to believe in, and He had already answered her prayers once.

"Little J, bring me the morning paper," Jason called to his son. He sat up against the headboard of the bed and waited. Little Jason's mother was in the kitchen cooking breakfast. Any minute she would come into her bedroom, with a plate piled high with food, smiling. Happy to have her with him the last month or so, Jason examined his thick arms to see if avoiding the gym had any impact on his physique. Hardly any. He would let her be happy until he was sure he could return home. He believed he put enough fear in Talya to keep her quiet, but he needed to be sure.

Little Jason climbed up on the bed and presented him with the newspaper. He was happy to have his father with them too. He was there when he went to sleep and still there when he woke up in the morning. He struggled to pull his pajama top over his head so that he could lean, bare chested, against the headboard, like Daddy.

Jason was aware his son sat beside him, copying his every move, but he paid no particular attention to him. He flipped the pages of the metro section. He'd found the first report of the shooting there. When Rizzo came rushing over to show him the article, he was floored. Mr. Suit and Tie really was rich. A multimillionaire. Owned some sort of real estate business. The police weren't going to sweep the shooting under the rug labeling it another inner-city violent crime for statistical purposes. They were investigating and searching for the shooter.

Jason tossed the unneeded portion of the paper onto the floor. "Take the paper back to your mother." Little J wouldn't stop chattering while he read the article.

Meridian was recovering. No mention of Talya.

He knew Talya had been discharged long ago from the hospital, but she wasn't at her apartment. Another week, and if no one came around asking questions, he would return home and continue trying to put his life back the way it was supposed to be. Him and Talya together and happy.

A return visit to the shelter and a meeting with her counselor gave Talya all the information she needed. She called the psychologist's number and made an appointment for the very next week. Meridian was released from the intensive care unit and could receive visitors again. Talya turned down Rena and Robert's offer to drive her to the hospital. She had things she needed to do first, she told them. Robert pushed his glasses back on his nose but didn't comment.

"Talya—" Bill rushed around his desk, arms extended—"how are you?"

Talya let him comfort her before she took a seat opposite his desk. He sat on top of his desk directly in front of her.

"I know I don't have the right to ask you for anymore favors, but—" She tore her eyes away from her hands and looked up into Bill's eager face. "I really want to keep my job. Is there any way you would consider letting me continue to work here?"

Bill's flawless face brightened. "Is that your favor? Did you really think you had lost your job?" He reached down into her lap and took her hand in his. "The job is yours, Talya. There was never a question otherwise."

Talya thanked him. She slowly pulled her hand away when Bill started stroking it.

"How about lunch?" Bill stood his full six feet and strutted around his desk.

"I've got some things to do." Talya stood, not wanting to waste any time. There was a lot to do.

"I hear Meridian is doing much better." He sat down in his custom-made leather chair and used the desk to pull himself forward. "Meridian and I have an unusual friendship, but I respect him and would never want anything to happen to him." His voice sounded sincere. "You take as much time as you need. I know you'll want to be with him until he's released. When you're ready, your job will be here."

Talya thanked him again and left the office.

The fragrance of fresh flowers drifted out into the hallway. Talya tapped lightly on the open door of Meridian's private room. He turned his head slowly from the television toward the sound. A smile lifted his beard.

Talya stepped into the room and closed the door behind her. The room was overrun by exotic flowers and cards. Talya examined the cards as she approached the bed. Friends, family, peers and employees had sent them.

"The nurse told me I could donate the flowers to the hospital, and the volunteer group would give them to patients who aren't lucky enough to have any visitors," Meridian said, breaking the silence. "I'll keep all of the cards."

Still thinking of others before himself. "I stopped by your house and brought you some books to read." Talya leaned against the siderail as she pulled two autobiographies of famous African-Americans from her purse.

Meridian examined them before he placed them next to him on the bed. "Thank you. The television is driving me crazy. I asked Robert to bring me some work to do, but he refused. Can you make sure that he does?"

Talya nodded. "I'll do it today."

Meridian returned her nod. The sweet odor of her perfume relaxed him. "Sit down."

Talya pulled up a chair next to his bed. She lowered the siderail, and ignoring the cord of the IV, took his hand in hers. "You know this was all my fault. I can see it in the way you look at me."

Meridian used the button on the call light to turn off the television before he answered. "I remember what happened. All of it. And I can see in the way you look at me that you remember too."

Talya gripped his hand over the IV tubing and bandage. "You haven't told anyone."

"Neither have you."

The panic rushed in on Talya. Every blink of her long lashes returned another forgotten memory. "Jason came to me in the hospital. He told me he would kill you if I told anyone what I remembered. If it were my life, I would have gone to the police right away, but you have risked enough for me—too much."

"What are you planning to do?"

Talya locked her eyes with his. "I don't know. I don't want you hurt." She lifted his hand and pressed it against her cheek. "Meridian, I—" She reached out and stroked his thick mustache and his full beard. "It's taken me a long time to realize how much I love you. I can't walk away from you, but I have no right to stay and jeopardize your life any further. Believe me, if I thought that Jason would have ever done anything like this to you, I would have left town a long time ago."

The nurse walked into the room with a small IV bag in hand. She attached it to one of the larger ones, adjusted the clamp, and left the room after asking Meridian if he needed anything.

"What do you want?" Meridian asked as soon as the door closed behind the nurse.

"I want you to love me like you used to. I want you to tell me that everything can be repaired between us. I want you to tell me that it's not too late for me to give you what you need from me."

Meridian fell back against his pillow and stared up at the white ceiling. His breathing came much easier now, but when Talya was near, she had the ability to make it catch. He lifted his head and found Talya watching his every move with tears in her eyes. "Do you mean, that after all of this time, all I have to do is say the word, and you'll be mine?"

Talya nodded.

"And all I had to do is get shot and almost die?"

She couldn't read his facial features under all of the dark, curly hair.

Meridian smiled. "Bad joke." He motioned for her to join him on the bed. "I'm saying the word."

Talya climbed into bed with Meridian, being careful not to disturb any medical equipment. She held his head against her breasts.

"I want you to go to the police," Meridian whispered against the warmth of her chest. "Tell them everything you remember. Don't stop to think about Jason's threats to me. The only way we're going to have a normal life together is to be rid of him forever."

CHAPTER THIRTY-EIGHT

"Talya, I'd feel better if you'd let me go up with you."

"You and Robert have done more than enough to help me. I've told the police everything; they'll have Jason in custody in no time."

Rena craned her neck around looking for strangers that might be lurking in the parking structure. "Stay with us until they've picked him up. We love having you."

"I couldn't ask for better friends than I have, but I've made up my mind. It's time for me to start living my life. Living unafraid of Jason. I'm moving back into my place. And I'm starting work at Bill's office first thing in the morning."

"I'm worried about you." Rena embraced Talya.

"Don't worry. Robert has taken care of security for Meridian, and the police promised they would provide surveillance on my building."

"Why are you being so brave?"

"Don't you think it's time? Rena, all these years I've cowered to Jason. If the past month won't make me stand up and fight him, what will? I owe this to Meridian, my friends and, most of all, to myself."

Rena relented. "If you need anything, call me or call Robert immediately."

"I will." Talya gathered her things from the car.

"Check in with me every day."

"I will." Talya stepped out of the car and into her independence.

Talya's hand quivered as she slid her key into the lock of her apartment. Bravado felt nice, but the underlying fear accompanying the horrific memories of the night Meridian had been shot stirred beneath the surface. Meridian got stronger every day. The counseling sessions were going well. She even called her mother and tried to mend their relationship. Of course, she couldn't believe that Jason would ever shoot someone unless he had been provoked. Talya separated her mother's beliefs from her own, attempting to put their past behind them. Instead of arguing, she told her mother she loved her and promised to visit soon. Meridian expressed his pride with the strides she was making. Life was beginning to be what it should be.

The afternoon sun still lit the sky, but Talya flipped on every light in her apartment. "Feeling uneasy the first time you go back to your place alone should be expected," the counselor prewarned. "Take it slow."

Returning to the bedroom was hardest. As promised, Robert had the landlord replace the carpeting. A new bed stood, bare of sheets, in the corner. No traces of Meridian's blood. She sat gingerly on the side of the bed. "Too soon," Talya whispered as visions of Meridian bleeding in her arms flashed in her mind. "I'll sleep on the sofa tonight. Take it slow. I'm here; I can do this."

"How are you doing?" Meridian's deep voice moved through the telephone line, covering Talya with a coat of sweet syrup.

"I'm sleeping on the sofa, but other than that, it's not too bad."

"Everyone would understand if you got in your car and drove to Robert's for the night. It might be too soon. I know I'd like knowing you weren't alone."

"I know, and believe me, I've been tempted about a hundred times tonight to leave. But, understand that I have to do this sometime, it might as well be now."

"It could wait until I'm out of the hospital, then I could be there with you."

"I have to do this alone."

Meridian hesitated. "I understand. I'm proud of you. I'm afraid for you too. I don't want anything to happen to you. If I couldn't get to you—"

"Meridian," Talya broke in, "don't scare me. I'll be okay. How many times have you called the police station today?"

"None." His laughter trickled from the receiver. "My mother took care of that. Can you see the police car?"

"No, but they told me it would be unmarked. Please, concentrate on getting better and coming home. Everything is under control here." As she assured Meridian, she began to believe it herself.

"What were you doing when I called?"

"Watching *I Love Lucy* reruns."

Talya predicted her mother's first phone call was to Jason.

"I told you I would kill him if you went to the police." Jason shoved her into the apartment. The door slammed behind him.

"I'm not afraid of you anymore, and neither is he." Her voice was loud and unrelenting, not giving away the fact that she was terrified. She expected to be the first time she saw him again, but she had already determined that her fear would no longer be in control.

"I have had it with you and your new attitude. It all ends now. No more stalling. No more excuses. This time you're leaving with me if I have to drag you through the parking lot to my car. Leave everything. You have everything you need at home." He grabbed her arm and started pulling her to the door.

His grip was so tight on her arm that she lost all sensation immediately. "Let me go." She fought wildly, landing one of her small fisted blows on the side of his face.

Jason froze, bringing his fingers up to his face in surprise. Once the initial shock wore off, he raised his hand and slapped her already scarred face. The fading scars would soon be accompanied by a purple-blue bruise. "What the hell is wrong with you?"

Jason yanked Talya's arm. She kept struggling, but her best fight wasn't enough to keep him from dragging her down the hallway to the elevator doors.

When the doors opened, two police officers—one plain clothed, the other in full uniform—were waiting with pistols drawn. "Freeze," they shouted in unison.

Thank God, Talya said to herself, they really were watching my apartment.

"Release Ms. Stevenson," the uniformed officer shouted in a loud, booming voice as he approached Jason. "Are you okay?" He glanced quickly down at Talya and then back up at Jason.

"Yes." Talya scrambled to get to her feet. She pulled her arm away from Jason. The plainclothes officer grabbed her around her waist, lifted her from her feet and pulled her a safe distance away. Simultaneously, the uniformed officer lunged at Jason, pinning his muscular body to the ground. He recited from memory Jason's Miranda rights as he applied the handcuffs.

Jason's eyes never left Talya's as he was ushered into the elevator, without her.

CHAPTER THIRTY-NINE

Early April

Meridian glanced to his right at Jennifer and the reverend. He never thought he'd see the reverend display his affection for Jennifer in public. Even if they were married. He looked over at Talya and wiggled his eyebrows.

Talya watched Robert and Rena, who were being as affectionate as the newlyweds. She touched Meridian's hand and nodded toward Robert.

Meridian shook his head. He leaned over to Talya's ear and whispered, "These married couples are terrible. They're going to get us kicked out of the restaurant."

Talya giggled nervously.

"Are you having a good time?" Meridian whispered.

Talya nodded.

"Did you like the watch I gave you for your birthday?"

Talya nodded again.

"The dress?"

Talya nodded.

"You seem preoccupied," he observed aloud, sitting up straight in his chair as the waiter arrived.

The couples ate their dinners in between carrying on lively discussions. Jennifer could not stop herself from giving everyone the details of her honeymoon—again. The intimate details of the honeymoon night had already been shared in private between Jennifer and Talya. Rena went on about the changes she was making to her house in anticipation for the baby she expected by the end of summer. Robert smiled proudly, squeezing her hand on top of the table. Everyone wanted to know how Meridian was recovering from his injuries. He had been out of the hospital more than two months and was getting stronger every day. Soon enough, the couples paired off in their own private conversations.

Meridian paid the check for Talya's birthday dinner celebration. They planned to go back to his house for a special dessert Mr. Martin had prepared. The cake wasn't finished baking when Meridian left the house, he hoped that Mr. Martin met his specifications exactly. Fond memories lifted his mustache when he recalled the cake Talya had baked him for his birthday.

Talya stopped Meridian as he stood to leave. "I want to ask you for one thing for my birthday."

Meridian settled back into his seat. "Do I know what that is?" He remembered the present she gave him after the birthday cake. He let his finger stray down the deep opening in the back of her evening dress.

Talya grinned nervously. Their relationship was stronger now than it had ever been. Being intimate had its restraints because of Meridian's lingering injuries, but neither complained. They spent most of their time talking, touching and kissing. Meridian insisted that Talya indulge him occasionally, and she happily gave in. But she was very careful with him. Meridian whispered many promises in the dark of what was to come once he healed completely.

During their lovemaking, the urgency that had once owned his body and his mind ignited. The urgency remained, but could no longer control him. He knew he had what he needed, whenever he needed it.

Meridian watched Talya's face. She had been unusually quiet since he picked her up at her apartment. He didn't remark when she finished her second glass of wine at dinner. Something played on her mind, but he'd learned to let her come to him when she was ready to talk. Probably something to do with Jason. After the trial, he was locked away at Jackson Prison. He had lied, denied and threatened all the way there, but Talya handled it like a trouper; he was proud of her.

Jason used his first phone call to reach Talya. Meridian wanted to strangle him with his bare hands as he listened to Talya on the phone. He still wanted Talya to change her recollection of the night of the shooting. Some scheme he had thought up with his crazy friend. He threatened her, and he threatened Meridian. Meridian stood to approach Talya with the intent of snatching the phone and offering Jason an opportunity to try and carry out his threats. He stopped before he reached Talya when he heard the strong words she said to Jason. She held her ground as she told Jason that if he came near Meridian she would kill him herself. Meridian almost literally burst at the seams. If he ever had a doubt about Talya's love for him it disappeared at that moment. Of course he scolded Talya for being crazy enough to taunt Jason, but he sure did love hearing it.

Meridian was doing much better since the shooting, but sometimes he grimaced just to get some attention from Talya. He would let her dote over him and adore every minute of it. She would catch him grinning at her and then she would light into him. They would always make up with one of those jolt-producing, urgency making kisses.

Talya had established a name for herself at Bill's firm, and Meridian was proud of that too. She never missed a counseling session and had started attending the reverend's church with a degree of regularity. Meridian always accompanied her, and as their faith grew in a higher power, so did their faith in each other. The final signal to Meridian that let him know Talya was now a recovering survivor of domestic abuse came the day she asked him to fly to Tennessee to meet her mother. He cleared his calendar—they would be traveling together next month to try to repair the broken relationship.

Meridian touched Talya's face lightly and waited for her to continue.

The gruff exterior Talya had grown used to during Meridian's hospital stay had disappeared. Back were the expensive suits that fit his trimmed-down body perfectly at every ripple and groove. His appetite returned now that she sat with him at every meal and encouraged him. The weight would come back soon, returning him to his slender, but firm, stature. Mr. Martin whispered to her that Meridian's appetite was fine, he suspected that he wanted her company. She was happy to give it.

The full mustache and beard were replaced by the faint shading of well-sculpted facial hair. Observing his handsomeness made her unconsciously touch the scar above her right eye. Meridian smiled as he removed her hand, still waiting for her to continue their conversation and make her request known. He had offered to pay for plastic surgery. Her counselor suggested the removal of the scar might help her to forget. Talya turned down Meridian's offer when he said he loved the scar as much as he loved her freckles. He removed any doubts that the statement was true when he kissed and stroked and licked the scar along with every freckle on her face.

He had stood from the sofa and raised his shirt exposing his own wounds. "If you can love me with this then I can surely love you with that."

Those kinds of gestures made her love him every day. It wasn't that he said such wonderful things. He was always doing such wonderful things. He never blamed her for what happened. He never gave her accusing glares when he grimaced from the painful scars left near his ribs, across his abdomen. There were only special gifts and loving caresses.

Talya strove to make him happy. She was proud of being able to possess what he needed to make him feel so delighted with his second chance at life. She promised to be there for him, doing little things that he could do for himself. It pleased him to see her dote on him. It took him weeks to admit that he didn't need any help undressing for bed.

Meridian pleaded with her while he was still in the hospital, "No one will walk in. I told the nurses that I needed my privacy with you today."

Her own body healed quickly; it was used to suffering abuse, having to rebound and return to her duties around the house. Jason's concern and caring attitude only lasted a matter of days.

Talya's mouth dropped. "You told them that—?"

Meridian nodded proudly, tugging at her arm, trying to pull her into bed with him. "These people are medical professionals. They understand the needs of a man."

"Oh, brother. You've got to be kidding." Talya rolled her eyes as she let him pull her down next to his battered body.

"Do you have any idea how long it has been." He guided her hand under the crisp hospital sheets.

"I know exactly how long it has been." She surprised him with the correct answer.

"And that's waaaay too long." His lids drooped slowly, and his body settled into a rhythm that matched her gentle, stroking fingers.

Meridian was famished by the time Talya gave in to him. He had pretended to be helpless for so long it backfired. She feared he was too weak and she might reinjure to his thinned body. He had to confess that his need for her assistance was not always necessary, but desired. She socked him in the arm, and he fell away on the bed. When she leaned over him, to be sure he was okay, he grabbed her around the waist and pulled her to him.

◆

"Talya?" Meridian touched her face, bringing her out of her trance. "What did you want for your birthday?"

Talya went into her purse and retrieved a small black velvet box. She placed it on the table and slid it over to him, slowly, using only her index finger.

"You're not supposed to give me presents on your birthday."

Talya blushed from recognition of the words she spoke to him on his birthday last year. She nodded toward the gift.

Meridian lifted the box, glancing down into her eyes before opening it. He lifted the lid while watching her. He stared, openmouthed, at a gold band with small diamonds surrounding it.

He leaned over so that his face almost touched Talya's. "What is this?"

Deep breath. "Will you marry me?"

Meridian's heart beat so hard and so fast he instinctively placed his hand there to stop the gallop. Unbelievable, the woman he loved, who still refused to move in with him, would be so bold as to ask him to marry him. Talya steadied his hand by covering it with her own. She worried he may have another setback. He gave a reassuring smile; she removed her hand.

Talya averted her eyes to her lap. "Well?"

Meridian lifted her head with his finger. He handed Talya the ring and held out his finger. He waited patiently, through ragged breaths and trembling fingers, for her to slide it into place. Once the ring was where it should be, Meridian leaned over and kissed Talya. Pressing his lips to hers, answered her question. He let her kiss him, and the urgency floated away from his body.

ABOUT THE AUTHOR

Kimberley White is a multi-published romance author. A Detroit native, she uses her nursing experience to address controversial topics in an entertaining, and informative manner. Please send your letters to: kwhite_writer @ hotmail.com

P.O. Box 672
Novi, MI 48376

2007 Publication Schedule

January

Rooms of the Heart
Donna Hill
ISBN-13: 978-1-58571-219-9
ISBN-10: 1-58571-219-1
$6.99

A Dangerous Love
J. M. Jeffries
ISBN-13: 978-1-58571-217-5
ISBN-10: 1-58571-217-5
$6.99

February

Bound By Love
Beverly Clark
ISBN-13: 978-1-58571-232-8
ISBN-10: 1-58571-232-9
$6.99

A Love to Cherish
Beverly Clark
ISBN-13: 978-1-58571-233-5
ISBN-10: 1-58571-233-7
$6.99

March

Best of Friends
Natalie Dunbar
ISBN-13: 978-1-58571-220-5
ISBN-10: 1-58571-220-5
$6.99

Midnight Magic
Gwynne Forster
ISBN-13: 978-1-58571-225-0
ISBN-10: 1-58571-225-6
$6.99

April

Cherish the Flame
Beverly Clark
ISBN-13: 978-1-58571-221-2
ISBN-10: 1-58571-221-3
$6.99

Quiet Storm
Donna Hill
ISBN-13: 978-1-58571-226-7
ISBN-10: 1-58571-226-4
$6.99

May

Sweet Tomorrows
Kimberley White
ISBN-13: 978-1-58571-234-2
ISBN-10: 1-58571-234-5
$6.99

No Commitment Required
Seressia Glass
ISBN-13: 978-1-58571-222-9
ISBN-10: 1-58571-222-1
$6.99

June

A Dangerous Deception
J. M. Jeffries
ISBN-13: 978-1-58571-228-1
ISBN-10: 1-58571-228-0
$6.99

Illusions
Pamela Leigh Starr
ISBN-13: 978-1-58571-229-8
ISBN-10: 1-58571-229-9
$6.99

2007 Publication Schedule (continued)

July

Indiscretions
Donna Hill
ISBN-13: 978-1-58571-230-4
ISBN-10: 1-58571-230-2
$6.99

Whispers in the Night
Dorothy Elizabeth Love
ISBN-13: 978-1-58571-231-1
ISBN-10: 1-58571-231-1
$6.99

August

Bodyguard
Andrea Jackson
ISBN-13: 978-1-58571-235-9
ISBN-10: 1-58571-235-3
$6.99

Crossing Paths, Tempting Memories
Dorothy Elizabeth Love
ISBN-13: 978-1-58571-236-6
ISBN-10: 1-58571-236-1
$6.99

September

Fate
Pamela Leigh Starr
ISBN-13: 978-1-58571-258-8
ISBN-10: 1-58571-258-2
$6.99

Mae's Promise
Melody Walcott
ISBN-13: 978-1-58571-259-5
ISBN-10: 1-58571-259-0
$6.99

October

Magnolia Sunset
Giselle Carmichael
ISBN-13: 978-1-58571-260-1
ISBN-10: 1-58571-260-4
$6.99

Broken
Dar Tomlinson
ISBN-13: 978-1-58571-261-8
ISBN-10: 1-58571-261-2
$6.99

November

Truly Inseparable
Wanda Y. Thomas
ISBN-13: 978-1-58571-262-5
ISBN-10: 1-58571-262-0
$6.99

The Color Line
Lizzette G. Carter
ISBN-13: 978-1-58571-263-2
ISBN-10: 1-58571-263-9
$6.99

December

Love Always
Mildred Riley
ISBN-13: 978-1-58571-264-9
ISBN-10: 1-58571-264-7
$6.99

Pride and Joi
Gay Gunn
ISBN-13: 978-1-58571-265-6
ISBN-10: 1-58571-265-5
$6.99

Other Genesis Press, Inc. Titles

A Dangerous Deception	J.M. Jeffries	$8.95
A Dangerous Love	J.M. Jeffries	$8.95
A Dangerous Obsession	J.M. Jeffries	$8.95
A Drummer's Beat to Mend	Kei Swanson	$9.95
A Happy Life	Charlotte Harris	$9.95
A Heart's Awakening	Veronica Parker	$9.95
A Lark on the Wing	Phyliss Hamilton	$9.95
A Love of Her Own	Cheris F. Hodges	$9.95
A Love to Cherish	Beverly Clark	$8.95
A Risk of Rain	Dar Tomlinson	$8.95
A Twist of Fate	Beverly Clark	$8.95
A Will to Love	Angie Daniels	$9.95
Acquisitions	Kimberley White	$8.95
Across	Carol Payne	$12.95
After the Vows	Leslie Esdaile	$10.95
(Summer Anthology)	T.T. Henderson	
	Jacqueline Thomas	
Again My Love	Kayla Perrin	$10.95
Against the Wind	Gwynne Forster	$8.95
All I Ask	Barbara Keaton	$8.95
Ambrosia	T.T. Henderson	$8.95
An Unfinished Love Affair	Barbara Keaton	$8.95
And Then Came You	Dorothy Elizabeth Love	$8.95
Angel's Paradise	Janice Angelique	$9.95
At Last	Lisa G. Riley	$8.95
Best of Friends	Natalie Dunbar	$8.95
Beyond the Rapture	Beverly Clark	$9.95
Blaze	Barbara Keaton	$9.95
Blood Lust	J. M. Jeffries	$9.95

Other Genesis Press, Inc. Titles (continued)

Other Genesis Press, Inc. Titles (continued)

Eden's Garden	Elizabeth Rose	$8.95
Everlastin' Love	Gay G. Gunn	$8.95
Everlasting Moments	Dorothy Elizabeth Love	$8.95
Everything and More	Sinclair Lebeau	$8.95
Everything but Love	Natalie Dunbar	$8.95
Eve's Prescription	Edwina Martin Arnold	$8.95
Falling	Natalie Dunbar	$9.95
Fate	Pamela Leigh Starr	$8.95
Finding Isabella	A.J. Garrotto	$8.95
Forbidden Quest	Dar Tomlinson	$10.95
Forever Love	Wanda Y. Thomas	$8.95
From the Ashes	Kathleen Suzanne	$8.95
	Jeanne Sumerix	
Gentle Yearning	Rochelle Alers	$10.95
Glory of Love	Sinclair LeBeau	$10.95
Go Gentle into that Good Night	Malcom Boyd	$12.95
Goldengroove	Mary Beth Craft	$16.95
Groove, Bang, and Jive	Steve Cannon	$8.99
Hand in Glove	Andrea Jackson	$9.95
Hard to Love	Kimberley White	$9.95
Hart & Soul	Angie Daniels	$8.95
Heartbeat	Stephanie Bedwell-Grime	$8.95
Hearts Remember	M. Loui Quezada	$8.95
Hidden Memories	Robin Allen	$10.95
Higher Ground	Leah Latimer	$19.95
Hitler, the War, and the Pope	Ronald Rychiak	$26.95
How to Write a Romance	Kathryn Falk	$18.95
I Married a Reclining Chair	Lisa M. Fuhs	$8.95
Indigo After Dark Vol. I	Nia Dixon/Angelique	$10.95

Other Genesis Press, Inc. Titles (continued)

Other Genesis Press, Inc. Titles (continued)

Other Genesis Press, Inc. Titles (continued)

Path of Thorns	Annetta P. Lee	$9.95
Peace Be Still	Colette Haywood	$12.95
Picture Perfect	Reon Carter	$8.95
Playing for Keeps	Stephanie Salinas	$8.95
Pride & Joi	Gay G. Gunn	$15.95
Pride & Joi	Gay G. Gunn	$8.95
Promises to Keep	Alicia Wiggins	$8.95
Quiet Storm	Donna Hill	$10.95
Reckless Surrender	Rochelle Alers	$6.95
Red Polka Dot in a World of Plaid	Varian Johnson	$12.95
Reluctant Captive	Joyce Jackson	$8.95
Rendezvous with Fate	Jeanne Sumerix	$8.95
Revelations	Cheris F. Hodges	$8.95
Rivers of the Soul	Leslie Esdaile	$8.95
Rocky Mountain Romance	Kathleen Suzanne	$8.95
Rooms of the Heart	Donna Hill	$8.95
Rough on Rats and Tough on Cats	Chris Parker	$12.95
Secret Library Vol. 1	Nina Sheridan	$18.95
Secret Library Vol. 2	Cassandra Colt	$8.95
Shades of Brown	Denise Becker	$8.95
Shades of Desire	Monica White	$8.95
Shadows in the Moonlight	Jeanne Sumerix	$8.95
Sin	Crystal Rhodes	$8.95
So Amazing	Sinclair LeBeau	$8.95
Somebody's Someone	Sinclair LeBeau	$8.95
Someone to Love	Alicia Wiggins	$8.95
Song in the Park	Martin Brant	$15.95

Other Genesis Press, Inc. Titles (continued)

Soul Eyes	Wayne L. Wilson	$12.95
Soul to Soul	Donna Hill	$8.95
Southern Comfort	J.M. Jeffries	$8.95
Still the Storm	Sharon Robinson	$8.95
Still Waters Run Deep	Leslie Esdaile	$8.95
Stories to Excite You	Anna Forrest/Divine	$14.95
Subtle Secrets	Wanda Y. Thomas	$8.95
Suddenly You	Crystal Hubbard	$9.95
Sweet Repercussions	Kimberley White	$9.95
Sweet Tomorrows	Kimberly White	$8.95
Taken by You	Dorothy Elizabeth Love	$9.95
Tattooed Tears	T. T. Henderson	$8.95
The Color Line	Lizzette Grayson Carter	$9.95
The Color of Trouble	Dyanne Davis	$8.95
The Disappearance of Allison Jones	Kayla Perrin	$5.95
The Honey Dipper's Legacy	Pannell-Allen	$14.95
The Joker's Love Tune	Sidney Rickman	$15.95
The Little Pretender	Barbara Cartland	$10.95
The Love We Had	Natalie Dunbar	$8.95
The Man Who Could Fly	Bob & Milana Beamon	$18.95
The Missing Link	Charlyne Dickerson	$8.95
The Price of Love	Sinclair LeBeau	$8.95
The Smoking Life	Ilene Barth	$29.95
The Words of the Pitcher	Kei Swanson	$8.95
Three Wishes	Seressia Glass	$8.95
Ties That Bind	Kathleen Suzanne	$8.95
Tiger Woods	Libby Hughes	$5.95

ESCAPE WITH INDIGO !!!!

Join Indigo Book Club©
It's simple, easy and secure.

Sign up and receive the new
releases
every month + Free shipping
and
20% off the cover price.

Go online to www.genesis-
press.com and click on Bookclub
or
call 1-888-INDIGO-1

Order Form

Mail to: Genesis Press, Inc.
P.O. Box 101
Columbus, MS 39703

Name _____
Address _____
City/State _____ Zip _____
Telephone _____

Ship to (if different from above)
Name _____
Address _____
City/State _____ Zip _____
Telephone _____

Credit Card Information
Credit Card # _____ ☐ Visa   ☐ Mastercard
Expiration Date (mm/yy) _____ ☐ AmEx ☐ Discover

Qty.	Author	Title	Price	Total

Use this order form, or call 1-888-INDIGO-1	Total for books _____
	Shipping and handling: $5 first two books, $1 each additional book _____
	Total S & H _____
	Total amount enclosed _____
	Mississippi residents add 7% sales tax

Visit www.genesis-press.com for latest releases and excerpts.